STOLEN FUTURE

What Readers Are Saying
About Stolen Future

LOVED it! It was the best one yet! Honestly they just kept getting better!

Mary Beth

My heart is racing. I have smiled, prayed, cried, held my breath, and rejoiced.   *Karen*

I have been waiting for the third book of this series! I can't believe how much I enjoyed it! This series just keeps getting better and better!   *JD*

Kimberly Rae is such a compelling author and has such a tasteful and classy way of dealing with a very unpleasant topic - human trafficking. Her books are full of suspense, drama, and romance, and hard to put down. I like to think of these books as entertainment with a purpose. It would probably be a great stand alone novel, but I recommend reading the first two in the series, Stolen Woman and Stolen Child if possible. Another great read from one of my favorite authors!   *Sue*

Kimberly Rae has done an excellent job in this entire series by creating interesting characters you fall in love with, exposing the dark story or human trafficking, and wrapping it all up in the restoration only available through Jesus Christ. Well done!!!! I am inspired, challenged and encouraged all throughout this series. This last book was definitely an excellent conclusion to the series. I couldn't put it down. Wish there were more to come!   *JCG*

…great conclusion to the series.   *Kimberly*

This is the third in the Stolen series!! Kimberly Rae has proven so far to be a most excellent writer. I read the first two in the same day I started them!!

Lyvonda

As a busy mom with three young children I rarely even have time to read. The story line kept me wanting to come back whenever I could get a moment to read it! Great suspense and drama! The short chapters allowed me to feel like I was able to catch a quick 10 minutes here and there when I could squeeze them in and not feel like I was having to stop right in the middle of something. I haven't read the other books in the series, but I want to now. I also feel I was able to pick up this book and not be lost with the characters even though I haven't read any of the other ones. I would definitely recommend it! It may even motivate you to get involved with programs helping stop human trafficking. We could definitely use more awareness with this subject! Great job to the author of this book. LOVED IT!   *Jodi*

It was amazing - I couldn't put it down (...I missed a lot of sleep!). It was awesome and such an encouragement.

Leanne

LOVE these books!!!

Judy

Kimberly Rae's finale to the Stolen series was truly worth waiting for... The romance was so touching and warm and the suspense kept me from putting the book down until I finished it! I would recommend reading the Stolen Woman and Stolen Child books first to build background and to understand the relationships more fully... but if those aren't available, Stolen Future can stand on its own! Human trafficking is horrible... and yet, Kimberly Rae handles it expertly. She provides background to help us understand what is happening around the world in a way that exposes the horror without horrific/sexual details... so the book is appropriate for teens and adults as well. Underlying the whole story is the love of Asha and Mark, and even more important their desire to help others and show the world Jesus' love!

Sawmillsmedia

...it was excellent.

Helen

...absolutely LOVED it!

Kelsey

I enjoyed it...realistic, well-developed characters and plot. Educates about human trafficking while entertaining. Looking forward to seeing what Kimberly writes next!

Donna

I am absolutely amazed at this book! I can't wait to see what God will do through it... This book makes me want to do more, to really make a difference.

Kim

...an exciting romance with danger and adventure and dreams come true.

Shawne

I have to say that this book is my favorite of all 3 in the Stolen series. This book brings you to many difficult places, places that we would rarely chose to go to on our own and shows that even in the darkest of moments that God's Love is more powerful than all the evil in the world. The relationship between Asha and Mark is beautiful and is a shining example of Christ's love for us. That He desires, protects, seeks us out and will never leave or forsake us. After reading this book I feel like I have taken a trip to India and I am already ready to go back!

Amy

...an amazing ending to the series.

Jennifer

I love the book!!!!... What an awesome series! Full of hope and love.

Lori

Oh my, it was excellent!!

Amy

Printed in South Carolina, the United States of America

The characters and events in this book are fictional. The author takes
full responsibility and apologizes for any mistakes in cultural
understanding or expression.

STOLEN SERIES, BOOK 3

STOLEN
FUTURE

KIMBERLY RAE

Dedicated to Sweetie, the baby tied to a pole so she can't get away.
I pray for you, precious child, and those like you who are trapped.
I pray true freedom for you, and lasting hope,
and that you may know that you are loved.

Character Guide:

Shazari (Shah-zah-ree)—Asha's biological mother

Neena (Nee-nah)—Asha's biological father's second wife

Ahmad (Ah-mahd)—man who stole Asha as a baby

Rashid (Rah-sheed)—Ahmad's younger brother

Milo (Mee-low)—former street kid, now lives on compound

Dapika (Dah-pee-kah)—girl growing up in red-light district

Amrita (Ah-mree-tah)—trafficking victim

Didi (Dee-dee)—Bengali term meaning "Big Sister"

Dada (Dah-dah)—Bengali term meaning "Big Brother"

Didi-Ma (Dee-dee-mah)—Bengali term meaning "Grandmother"

Places:

Sonagachi—largest red-light district in Kolkata

Scarlet Cord—safe house outside city, named so from the Biblical story in Joshua 2 of the red rope used to rescue Rahab when Jericho fell

PROLOGUE

Neena shrank back but Shazari stood firm. "Get away from us," she hissed.

Ahmad continued toward them, laughing off Shazari's fury. "Your husband is dead. You have no income. Soon you will have no food."

His grin was sly, evil. "You know you have no other choice."

Neena backed against a large tree, trembling. "I will never marry you!" she shrieked. She flung an arm up to shield her face from his sight. "How could you even think I would want to marry you?"

"Want to?" Ahmad shoved Shazari aside. She pummeled him with uselessly small fists as he drew closer to Neena, close enough for Neena to feel his hot breath against her.

"It is completely unimportant to me what you want."

Neena was shaking violently. Her voice came out in a desperate whisper. "Then . . . why?"

He gripped a handful of her long, silky hair. "I want to own you," he said. His chest heaved. "I want your husband's daughter to know that I won."

His voice rose. "I will exact my vengeance on her by destroying your future."

Neena slumped down against the tree. Where had Shazari gone? Where had God gone?

"Let her go."

Neena's head shot up. Rashid stood behind Ahmad, feet planted, a weapon in his hand.

Shazari stood directly behind him. Her chin was up. Her eyes shot sparks. "We are not as helpless as you think."

Ahmad burst into laughter. "You think my weak little brother, who has never stood up for anything in his life, is going to help you?"

Rashid pointed the gun at his brother. "Let her go, Ahmad. You have made my life miserable since I was a boy, but I will not let you do that to them. I've had enough."

Ahmad's eyes blazed, but his gaze failed to force Rashid's submission.

Very slowly, Ahmad's hand released Neena. She rushed around him to Shazari's side. Both women huddled behind Rashid, taking small steps backward toward the path that led away from the village.

Rashid backed away with them. "I will take you away from here," he said. "I will stay with you until I am certain you are safe."

Neena, Shazari and Rashid fled the village. "We'll go to Asha," Shazari whispered to Neena. "She rescues women in danger. She will have a place for us."

"You will never be safe," Ahmad called after them. "Do you hear me, Rashid? I will find you!"

He slammed his palm into the tree, shouting words raw with hate. "No matter where you go, or how far, you will never get away from me."

STOLEN FUTURE

Part One

He looked for justice,

but behold, oppression;

For righteousness,

but behold, a cry for help.

Isaiah 5:7

KIMBERLY RAE

CHAPTER ONE

"*I* give you good price! Good price for mother of groom!"

Asha fingered the beautiful silk sari. "Ironic, isn't it, that he's speaking Bengali to me, but every time he talks to you he tries to speak in English?"

Eleanor Stephens smiled. "Well, you do look much more Bengali than I." She put her arm against Asha's, her own pale skin nearly transparent with age, a vast contrast to Asha's dark brown.

"We would like to see your best wedding saris," Eleanor told the shopkeeper in Bengali. "And I'm the grandmother of the groom, by the way." Her smile widened when the man ran off a stream of Bengali so rapid Asha had a hard time keeping up.

"What's he saying?"

"He wants to know if this will be a Western-style wedding or an Indian-style one. Traditionally, Indian brides wear red." She smiled. "And he apologized for thinking I was younger. We white people all look the same, he says."

"Red is the color of joy," the shopkeeper interjected.

Asha looked around the shop at row upon row of bright-colored saris edged with intricate embroidery. She looked toward her future grandmother-in-law. "I read somewhere that the groom's family chooses the sari, but if you don't mind, I'd really like red."

"Of course, dear." Eleanor grasped Asha's hand and gave it a warm squeeze. "That's why we are here together, so you can choose your own sari." She chuckled. "We won't be doing everything the traditional route."

The shopkeeper sent an employee into the stock room for their best red saris. Asha motioned Mark's grandmother toward a stool to sit on, then settled herself in a cross-legged position on the floor nearby.

Her mind was immediately taken back to over a year ago, sitting in that exact same position as she talked with Rani about her plans to escape a life of forced prostitution. It was a rare blessing that Rani's mother and sister in Bangladesh had welcomed her back home, but Asha missed her.

"I appreciate you being willing to come to this particular shop," Asha said.

"It was an unusual choice, I'll admit."

Asha nodded. "I know. But I got a letter from Rani last week and she asked me to come back here. She told me to go to our sari shop and remember her when I got measured for my sari blouse. She said, 'Think of me and the others to follow.'"

"I wonder why," Eleanor mused as the red saris were brought into the shop. The shopkeeper pulled the top one from the employee's arms and flung the six yards outward with dramatic flourish.

"Beautiful!" he said, holding the sari up to model it against his own body.

Asha swallowed a smile. She never would get used to men having all the jobs, even the ones in women's clothing. She reached out and touched the soft material. "I don't know why Rani wanted me to come back here. I had written her saying we—" She stopped herself. Edging toward the door to the shop, she looked outside down the narrow street. It was empty. She switched to speaking in English. "I told her I was trying to figure out some kind of strategy for rescuing girls. Every time one is ready to get out, we have to come up with a new plan. That won't work if we're to have a consistent ministry. I want to be able to do more than rescue one or two every few months."

Eleanor stood and motioned a request to see the sari in the middle of the stack. The shopkeeper quickly threw the first back toward the employee as he pulled out the middle sari. The employee struggled to hold the rest of the pile while getting the discarded sari off his head where it had landed.

"Did Rani write back with any ideas?"

"That's the thing," Asha said, also standing to better see the sari Eleanor was considering. "She didn't say a word about that. All she wrote about was how things were going, and that I should come here."

Eleanor held the sari up below Asha's chin. "This is the perfect shade of red for your skin. Kind of crimson, wouldn't you say? So you think she didn't have any ideas?"

"I don't know." Asha turned to view the sari on herself in the small, slightly cracked mirror. "I think she would have said so if she didn't. It's strange. I remember after she was rescued, she didn't want to have anything to do with coming back here. That's why I was so surprised that she asked me to come back to this particular shop, right down the road from the red-light district."

Asha looked over the rest of the pile of saris, then back toward Eleanor. "I like this one best."

Eleanor nodded, her eyes shining. "Me too."

"Let's check the others just in case." Asha asked for the rest to be shown, but kept the crimson one in her hands. "I'm so excited about this wedding—getting my hands painted and having roses all over the car. Will Mark be wearing red, too?"

Eleanor helped Asha fold the long yards of sari material. "No, he'll be in a more neutral color. My grandson will be much less elaborately decorated than you." She grinned. "You'll be decked out with costume jewelry in your hair and bracelets all up your arms, and your hands and feet and perhaps even your forehead painted with designs. And before the wedding ceremony, you'll have all sorts of people hovering over you, feeding you and pampering you to your heart's content—and then some!"

Asha held up the folded sari and considered it in the mirror again. "Sounds like fun. And what about this hol . . . this hol-loo party I've heard about?"

Eleanor laughed. "The *Gai Holud* party. That will happen the evening before the wedding. Friends and family will come and smear your face with turmeric, and—"

"Turmeric? The yellow cooking spice?"

"That's the one. People will come up one at a time, dip their fingers into a paste of the spice mixed with water, and smear it on your face."

Asha's nose scrunched up. "What for?"

"To make your skin glow for the wedding. The groom's family brings the turmeric. That is also the time you will be officially presented with your wedding sari as a gift from the groom's family. You'll be given other gifts as well. Sometimes they even bring two large cooked fish decorated like a bride and groom!"

Asha laughed. "I am going to love sending pictures of all this back to my friends in North Carolina."

A moth landed on the sari Asha held. Eleanor brushed it off. "*Gai Holud* is a fun ceremony for everyone, except sometimes the bride—which is understandable if she is leaving home to marry a complete stranger. I went to one where she cried the entire time."

Asha smiled dreamily. "Well, I won't be crying." She pictured herself walking down the aisle toward Mark. Turning to look in the mirror one last time, she said, "This is definitely the right sari."

"Let's get it then!"

Though they spoke in English, the shopkeeper could tell the choice had been made. He sent his employee scurrying to fold the other saris, while he ushered Asha and Eleanor into the small room adjoining the sari shop. "You need to be measured for your sari blouse."

"I got measured a year ago," Asha muttered in English, "but with the way they make the blouse arms so tight, if I've gained half a pound since then, I don't think I'd have any circulation in my arms."

The man opened the door and gestured her in.

"Besides," she added, "Rani told me to remember her in the little measuring room, so here I go."

She ducked through the small door into a tiny room, barely big enough for her, Eleanor, and the tailor to stand without touching. The room was conveniently placed. The sari shop faced the street near the brothel where Rani had been taken after being trafficked. The tailor shop was on the next street over. The small measuring room joined the two shops together, back to back.

The employee, with several gestures of humble apology, hunched into the tiny room. Eleanor exited the room to give more space.

Asha was remembering Rani, her eyes bright on the day she was freed from a lifetime of slavery, while the employee opened a panel in the wall and stepped inside to place the remaining red saris on an empty shelf.

Asha's eyebrows rose. She had never noticed that panel—just one of many that lined the wall. It was totally camouflaged.

And it had enough room inside for one person, maybe two if they were small.

A small, hidden room.

Camouflaged, and accessible from two directions.

Just the right size for one or two escaping girls.

"Rani, you're a genius!"

Asha clapped her hands. The tailor at her elbow, busy measuring her arms, jumped, the pins clamped between his lips dropping all around his feet, jingling against each other and onto the cement floor like the ring of a hundred miniature bells.

"Oh, sorry!" Asha started to help pick up the pins. "Mrs. Stephens—*Didi-Ma*!" She handed a few to the tailor, then rushed through the door into the sari shop to whisper, "I've got it! Rani *was* giving me an idea, and it's perfect! We're going to be rescuing more girls very, very soon!"

CHAPTER TWO

Sonagachi. The sight brought chills to nearly everyone who approached, but the feeling that crept up Ahmad's spine was undiluted pleasure. An entire city block. One massive cage of human flesh, full to overflowing with women and girls.

Ahmad focused and observed. He had to learn a great deal in a small amount of time. Rashid would arrive with Asha's mother and Neena any day now.

Fools. Ahmad snarled. Did they really think he wouldn't know they would come straight to find Asha? Rashid had not even had the good sense to steal money from their parents before he abandoned the village. They would have to walk or hitchhike all the way to Chittagong, ride the lowest-class section of the train to the capital city of Dhaka, catch a bus to the last stop-off before walking across the Indian border, then try to find another bus to get them to this area of Kolkata.

Ahmad almost chuckled. What a life Rashid had chosen for himself. And he had the gall to think it better than Ahmad's.

Well, he would pay for his choice.

Huge buildings towered over Ahmad's head as he walked. He stepped over a pile of shattered glass, the broken window above him testifying to a violent night. A woman approached from the side and touched his arm. At his throaty growl she backed away, rejoining the others in the line that stretched down the road, past building after building, as far as Ahmad could see.

He was grinning, but it was not an expression that made anyone around him feel pleasant. The women began edging away at his approach, sighing in relief when he passed by without noticing them.

At the corner of the street near a small fruit market, Ahmad stopped. What he needed was a plan. A plan both successful and shady. He needed to keep his identity a secret if he wanted to continue in the trafficking business.

And he wanted to. He could make more money here in Sonagachi than he'd ever dreamed of back in that insignificant village in Bangladesh.

This was a much better idea than the child trafficking he had been doing or even the drug dealing he was considering. Drugs could be sold only once. A human body could be sold again and again.

He would trap and sell women.

And one of the women he trapped would be Asha.

Maybe her little friend, Neena, too. The image of his brother protecting the young beauty soured deep in his gut. No, he would think of something special for her. Something that would keep Rashid's betrayal of him forever before his face.

"Stop! Wait for me!"

Ahmad looked across the street as a young girl, around ten or eleven years old, darted out into the road from the facing sidewalk. An older woman called out to her but she raced on, dashing right in front of a taxi. The driver honked loudly as the girl jumped out of the way. She laughed.

Unlike the hundred women he had just passed, her face was unpainted and her skin fresh. She wore a long shirt over baggy pants and her hair lay in strings down over her ears. She was messy and dirty, but her eyes shone.

Suddenly she was standing right next to him. "What is your name, child?"

The girl looked up and the laughter died from her eyes. Her chin went up and her eyes flashed defiance. "My mother may have to talk to men like you, but I don't."

He reached to grab her arm, but quick as lightning she stomped on his foot, hard. With a curse he bent over. He looked up to see her running down the side street at the edge of the block. In her place now stood the older woman, chest heaving from running across the street.

"What are you doing, talking with my daughter?"

Ahmad looked directly into the woman's eyes. She looked back at him, a sure sign she was no stranger to this area and its workings. In her eyes Ahmad saw anger, and fear. He could use that to his advantage.

"Pardon me," he said with mock humility. "I only wanted to know her name."

The woman looked down. Her shoulders sagged. From her faded sari to her torn handbag and unkempt hair, everything about her looked worn. Defeated. "I'm not that stupid," the woman said dully.

She walked away, not noting the intense eyes that watched to see exactly which path she took. When she was several yards away, Ahmad followed, remaining far enough behind that the woman never noticed.

He turned left after she did and found himself standing in front of yet another filthy building. Mounds of trash stood like lopsided pillars between the building and the sidewalk. Only half of the steps to the building remained, and they were rotting. A rat scampered around a trash pile, knocking it over, scurrying toward an orange peel near Ahmad's foot. Ahmad kicked at the rat in disgust. The rat, not intimidated, remained beside the orange peel, looking over at Ahmad as if in recognition of a fellow scavenger.

Ahmad stepped around the trash piles, sure to steer clear of the rat, and approached the building. He tried the door and, finding the lock rusted and broken, he pushed the door open and stepped into a hallway.

The smell inside was worse than outside. A small, skeletal woman emerged and gave a shriek when she saw Ahmad. "What are you doing here? The men don't come here! You stay on the other street—I bring the women there!"

She pushed Ahmad backward. The woman opened the door and tried to shove Ahmad out, shouting, "Are you stupid? Can't you see the line is not on this side? The line is on the other street. Go there."

She gave him one last shove, but her arm missed and she nearly fell past him out the door. Ahmad caught her by the arm, but held her away from him, as if as disgusted by her as he had been earlier by the rat.

"Are you the owner of the women in this building?" he said, his tone harsh and authoritative.

The woman was not impressed. "Of course I am. Now get out!"

"The children, too?"

The woman stilled. "There is only one child in this building. One who eats my food but brings in no money. I am going to sell her as soon as I find someone who will take her across the border. Her mother is very protective and wants to keep her off the line for good. But she's my property, not hers!"

Ahmad's lips curved into a smile again. "I think I might be able to help you. Let me talk with the mother."

"No! I get the money. You talk to me."

"You'll get the money," Ahmad said, making his way back down the hall toward the rooms. "But I do the negotiating."

"Negotiating? For what?"

"For the daughter's help with a little trap I want to set. I need to use the girl as bait. Bait for a very important, very specific prey."

CHAPTER THREE

"Well, what do you think?" Mark looked down to the silky, cocoa-colored skin of Asha's face.

She bit her lip unconsciously. "It needs a lot of work." Her eyes lit as they lifted to his. "But you're right; the location's perfect."

He smiled. "Let me show you around."

"Don't forget about us." John Stephens, Mark's father, emerged from the vehicle. "Just because you're in love and all doesn't mean you can just leave us old folks behind."

"Stop teasing." Eleanor Stephens, Mark's grandmother, gingerly stepped down behind her son, using a cane to steady herself. "Look, you're making the poor girl blush."

"Never knew a Bengali in my life whose brown skin could turn as red as yours, little lady." John Stephens chuckled as Asha's cheeks flamed even more.

"Well, maybe that's just because you don't pick on the other Bengali girls as much as you do me." Asha held her breath. Had that been disrespectful? She was still wading through this new idea that teasing could be a sign of affection.

Her future father-in-law shot out a burst of loud, uninhibited laughter. "You got me there!"

"Bravo, dear." Eleanor approached and patted her arm. "Don't let those boys gang up on you."

"Hey, I didn't say a word." Mark's hands were up in mock surrender. He grinned down at Asha. "I'm not risking making this beautiful woman mad at me."

She beamed at him until his sudden grimace brought her eyebrows high in question.

"Well, except there is something we need to talk about that I'm afraid you won't like."

Unease twisted deep in Asha's stomach. "What is it?"

Mark looked over at his grandmother, who looked over at her son. "John, don't we have church friends in this area that we have not visited in some time?" Eleanor questioned. "Why don't you and I go visit them, and leave these children to tour this facility and have their discussion in private?"

"But maybe we can help come to a solution and—"

"John, dear, when you and your future wife were courting, did you want your father's presence in your wedding discussions?"

John Stephens chuckled, his belly bouncing over his belt. "Okay, Mother. Let's go." He looked back at Mark and Asha. "We'll be back in less than two hours." He climbed into the Land Rover. "Who are we going to visit?"

Mark watched the vehicle bump away over the potholed roads before he turned to Asha. "Well, this is a pleasant surprise. A whole two hours with you all to myself."

Asha smiled. "Like a date—to a run-down, needing-work mess of a place. How romantic."

"Wait till you see the abandoned chicken coop. That'll really make you feel warm and fuzzy."

"Sure. All those warm and fuzzy feathers."

He laughed. "I know it's a mess, but I think it would be the perfect place for the second site of the Scarlet Cord."

Asha's gaze swept the area. Several acres stretched out behind the mud buildings, perfect for farming rice and other food to sustain the women, and perhaps enough to make some money to help the work of the Scarlet Cord. Standing in front of the fields, like a set of guardians, stood two mud buildings. "The one building over to the right could be a home for the girls who come to work on the farm. The smaller building to the left could house the couple who would run the farm."

"If God sends a couple out. You didn't get any interest from the newsletter you sent out in America?"

"Not yet." Asha started down the dirt path toward the chicken coop. "But I keep praying. Who knows what God will do?"

"I hope He does it soon." Mark opened the door to the coop and looked inside. He sneezed, then closed the door and grinned back at Asha. "You don't want to look in there."

They wandered back to the larger building. "The mud walls are sturdy enough, but it needs a whole new roof, not to mention doors. And windows."

"Maybe a floor?"

Mark sighed, putting a hand to the window opening. "The price is just what we'd hoped, but like you said, it needs a lot of work." He looked over his shoulder to where Asha stood. "That's what I need to talk to you about."

"I can tell." She walked toward him, slipping a hand through the crook of his arm and smiling up at him. "You keep doing that quiet, thinking thing." She squeezed his arm. "Just spit it out already."

He leaned his head down until his forehead touched hers. "Have I mentioned that I love you?"

"Not yet today." She kissed his cheek. "I love you too. Now what's the problem?"

He turned back to look out the window. "You know we need a second site for the Scarlet Cord work. There are too many girls, and more ready to come if we had a place for them."

"Mark . . ." Asha pulled on his arm a little. "I know all that. That's why we're here looking at this place. If we can rent it, more girls can be rescued. The ones who don't want to or can't sew at the Scarlet Cord can come and farm here. Hopefully in time, we'll get an income from the eggs or the chickens or the food, enough for this site to sustain itself and those who live here."

"Right."

"So where does the problem come in? Not having a couple to run it?" She grinned. "That's not a big deal right now. It would be a problem if people were ready to come since this place needs so much work."

"True. But I'd like it to be ready soon. If it were ready, and we had girls needing to stay here, maybe you and I could live here until someone came to take it over—after we're married of course." He kissed her small, round nose.

"But what about the house you're going to build for us? Off the compound?"

Mark ran a hand down the smooth length of her hair. "That's the problem. There are only enough workers for one place at a time. If we decide this site is the right place . . ." He grimaced. "I know we'd both hoped to have our own home by the wedding, but I can't do a house for us and this place too."

"Oh." Asha looked down. "I see."

She meandered through the building, then exited through the open doorway and toward the smaller mud home. Inside it, she looked around the one room and tried to smile instead of sigh. "This would be a good place to start our married life, wouldn't it? That way, wherever we moved afterward would be an improvement." She looked to where Mark stood in the doorway. "Unless you were planning to build us a bamboo shack?"

He came close to cup her cheeks with both hands and kiss her softly. "I'd build you a palace if I could." His gaze caressed her face. "Would you really be willing to live here? Just for awhile?"

Her slim hand reached up to touch light fingertips to his lips. "I love you. And I love this work. Why wouldn't I be happy to sacrifice a little for these girls who've suffered so much?"

She smiled, but then her face fell a little and Mark dipped his head to catch her gaze again. "What is it?"

She lifted her face. "You're not the only one with a tough question to ask."

Mark smiled tenderly. "So it's your turn, then. What is your worrisome problem?"

Asha looked down, biting her lip.

"Our honeymoon."

John Stephens maneuvered into a cross-legged position and helped his mother as she also lowered herself to the ground.

"My bones are getting too old for this sitting on the floor stuff," Eleanor muttered in English. She looked up when the Bengali family entered the room.

"John, I'd like you to meet Paul and Silas, and their parents." She had switched to speaking Bengali, but added in English, "The parents are Christian so the boys got Bible names instead of Bengali ones."

The two young men and the older couple behind them lifted their hands, palms together, and touched their foreheads in the usual greeting. "We welcome you to our home."

While the parents went to prepare food for their guests, the two men sat across from John. "We will be joining your work soon," the eldest, Paul, said.

"Really?" John looked to his mother.

"Indeed. These young men, along with one other, are the ones who got jobs working the night shift at the sari shop and tailor shop out near the red-light district. They will be making our rescues possible." She smiled her approval. "It's a wonderful ministry. I am so thankful for you."

John's eyebrows rose. "How did you manage to get those exact jobs in those exact places? Jobs are hard to get around here."

Silas, the younger brother, smiled wide, his white teeth gleaming against his dark skin. "When we offered to work for very low wages, it was easy to see the owner assumed we were from the country and did not know to ask for higher pay."

Paul also smiled. "He thinks he is taking advantage of us, but the advantage will be ours instead."

John laughed. "Brilliant!" He put his head down, then up in a respectful bow. "I honor you. It will be a blessing to know my future daughter-in-law will be watched over by such men as yourselves."

Eleanor's soft voice floated between them. "Please don't mind, but may I ask why you chose to do this work?"

"Not for the pay, obviously," John quipped.

Both men shook their heads. The elder spoke. "We had a cousin who was taken. She met an older boy who was not a believer. Her parents warned her. They were already arranging a marriage for her to a good man, but she went and met this other man without a chaperone. He gave her drugs."

When Paul fell silent, Silas continued. "We were very young, but we remember our family's pain when she ran away to be with him. Her heart had no room for love of family or love of God. She only wanted more drugs, and to be with this man."

"Our father and her father tried to find her, but when they searched, they found out the man had done this before to others. Many others. He promised girls love, gave them drugs, then once they were willing to run away with him . . ."

Eleanor dipped her head, looking away as Silas concluded.

"He sold them all. He sold her. Our fathers were never able to find her again."

John shifted his position on the ground and cleared his throat. "I'm so sorry for your family."

With a lift of the chin, young Silas looked more man than boy. "We will work in the shops at night, and help you rescue other girls who have been sold. Even if she might never be one of them, if we can rescue some, other families will not suffer as ours has."

The conversation ceased as the parents entered the room with snacks and tea. After eating and visiting awhile, Eleanor rose to go. "God bless you," she said, her eyes finding the two sons. "God bless you all."

"Well, it's time to get going." John huffed as he lugged his body from the ground into a standing position. "We've got to get back to pick up—"

"It was so nice visiting with you," Eleanor interrupted. "*Pore Dekha hobe.* See you later."

Outside the home, John helped his mother into the vehicle. "What was that all about?"

She gestured toward the house with her cane. "You were going to tell them that we'd left your son and his fiancé unchaperoned and alone. That in itself is scandalous here, but after their story . . ."

"Oh, hadn't thought of that." John turned the key in the ignition. "Well, if it's not appropriate, why'd you leave them alone like that?"

Eleanor had to raise her voice as they rode through the city with the windows rolled down. "They are both Americans for one. Just because they live here doesn't mean they should have to do everything the way it is done here. For another, I trust them to maintain Godly standards. And finally, good gracious, if I were planning to be married in two months, I'd certainly want a moment alone with the person I was in love with. Wouldn't you?"

John chuckled. "You're a hopeless romantic, Mom."

"Romantic, yes. Hopeless, not a chance." She stomped her cane against the floor of the Land Rover. "I'm not so old I don't remember what a good kiss feels like."

Her son laughed. "Well, then, let's get back there and see if we can catch them kissing. Sure is fun, watching that girl turn beet red like she does."

"John Stephens, you sound like an unruly teenager. I wish your wife was still here—she'd keep you in line."

John sighed. "I wish she were, too. She would have loved to be part of planning this wedding, seeing our son so happy."

Eleanor put a soft hand on his arm. "I miss her, too. And your father." She looked out the window and up into the clouds. "Maybe God will let them watch the wedding from heaven."

John chuckled. "If He does, I know Susan will be sitting up there fuming at all the things I didn't get right about the ceremony! As soon as I die, she'll be waiting to let me have it."

Eleanor laughed. "Well, we'll just have to do our best then."

John's face grew serious. "I'm glad you're still around, Mom."

She reached over and poked him with her cane. "Don't start getting all sentimental on me, boy. Makes me think I'm going to die or something. Now get a move on it so we can get back to that farm and catch those two kissing!"

CHAPTER FOUR

Mark laughed out loud. "Our honeymoon is a problem?" His eyes looked down on Asha with such love, it took her breath away. "I have absolutely no bad feelings whatsoever regarding our honeymoon."

"Oh, Mark." She stepped forward and offered herself to his embrace. His arms wrapped around her and he rested his cheek against her hair. She nestled her head into the curve of his shoulder, made perfectly for her, and sighed with contentment.

At that moment she did not care if they lived in a mud hut or a bamboo shack, as long as they were together.

Mark pulled back and looked down into her face. He lifted her chin with his hand. "So what is it?"

"It's my parents. They're coming for the wedding."

"I know."

"Both my parents are using their vacation time, but with it taking three days to get here and three days back, they will only have three or four days here."

"And?"

Asha pulled away and walked around the mud room, running a finger along the wall, watching the dust flare up and dance in the sunlight. "Well, there are ceremonies and things before the wedding that they are supposed to be here for, but then I heard that traditionally, here, the couple usually stays with the bride's family after the wedding for awhile."

"We don't have to do everything the traditional way, you know."

"I know." She wrapped her arms around herself and bit her lip. "I feel really torn, and I don't know how to say it because I don't want it to sound like I want to skip our honeymoon or—"

"Whoa, wait a minute. You don't want to skip our honeymoon, do you?"

She grinned. "You know I don't."

He wiped his brow in relief. "You had me worried."

With a playful slap at his arm, she said, "Stop. I'm being serious."

In response, he stood right in front of her, placed both hands on her shoulders, and put on his most serious face. "Okay, I'm ready."

Laughing, Asha pushed him away. "The thing is, if my parents come before the wedding, they'll get to enjoy all those activities, but we wouldn't get to spend any real time with them. And they barely know you. And we won't see them again until we go back to America six months later for the big reception they're planning for us there."

"Asha." This time Mark's face genuinely was serious. He again placed his hands on her shoulders and added a smile. "You want them to come after the wedding so we can make the most of their visit."

"I do, but I don't," she almost wailed. "I want to have an amazing, memorable honeymoon with you all to myself, but I also don't want to miss you getting to know my parents the one time they will be here." She threw her hands up. "Why does it have to take so long to get here?"

One side of Mark's mouth tipped up. "I could give you a geography lesson to answer that, but I have a feeling you wouldn't find that helpful."

She rolled her eyes at him.

"Come here, Beautiful."

Asha came. Mark leaned back against the mud wall and pulled her against him, his arms strong and sure around her. "Here's what we can do. Why don't you have them get here in time for the wedding—I know your mom wouldn't miss that for anything—and then you and I can have that first night to ourselves while your parents stay on the compound and get to know my dad and Grams and Milo and everybody. Then the next day we come back and spend time with them, and have our official honeymoon after they're gone."

She lifted her face to search his. "Really? You would do that for me?"

His eyes on hers were gentle and loving. "I get you for the rest of my life," he said. "And even though I'm counting the days till that rest-of-our-lives part starts, a few more days of waiting will be worth it to make this whole wedding experience, not just the ceremony, as beautiful and wonderful as you are."

Asha pulled away enough to get her arms free, then threw them around his neck and held tight. "Thank you," she whispered.

"So . . ." He spoke against her hair. "If we only get one night, we should go someplace amazing. Where would you like to go most in the world? Within a reasonable distance, that is." She felt his smile. "I'd take you to our banyan tree, but there's no bed or breakfast there." He pulled back to look at her. "I want it to be perfect. So tell me, where would be perfect?"

Asha was still wiping away tears that dripped over her smile. "I know it isn't possible anymore, but I had hoped that our house would be finished by the wedding so we could spend our first night there." She placed a soft palm against his cheek. "I couldn't imagine any place more perfect for us to spend our first night than in the place we will call home."

Her slim fingers pushed his frown into a smile. "But since that's out, we'll just have to think of someplace else."

"I love you, Asha. I couldn't care less if we stayed on the compound, so long as I had you." He thought for a second. "Well, actually, now that I think about it, I wouldn't really want to stay on the compound. After all—"

Her smiling lips stopped his words with a kiss. He was wrapping a hand around her waist to pull her closer when his father's gleeful voice right outside the window broke them apart.

"Hah! Caught you!" John Stephens laughed loudly and Asha was mortified to see even Mrs. Stephens giggling behind him.

"Look, there she goes!" Mark's father pointed toward the red hue creeping up Asha's neck and across her cheeks.

Mark just smiled, pulled Asha's hand into his own, then leaned down to say as they left the mud home, "We are definitely not spending our first night on the compound."

Shazari was the first to step from the bus. Neena followed, Rashid behind her.

Each walked far enough from the loud, honking beast to allow the others to disembark, but then all three stood still, staring.

The city of Kolkata. Noisy, polluted, crowded, and colorful, it was everything their quiet little village was not. People pushed passed them, crowding forward toward the ticket line, or over to a different bus. A barely clad child held out empty hands to tourists and new arrivals. Several beggars slept under the awning near the ticket counter, travelers stepping around or over them where they lay.

A man walked by. He dropped his cigarette to the ground. Another man, a beggar, picked it up and put it to his mouth.

Neena was the first to speak. "I wish we could go home," she said, her voice muted, her eyes huge as they took in this strange new world.

"Well we can't," Shazari snapped. "So no sense crying about it."

"I wasn't crying." Neena sniffed.

Rashid swept keen eyes around the area. Checking. Searching.

"What are you looking for?"

Neena's eyes, so pure and young, caused his throat to clamp up with feeling. Did she know how her beauty moved him? Did she know the purity of her soul made him want to be a better man, a man worthy of her?

"I'm—checking to see where we should go." He would not tell her he was making sure Ahmad was not nearby. Sneaking. Sulking through the shadows. Waiting to punish him.

Rashid was sure he was out there somewhere. He prayed to any and every god that Ahmad would not have figured out some way to follow them. He had checked every bus before they took it. Walked through it, even looked under the seats to make sure his brother had not somehow discovered their way and come after them.

He would not breathe securely until they were out of the city. Shazari had mentioned a place where Asha took rescued girls. A safe house, she had called it. That is exactly what they needed.

"I'm hot, and standing here is not helping any of us." Shazari's voice was tight with fatigue and worry. "Let's show somebody the address Asha wrote down and get there before it gets dark."

"Oh, but we can't." Neena's voice held anxious fear. She looked with apology toward Rashid. "What if he followed us? We can't lead him right to her! You know he hates her. He might kill her!"

"If we didn't come to find Asha, then what are we doing in Kolkata?" Shazari reached a palm up to strike the girl, then forcefully lowered it. "Sorry," she grumbled, "old habit."

"I sent her a letter," Neena said. "I sent it awhile ago. If she has received it, she knows we are in trouble. I know she will help us, but I don't want to put her in danger." Near tears, she focused on Rashid. "What should we do?"

Her face, looking up at him, was as trusting as a child, and filled him with fear. She should not trust him. She should not look at him as if he were good, and wise, and helpful. He had lived a lie since boyhood.

"Well?"

The sharp voice brought his focus from Neena's beautiful young face to Shazari's weathered and wrinkled one.

"I don't think we should go straight to Asha's compound," he said. "If Ahmad did somehow figure out where we were going, we would not want to lead him directly to her. Also, if Ahmad somehow knows where her compound is and is waiting there for us, we would not want to reveal ourselves either."

Shazari's shoulders slumped. "So what do we do?"

"Let's find a safe place to spend the night, then in the morning we'll think of a way to get a message to Asha and tell her where she can meet us. She probably has access to a car, and can take us directly to the safe house."

Neena sighed in relief. "That is a good plan. Thank you, Rashid."

He looked down at her face. *I would do anything for you*, he wanted to say. *I would give my life to protect you.*

Instead, he nodded silently. Looking around, he randomly picked a road, and led the two women, his new charges, on a route he was choosing step by step as they went, looking for a place where three homeless people on the run could safely spend the night.

CHAPTER FIVE

Asha hopped on her heels. "It's tonight, the first rescue at the sari shop. I'm so excited I can't stand it."

Mark smiled from where he lounged on the couch in his grandmother's living room. "You know you're going to need to start sending other people in to do these. You can't do them all; your face will get familiar and it will blow your cover."

"I know. But I can't miss this first one. I want to make sure everything goes perfectly."

He grinned. "Admit it. You just want to be involved."

"Hey now!"

Mark put a finger to his lips, a reminder that his grandmother was napping.

"Sorry, I forgot," she whispered, then put her hands on her hips. "Okay, you're right. I admit it. I can't stand the idea of not being part of it."

He rose. "I just want you to be safe," he said quietly.

"Tell you what." She smiled up at him impishly. "I'll wear a *burkah* tonight. It will cover me in black from head to toe and no one will be able to see me. Will that make you feel better?"

"Yes." His response was serious. "But I'd feel even better if you'd let me teach you some basic self-defense moves."

"You gave me that DVD on self-defense a week ago, remember?"

"Have you watched it?"

Her lips pursed. "Well . . . no. I was busy Skyping with my mom about wedding plans."

His eyes reproached her.

"Okay, okay. You can teach me a couple of moves." She grinned. "Can you really see me using them, though? Some guy comes up to mug me and I flip him over in the street?"

"It's not a mugger I'm worried about."

"Maybe you worry too much." She stood up on tiptoe and kissed his cheek.

His frown deepened. "Would you just humor me? Just learn the basics. If you're going on a rescue tonight, I'll feel better if you know some simple moves to defend yourself if, God forbid, you need to."

With a resigned sigh, Asha placed herself in the middle of the room, feet planted apart, waiting. "All right, Mr. Expert, show me what to do."

For several minutes, she obediently modeled the various techniques Mark demonstrated.

"Now we role play."

At this, Asha grinned. "That's the part I've been looking forward to, getting to pretend you're the bad guy and I flip you over."

She stood showing her toughest stance and Mark laughed.

"Don't mess with me." She put her fists up.

He grabbed them and kissed each one. "You make even my heart smile."

She stuck her tongue out in mock annoyance, then turned her back. "I'm ready for you, Bad Guy."

He approached from behind, wrapped both arms around her and lifted her into the air, swinging her around.

"Put me down!" She kicked and squirmed furiously.

"You're tougher than you look," he said, admiration in his voice. Setting her feet back on the ground, he planted a kiss on the back of her neck.

It was the first time he had ever done so. Asha shivered despite her feigned irritation.

"Okay, my turn," Mark said. "Now you're the bad guy. Or should I say the bad girl?"

"Your turn?" Asha huffed. "How come you get a turn when I didn't even get to—"

Before she had finished her sentence, he had kneeled, deftly knocked her off her feet, and pinned her to the floor. At her look of shock, he grinned down at her. "Guess I never mentioned I did a little wrestling during my seminary years."

She struggled to free herself, twisting her body, but to no avail. When she wrinkled her nose at him in frustration, he laughed.

"Well, I guess you get points for knowing how to sweep a girl off her feet," Asha said wryly.

Seconds passed as he looked down on her with affection. Then gradually, the air around them changed. Mark's eyes darkened, and Asha felt her breathing quicken. Blood rushed through her veins.

Though the only actual touch between them was his hands holding her wrists captive above her head as she lay flat on the floor, her whole body came alive at the nearness of him. When she sucked in a gasping breath, his eyes went to her lips, then her neck.

His head bent toward hers. Asha's flesh cried out to give in, even as her spirit whispered to flee.

His breath, ragged, was on her face. She closed her eyes as his lips ran across hers in a caress as soft as butterfly wings.

Flee . . .

Stay . . .

She whispered his name. His hands tightened on her arms.

Then suddenly, before she had a chance to beg him to leave, he was gone.

After Mark fled the room Asha lay still, almost numb, flat on the floor for several minutes, waiting for her breathing to calm and this new, frightening rush of feelings to fade.

By evening, they almost had. Right before supper, however, when Mark ushered her into his grandmother's kitchen, asking if they could talk, the moment they were alone again the emotions came flooding back. They washed over her, engulfed her.

He had approached to take her hand, but as the space between them filled with electricity, she saw him take one, then two steps back. When the entire room was between them, and each had a back to an opposing wall, Mark finally spoke.

"I don't think we should work on the self-defense stuff together any more for awhile." His voice was husky and he cleared his throat. Then he grinned. "At least not until we're married. It'd be fun to do after we're married."

Asha felt her face flame.

"I had no idea it would be this hard." He was walking toward her without even realizing it. "You know I love all of you," he said, his hand running along the kitchen counter. She watched it as he continued speaking. "I love your heart, and your mind, and your compassion for people." He grinned. "I love your spunk and your drama."

He chuckled, then heaved a deep breath. "But the fact is, I love all of you." He emphasized the word "all," and Asha felt a heat rush through her.

He looked her in the eye. "Can I speak plainly?"

She nodded mutely.

His gaze went down to his hand on the counter and he spoke as if to it. "I want you. That's just the truth." A crooked smile crossed his face. "And I know that will be a gift from God once we're married, but for now . . . um . . ."

Her toes were curling and she felt she could not get enough breath. Was this how married people felt about each other? How did they stand it?

"For now I need to keep some space between us. Some boundaries." He looked at her then and her breath escaped entirely. "I am committed to honoring God and his rules because they are for our good. And I have absolutely no doubts that we'll be thankful we followed God's way. But I can only handle so much temptation—and you are—you are—"

Asha felt her whole being responding to the look in his eyes. She gave up a silent prayer of thanks that this man, her future husband, cared more about doing what was right in God's sight than what either of them wanted.

He came close enough to take her hand. "Well, let's just say that I'll need your help." He kissed her palm. "For you are more temptation than I can handle."

Her eyes filled with love for this honorable man. A man she could trust not only to protect his own purity, but hers as well.

The sigh that escaped him sounded more like a groan. "And looking at me like that won't help a bit," he said half-teasing. He leaned in to kiss the tip of her pert nose, then backed away. "Let's plan to have a talk about what our boundaries will be," he said, taking another step away. "But in some public place, like outside or something."

Again, she nodded silently, and he turned away, opening the door leading to the dining room.

Then he stopped, turned his head back, and threw a grin her way. "Unless you want to get married, say, this weekend?"

She laughed then, feeling the tension crumble and fall all around her. "If my parents didn't already have their plane tickets for two months from now, I'd seriously consider it."

His smile toward her was all love. He quickly crossed the room toward her again, took her face in his hands, kissed her till she could no longer breathe, then found the nearest exit and took it.

Asha sighed. She felt like a blob of melted butter.

Before today, two months had not seemed like enough time to plan a wedding in India.

Now, suddenly, two months seemed very, very long.

Asha snapped the gown of the *burkah* into place over her clothing. "I'll put on the head-covering part when I'm nearly there, in the rickshaw."

Mark frowned at her.

"All right. I'll put it on now." She grinned in his direction and picked up the black veil.

"Oh, gracious me, I can't believe I forgot." Eleanor Stephens reached behind her to a small table near the door. "My dear, there was a letter for you today. It came right before I went up for my nap and completely slipped my mind since."

Eleanor Stephens handed over the crinkled, cheaply made paper. Asha dropped the head-covering and took the letter without looking up, her mind suddenly replaying what had happened while Eleanor was napping.

"Thanks," Asha squeaked out. She cleared her throat and kept her head down, knowing she was blushing. "Thanks," she said again, her voice more controlled.

She opened it and smiled. "It's from Neena!" As she read, her hands began shaking and she sank into the nearest chair.

"What is it, dear?"

Asha looked from Eleanor to Mark. "My biological father has died. They are running out of money. And Ahmad—" She choked on her distaste for the name. "Ahmad is pressuring Neena to marry him."

"Ahmad?" Mark stepped forward.

Asha stood. "Marry Ahmad—impossible!"

Eleanor sat on the couch. "Isn't he the man who stole you as a baby, the one you discovered had been trafficking children for years from your village?"

"Yes. He would be a cruel, horrible husband. Neena is very beautiful, and I can only imagine he is using their lack of money as a way to trap her." Asha started toward the door. "I have to go help them!"

Mark was reaching out for her arm when she stopped. "But I can't! I have to go do this rescue." She pivoted. "What if she's in trouble, Mark? What if he's already forced her to marry him? I need to go get them and bring them back here!"

Eleanor looked up. "Them? Neena and Ahmad?"

"No!" Asha gripped the paper hard. It crackled as her hands shook. "No, I never want to see that man again in my life. No, Neena was my biological father's wife, but my father was also married to my biological mother. Her name is Shazari. I need to go get them both and bring them here. There is no other family in the village that can take care of them. Maybe that one aunt could, but she's even poorer than they are."

"They would need passports and visas for you to bring them back," Mark reminded her.

"That's a problem," Eleanor commented.

"No, actually that is taken care of, thank God," Asha said. "Mark, do you remember the clinic near their village, the one with the nurse who got me in touch with my biological family?"

Mark nodded.

"They've been helping me get passports and visas for both my mother and Neena to come to the wedding. I know it takes awhile sometimes, so we started weeks ago. And I sent enough money for them to buy plane tickets to come, so we could use that money to bring them back here now instead." Asha frowned. "Maybe they got their passports already and that's what pushed Ahmad into threatening them."

She went to Mark, her eyes pleading. "I have to go and see what I can do to help them. They have nothing."

He gripped her shoulders and looked into her face. "Of course you do. We'll go first thing in the morning and see about getting plane tickets to get you there as soon as possible."

"The ticket places wouldn't be open at this time of night anyway, dear," Eleanor added.

"You're right." Asha lifted the head-covering toward her face, but her hands fell and the material floated down around her feet. "But what if they need help now?"

Mark stuffed his hands into his pockets, but his words reached out to her. "You're going to get tickets in the morning to go get them. There's nothing you can do until then. Right now you need to focus on this rescue. You can't afford to not be paying attention."

Eleanor walked around Mark and embraced Asha. "He's right. And in the meantime, we will be here praying—for you and for them."

Asha hugged her back. "Thank you. Okay. Yes." She looked around the room then down, picking up the head-covering. "Yes, I'll go get tickets tomorrow. Tonight, the rescue."

Her eyes lifted across the room to Mark. "See you later?"

He nodded. "You know I won't be able to sleep until you're safely back here."

Eleanor looked from one to the other. "I'll just go in the kitchen and give you two some time."

"No, that's okay," Mark said quickly. At his grandmother's surprised look, he smiled sheepishly. "I just figured out today that the Bengali idea of having chaperones is a smart one."

Eleanor's eyebrows rose further still, and Asha blushed.

He approached and took one hand from his pocket to lightly caress Asha's cheek. "God go with you." His voice was husky at the moisture that suddenly brightened her eyes. "Be safe."

She nodded once, holding his eyes with her own. Slowly, she lifted the black material and placed it over her head, tying it securely under her chin, then letting the sheer black veil fall over her face.

Now a stranger covered in black, she nodded once more before turning away from them both, leaving the sanctuary of Eleanor's home for the dangers of the night.

CHAPTER SIX

Ahmad waited across the street from a sari shop near the red-light district. Since his arrival three days earlier, he had scoped out the district, discovered and made connections with several of the higher leaders within the system, and hired two generic hit men to be ready when called upon to service his plan.

One was already busy watching Rashid and his two helpless women. Ahmad had taken fiendish pleasure in watching Rashid scan the area after alighting from the bus earlier that day, looking for him. Did he really think Ahmad was foolish enough to allow himself to be seen? With a flick of his hand, the man he'd hired was on their trail.

The hired thug followed them until they chose a place to spend the night, then reported back to Ahmad. Ahmad sent him back to guard them, making sure they remained until the morning, at the specified time when Ahmad would arrive to watch as the man followed his instructions and carried out Rashid's punishment.

He rubbed his hands together in anticipation. The fact that it was only the first part of his plan was all the more delicious.

In the meantime, the contacts he had made, and the subtle—and not-so-subtle—questioning he had done of several of the more seasoned prostitutes had led him here, to a sari shop, where a girl had once brought up a conversation about escape. A girl who later had escaped, an occurrence rare enough to be remembered.

Whether that escape had anything to do with Asha, Ahmad did not know. Thus far, as Rashid had obviously become smarter over the years and not gone straight to wherever Asha lived, it was all he had to work with for now.

This was his third night standing across the street from the shop, waiting and watching. If nothing happened tonight, he would go back to working on his initial plan. Either way, the young girl he'd found would prove helpful. Her mother had foolishly believed his promise of buying her daughter's freedom were the girl to help him do this job. Women like her were the easiest to manipulate.

Ahmad dropped his used cigarette to the ground. His gaze latched onto a young woman, perhaps in her late teens, walking toward the sari shop. Her eyes darted back and forth as she walked. For one moment, her gaze locked with Ahmad's. She crossed her arms in front of herself and darted into the shop.

Ahmad found himself smiling. Maybe his stakeout would not prove a waste of time after all. He would wait for the girl to leave the shop and then follow her. He had no taste for the seasoned kind of woman in the district, the ones who approached him with their offers. No, it was the young frightened ones that were his favorite.

And she was alone, which was very unusual. And intriguing.

He lit another cigarette and drew in a breath. Letting it out, he watched through the rising smoke as the girl spoke with the shop employee. Even her actions with that man expressed fear. Vulnerability.

Yes, Ahmad decided, flicking ashes onto the pavement at his feet. Tonight would be a good night after all.

Kochi shuddered and cast a look behind her. The man remained standing across the street. His stare was bold. His eyes looked over her in a familiar way, one that sent chills throughout her body.

She looked up at the shop worker, trembling.

His eyes were vastly different from the men she was used to encountering. They held compassion, and something like courage, as if he were trying to share some with her. A quality she desperately needed.

"I am looking for a sari," she choked out, her voice hesitant, her hands clenched. "For a special occasion."

A second employee, sitting on the floor drinking tea, set his cup down and stood. "I think we have exactly what you are looking for," he said softly. "Red is the color of joy."

"Yes." Kochi's eyes filled with tears. "Red is pretty, but I want to wear white. White and gold."

The first employee nodded to the second, who pulled a sari from the shelf. "We have one sari that might suit you." He held the folded sari toward her.

Kochi's trembling increased as she looked at the white silk sari with gold embroidered leaves in the shape of an X, or a cross.

"Is this what you want?"

Unable to speak, she nodded. Yes. Yes, she wanted this.

"We are very glad." At the voice, Kochi looked up to see sincerity in the man's eyes. Her own overflowed.

The man's eyes looked out into the street, then quickly back to Kochi. "She needs to be fitted," he said suddenly. "Please go into the measuring room now."

Ahmad dropped another used cigarette and stomped it out with a growl. His patience was wearing thin.

The girl had disappeared at least fifteen minutes ago. How long did it take to get fitted for a sari blouse?

His eyes narrowed into slits. Or was something else going on here?

Pushing his body off the wall where he leaned, he set purposeful steps toward the sari shop. He walked inside with the confident bearing that got him both deference and answers in this status-based society.

The one employee did not rush to court his favor. Ahmad felt his face flush as the man gave him a lazy smile, then turned to climb a short ladder and re-arrange an already perfectly stacked row of saris.

"Where is your other employee?" Ahmad asked pointedly.

The man did not turn. "He is busy."

"I am here." The second employee suddenly returned from the measuring room.

"I want to see that white sari you had for sale," Ahmad ordered.

Taking slow, measured steps, the first man climbed down the ladder and faced Ahmad. "We have no white saris for sale."

"Don't play me for a fool!" Ahmad spat out. "I saw you just showing a white sari to a girl who came in here. Where is she?"

The first man said, "She is being measured," while the second simultaneously said, "We have no customers right now."

Clearly flustered, the first man pulled a bright purple sari from the shelf and modeled it. "Would you like to consider this color? Very bright. Very nice."

Ahmad pushed past the man and went to the shelf where the white sari had earlier been stacked. It was gone. He pulled several saris from the stack and threw them to the ground.

With both employees protesting in the background, Ahmad stepped on the saris as he made a direct path toward the small measuring room next to the sari shop.

"Sir, no!"

Ahmad flung open the door, only to find the room empty. Another door stood opposite the one he held open. He took the three steps necessary to cross the small area and pushed on the second door.

It opened to reveal a tailor's shop. Ahmad looked around. One man sat at a sewing machine, his foot pedaling to produce the power to run the needle over the material. A woman in a *burkah* stood admiring a bolt of cloth, but her one arm remained tight against her waist, as if she were concealing something beneath her long black gown.

The woman had not turned his direction, but he knew it was not the girl who had entered the sari shop. This woman was slightly taller, her movements more sure.

Ahmad retraced his steps back into the sari shop. "Where is the girl?" he shouted.

"What girl?"

"The girl who came in here looking at the white sari!"

"We have no white saris for sale."

Ahmad was fuming. "A girl came in here. Where did she go?"

The first employee gave an indifferent shrug. "As you can see, there is no girl here. Perhaps you are thinking of a different shop."

The employee finished folding the last of the saris Ahmad had thrown down. "Good night, sir," he said, his voice even, his eyes away from Ahmad's face.

Ahmad wanted to kick something. His night had been ruined.

Both employees kept a surreptitious eye on Ahmad. They glanced toward each other as Ahmad's face slowly changed, awakened. Suddenly, he ran through the shop again to the measuring room. Yanking the first door open, he rushed to open the second door.

The man at the sewing machine suddenly began pedaling at a furious pace, focusing on his sewing and keeping his eyes down on his work.

Ahmad ran across the otherwise empty tailor shop and into the street. The woman in a *burkah* was there, helping a young girl into a rickshaw. Ahmad could not see the girl's face, but her clothing was the same color as the young, frightened girl he had intended to pursue.

The woman in the *burkah* turned full circle before climbing into the rickshaw. When her eyes neared the tailor shop, Ahmad stepped under the one street light, allowing his face to be seen.

She jerked at the sight of him, backing away. Slim hands rose to ensure her veil was in place. She practically jumped into the rickshaw.

It sped away, and Ahmad made no attempt to follow. He did not need to. A triumphant smile spread his lips.

Never mind the girl. He had found something even better.

His night had turned out good after all.

CHAPTER SEVEN

Asha stopped frantically searching for her passport and looked across the room at Stacy Richardson, the missionary nurse. "Thank you for being willing to take Kochi to the Scarlet Cord so I can go get plane tickets this morning."

"No problem." Stacy smiled. "It will be good for Dr. Andersen to have to oversee the clinic on his own for a change—will make him appreciate me more."

"Well, I'm grateful. I want to get to Bangladesh as soon as possible. I'm so thankful we'd already set things up with Pastor Hamal's wife to do the rescue tomorrow night. I had planned to go along, but now, with needing to go to Bangladesh, it works out so well that she's already—"

"Asha!"

The loud yell, Mark's voice, brought both women immediately to their feet. Yelling was unacceptable unless you were a lower-class traveling salesperson, and the fact that he yelled her first name . . . Something must be very wrong.

Asha dropped the passport she had finally found and took off at a run.

"Mark?"

She burst through the front door of her little house on the compound, then pushed the screen door forward, letting it swing outward to bang against the wall, ignoring the harsh sound as she rushed forward.

"Mark?"

A scream, full of agony, came from near the compound gate. Mark was running toward her. "Asha, they're here. He's hurt her. It's acid."

"Who is here? Who hurt who?" Asha ran after Mark, who had turned the moment she was in view to retrace his route toward the compound gate. Halfway there he stopped. Asha, panting, stopped beside him, the screaming still filling the air around them.

"You go ahead. I'll get Dr. Andersen." Mark started running to his right.

"He's at the clinic," Asha shouted after him, "but Stacy is here. She was at my place."

Mark turned again, just as Stacy passed by Asha. "Did you say acid?"

Asha watched Mark nod, then her focus went to the trio of Bangladeshis who came into view. An older woman led the way, speaking rapidly. Behind her a man, tall and slender, carried a young woman. The woman in his arms had her hands on her face. Her mouth was opened and the horrifying, tortured screams were coming from her mouth.

Neena. Dear God, what has happened to her?

Asha nearly fell to the ground when her eyes lifted from Neena's face to Rashid's. What was he doing there? On their safe compound?

"What have you done to her?"

Neena heard Asha's voice and removed the hands from her face. Asha cried out. The skin on the right side of Neena's face was burning away. Tiny pieces of searing flesh actually fell from her face to the ground. The hands she pulled away peeled skin from her cheek and ear.

"What did you do to her?" Asha's voice was rent with pain. Neena's beautiful face. It was steaming, and the smell of her burning flesh brought such a wave of nausea Asha had to fight to keep from gagging.

Stacy literally shoved her way past Asha and did a quick assessment of Neena's face and neck, holding down Neena's hands with force. "Don't," she ordered. "It will only tear off more skin."

She looked up at Rashid. "Do you know what kind of acid was used?"

"No."

"How long ago did it happen?"

"Twenty minutes maybe?" Rashid talked, his voice coarse, as they rushed Neena toward Stacy's house. "We were several blocks away. We did not want to come directly here—did not want him to know this location . . ."

Asha looked back. One glance at his face and her body went cold. Ahmad. He was here. A wave of fear flooded over her. Had it really been him standing outside the tailor shop last night?

"But we had no money left for a hospital," Shazari interjected, her wrinkled brow tight with worry. "Someone stole the rest of our money last night while we slept. We had to come here when it happened."

Neena was carried inside Stacy's house. Asha gripped her mother's arm, keeping them both outside for a moment. "What happened? Was it Ahmad?"

"We were discussing how best to contact you so you could meet us in the city and take us to your safe place. A stranger came up with a tin cup in his hand. I thought he was a beggar."

"So it wasn't Ahmad?"

Shazari shook her head. "No, but Ahmad was surely behind the attack. The man walked straight up to Neena and threw the cup full of acid in her face."

Asha felt her hands involuntarily come up to her own cheeks.

Shazari opened the door to enter the home. "She had just turned to say something to me. If she hadn't, the acid would have covered her entire face. Her eyes."

A shriek of pain came from inside. Asha and Shazari hurried in. Asha looked inside the bedroom, but Stacy's bed lay empty.

The sound of running water brought her search to the bathroom. Stacy and Rashid held Neena down in the bathtub, running water over the right side of her face.

"I need to get my supplies," Stacy spoke back to Asha. "Come hold her down."

Asha stood in the doorway, stock still. She wanted to help, but could not get her body to move one step closer to the man who partnered with Ahmad to steal her as a child. How much responsibility did he hold in Neena's attack? Now that he was on the mission compound, were they all in danger?

Stacy sent a pointed look from Asha to Rashid. When Asha's eyes followed her gaze, she saw tears streaming unheeded down Rashid's cheeks as he helped hold down the thrashing young woman.

"Move!" Shazari elbowed Asha aside and went forward to do Stacy's bidding. "Tell me what to do."

"You must keep this water running over the burned skin until I return with my supplies," Stacy instructed Shazari and Rashid. "Do not change the temperature. The water must be lukewarm—cold or hot water would do more harm than good at this point. We must keep the water running over her skin for ten to twenty minutes."

"Will she die?" An ache spread through Asha at the heartbreak in Rashid's voice.

Mark entered, filling the small bathroom to capacity. He subtly touched Asha's hand. She backed away from her hypnotized stare at Neena's mutilated face.

Stacy joined them in the hallway, indicating they follow her. As they walked, Mark's voice was low for Asha's ears alone. "No matter what his past, he wouldn't have had any part in this."

"How do you know for sure?"

Mark looked over at her. "Asha, if you had seen him kick open the gate, carrying her, yelling desperately for help, you'd know."

Asha swallowed her doubts rather than voice them. Mark always believed the best in people. But Ahmad's brother turning into a good man? What if he was just really good at acting his part?

Stacy had them gather gauze, surgical tape and sterilized tools. The sight of a pair of medical scissors for cutting away skin had Asha fighting nausea again.

"Please set all of this up next to my bed," Stacy said, her voice as brisk as her stride back to the bathroom. Asha heard her speak to Rashid.

"I'm sorry I forgot to answer your important question." The water kept running. "From what I can tell, the acid—though it covered her right cheek, ear, neck and part of her forehead—I think it missed her eye, and it does not appear that any of it went into her mouth where more extensive damage would occur."

"Thank God." Mark had deposited his supplies and stepped into the bathroom to stand beside Rashid. "She will live."

He put a hand on Rashid's shoulder and with a voice strong and confident he thanked God for sparing Neena's life, and he asked God's help as they treated her wounds.

Asha watched all of this from the hallway, her arms still full of gauze, her heart filled with fear and pain. She, too, thanked God for saving Neena's life, but what would happen to her now?

And with Rashid's presence on the compound, and Ahmad's presence somewhere in the city, what would happen to them all?

CHAPTER EIGHT

The right side of Neena's face was covered in dampened gauze taped onto undamaged portions of her skin.

Asha had not been able to watch as Stacy cut away at the seared, tearing pieces of flesh on her dear friend's swollen face.

Fleeing the room, the sounds of Neena's pain, Asha ran down the hallway and outside to sit on the front porch steps, putting hands over her ears and hiding her face into her raised knees.

Shazari sat beside her and Asha lifted tear-stained eyes to her biological mother. "How could anyone do such a terrible thing?"

Shazari's voice was surprisingly gentle. "Unfortunately, it is a common crime in our part of the world."

"Common?" Asha ran a hand under her nose to wipe it. "But why? Why would anyone do something so . . . so hideous?"

"Usually it's a man bitter because a woman has rejected him. I suppose he decides if he can't have her, he will destroy her beauty and no one else will enjoy it either."

Asha's hands, still against her ears, clenched into fists. "That is evil. It is sickening. It makes me want to . . . want to . . ." She left her sentence hanging, anger leaving no room for more words.

Shazari's head hung low. "All my hopes for us are gone. Neena's beauty gave us a chance that a man of means might want her for his bride. Were that to happen, I know she would have taken me in with her. Now we are both destitute." She grimaced. "Even our rescuer has nothing, except courage."

"Did he really stand up to Ahmad to protect you?" Asha lifted her head to see Mark stride toward them.

"He did. It was fortunate that he already had a passport. We were able to leave the village together after Ahmad—" Shazari stopped when Mark came close enough to hear. She flung a hand in his direction. "Has this man with sunshine hair made you his bride yet?"

Asha blushed and almost smiled. Neena's cries had calmed and Asha's insides were beginning to uncoil. The medication Stacy administered must finally be helping. "Soon. In two months."

"Hhmph. Should have been two weeks ago, if you ask me."

Asha dried her tears. "I think I agree with you." She smiled at Mark. "But we have to plan a wedding, and my father has to come out to give me away."

"Give you away? Your dowry is what he is giving away. Of course, your American parents are rich and can afford the high dowry an American man would surely require."

"No dowry is required." Mark's words were for Shazari but his gaze was for Asha alone. "She is a priceless treasure. A gift from God to me, far better than any money."

Shazari snorted. "Would God had sent such a man to love Neena and desire no dowry, for I have none to give, and her parents certainly have none to pay a second time." The aging woman sighed and spoke, her eyes down on the ground at their feet. "My daughter, your father is dead, probably from all those years of smoking cigarettes instead of selling them. He left us with only enough to pay off the debts in his store. We sold the store to get food for awhile, but it did not last. If you had not sent us money for plane tickets, I do not know what we would have done."

Asha wanted to hug the grieving woman, but knew it was not the Bengali way. Instead, she wrapped her hand around the work-hardened arm. "Did he . . . did he ever accept Jesus before he died?"

Shazari's eyes lifted, looking past both Asha and Mark. "I do not know." Her voice became unusually soft. "We never spoke of such personal things." She turned to Asha. "However, I heard from the village elders that, as he lay dying, he told the elders everything. He confessed to allowing you to be taken, and that Ahmad was the man who had taken you and the other babies. The villagers were deciding what to do about Ahmad when he started pursuing Neena."

Mark frowned. "Maybe he thought if he married into your family, the village would let him stay."

Asha's frown was even deeper. "Or maybe he just wanted to make you both miserable."

Shazari's head tossed to the side in agreement.

Asha sighed and rose. "I should go see if Stacy needs any help."

"I'll go, too." Shazari also stood.

Mark held the door open for them, speaking to Asha. "I told the girl you rescued last night that our trip to the Scarlet Cord was going to be delayed awhile. She was pretty scared with all that yelling. I found her hiding in your closet."

"Oh!" Asha's hands flew up to her cheeks. "I forgot about her, the poor girl. Thank you, Mark. I'll talk with her soon and let her know we'll leave for the Scarlet Cord when we can. With Ahmad out there somewhere, we should take Neena and my mother there as soon as possible—maybe late tonight when it's least likely he'll be watching." She shook her head and walked into the house. "I'm having such a hard time believing this day is really happening. Neena . . . and my biological father dying . . . Ahmad . . ."

Rashid stepped into the hallway.

"And him being here."

Mark spoke softly behind her in English. "I'm certain he means you no harm."

"I want to believe you. I just . . ." Asha bit her lip. She slipped quietly into the bedroom and looked down on Neena's bandaged face. Rashid and Stacy were speaking in the hallway, so Asha turned and implored Mark in English, "Please, could you keep him here or somewhere while I take my mother and Neena and Kochi to the Scarlet Cord? I don't want him there."

"Don't you think he has the right to be near Neena as she recovers?"

Asha's brows came together. She touched Neena's hand on the bed. "Right? I appreciate that he helped, but I just can't focus with him around. It brings up too many questions. And I don't want him knowing where the Scarlet Cord is, just in case."

Mark stood at Neena's bedside and considered Asha's words. "Well, there was a trip to several villages I'd planned to take in a few weeks. I could go now and take Rashid with me, if he were willing to go."

"Would you? That would be great."

Mark half-smiled. "You're excited to get rid of me already? We're not even married yet."

Asha started to reach for Mark, but dropped her hands as Shazari, Stacy and Rashid entered the room. Stacy started explaining to Shazari how to change Neena's bandages and clean her wounds.

Backing away from the bed slightly, now whispering as Neena had fallen into a fitful sleep, Asha turned to Mark. "You know I'll miss you terribly. But right now I feel like so many people need me. I want to get Neena and Kochi, and my mother, to the Scarlet Cord safely and help them begin to heal."

"No time for your future husband already," Mark teased, then at the distress on her face, his voice softened. "I understand. And it will actually be a good thing to have Rashid along on this trip. I could use his help, if he'll go."

"How long will you be gone?" Asha asked as Stacy herded them all from the room so Neena could rest.

"Likely only three to four days. Several villages in an outlying area started a new discipleship program and I want to check and see if they need any help with resources or more curriculum or anything."

When Rashid joined them on the porch, Asha backed away. Mark compensated by filling the space with himself, leading Rashid away to speak privately.

Stacy took in a deep breath. "She'll sleep for awhile now. I gave her a sedative. Acid burns cause excruciating pain and will scar her for life. She will have a difficult healing process, and I don't just mean her face."

Asha felt tears filling her eyes again. "I think . . . I think I'll just go stand outside her room and pray. Poor Neena. Poor beautiful Neena."

Stacy grasped her arm as she passed. "She has beauty beyond her looks. You will need to teach her that in the days ahead."

Shazari surprised Asha by linking her arm through Asha's. "We will go and pray together." Her smile was a flicker of light in the darkness. "I feel like all is hopeless, but I am learning that at just the times like these, the Creator God of your Holy Book loves to come through and do something amazing."

"Yes." Asha's throat clamped up. "Yes, that's true." They stepped inside the house, toward Neena's pain. Asha's heart had been praying for her friend since she had received Neena's letter. Now she added a prayer for herself. *God, increase my faith.*

CHAPTER NINE

Dapika winced at the grip on her arm. They were walking toward a small, bright green baby-taxi, called an auto. She did not know their destination and dared not ask.

She had never been more than a block from the tiny room she and her mother shared in Sonagachi. Her mother had never allowed her to wander far, worried something bad would happen.

Now her mother thought their problems were solved. Dapika knew better. She had watched the line and its workings for years. She could tell when a man felt ashamed or emboldened, secretive or power-hungry. Her mother never noticed such things, but Dapika had time for awareness.

When the man with angry eyes came into their room to talk with her mother, Dapika recognized him immediately. He was the one whose foot she had stomped on several days earlier. He was the one with eyes full of the kind of energy that enjoyed hurting people.

Dapika's mother believed his promise that he would buy Dapika's freedom if she helped him do a job. It was a foolish, simple hope. Perhaps her mother believed it because she had no choice either way.

By the time the auto arrived at the large metal gate, Dapika had been well instructed. She stepped down from the auto across the street from what the man called a compound. Dapika had never heard the word, but could tell it was a place closed-in by a tall concrete wall. It was small. Miniscule compared to Sonagachi. Only a few houses would fit inside the space.

Finding a tree to hide behind, Dapika waited as the auto sped away. She felt no regret seeing it go. The angry man in charge had hit another man in the taxi, yelling at him for falling asleep the night before and not seeing which direction the people had gone.

Dapika did not know to whom he referred, and did not care. She only knew her own instructions: find a way into the compound, tell her story, and convince someone to get a message to a woman named Asha.

Reaching down, the young girl rubbed handfuls of dirt onto her already dirty clothing and hair. She ran across the street and banged on the gate.

A Bengali man opened it and Dapika spoke in the breathy, rushed tones of distress. "Help me, please! I came from the red-light district. I need help!"

The man gave a quick look left and right, then pulled her inside the gate and closed it behind her. "What are you doing here? How do you know this place?"

Dapika cast a look around. Small homes in a U shape filled the enclosed area. Everything was clean. There was even a playground. It was a paradise.

She ignored the sudden hunger to run, to play, to be free, and tried to sound frightened. "I need to talk to Asha!"

A boy about her own age came toward her, deftly working a crutch and his one foot in a rhythm that told her he had been using the crutch for years. Just a boy; he was useless. She turned back to the adult. "I must see Asha! I don't have much time!"

"Why do you want to see Asha *Didi*?" the boy asked.

Dapika had no time for his curiosity. She remembered the moment when the man took her from the room with a rough hand on her arm and whispered as they walked from the building, "You will do what I say, exactly as I say, or your mother will suffer for it."

Dapika was certain if she did not do this man's bidding, he would kill her mother. It was easy enough to do in the red-light district. It happened when certain people were not obeyed, and the police refused to get involved in such inner workings of the district. Why bother? For every woman who disappeared, another girl soon took her place.

She had to do this job. Once done, Dapika knew he would not give her freedom. He would sell her. Men like him were predictable in their ambitions.

However, once she was sold, her mother would be safe.

Her mother would grieve when she realized the truth. But it had to be done. Dapika loved her too much to let her mother pay the ultimate price for a freedom her child would never know.

"I said, why do you want to see Asha *Didi*? I'm Milo, by the way." He looked her over. "You put that dirt on yourself on purpose. Why?"

Dapika felt the hairs on her arm stand up. "What are you talking about?"

"There are handprints that run down your shirt. It's okay," he grinned. "I used to do that, too. It got me a lot of free ice cream."

"Ice cream? Who cares about ice cream at a time like this?" Dapika let frustration fill her voice. "A man is going to sell me and my mother. I have to get help. I need to talk with Asha."

The man looked worried. The boy's eyes narrowed with wariness. "How did you know her name?"

"I just need to talk to her, okay?"

The boy came closer. Dapika put her head down so he could not look into her eyes. She had not expected to meet a street kid. They were smart.

"She isn't here," he said. "She left last night. But maybe you already knew that?"

Now he was very close, scrutinizing her. The man had disappeared somewhere.

Dapika felt panic rising. She had to do her job and get out of there. "Can you give her a message? Tell her I need her help?" Taking a deep breath, she lifted her face, now schooled into what she hoped was a look of honesty. "To be truthful, I was sent here by someone who wants to stop the work you all do here. The man beats me and has threatened to kill my mother. But I want to talk to Asha in person, so I can ask for her help to get away from him. I want to escape, so he can't control us any longer." She squeezed a fake tear from one eye and bit the edge of one fingernail. "It's so awful. You just can't imagine how awful he is."

Putting her head into her hands, she began sobbing, making her shoulders shake, peeking with one eye through her hands to see if it was working.

The boy's face changed from suspicion to concern. "You promise you're telling the truth?"

She choked down a cynical laugh. Her world was one filled to overflowing with lies and deception. He must have been off the streets for awhile to have forgotten so much. "I promise."

The man was coming back toward them, accompanied by an old woman whose skin was very pale. Dapika stared. She had never seen a white woman before. "Is that Asha?"

The boy laughed. "Of course not, I told you she wasn't here."

They were coming closer. Something about the woman's eyes seemed to see inside Dapika, seemed to already know her deception. "I have to go," she said quickly. Turning to Milo, she added, "Tell Asha I know about the sari shop rescues. The last woman that got rescued—I overheard her talking about it. I have to get back before they realize I'm gone and beat my mother, but my mother and I will both be able to get away two weeks from Tuesday. We will come to the shop that night, at nine o'clock."

She backed away and opened the gate, avoiding looking at the white woman again. "Tell her it is our only chance. And it has to be Asha who comes. I won't go with anyone else. I don't trust anyone but her."

The boy was asking more questions. The white woman was coming still nearer. Dapika slipped through the gate, shutting it behind her.

By the time the gate had been reopened and the faces of the man and woman appeared, Dapika had disappeared around the corner. She watched the adults look around, speak with one another, then step back into their safe, clean, perfect world.

Had they believed her? Would they get the message to Asha?

Dapika sank to the ground, waiting for the auto to return and the men to take her home. To a place that would only be home for two and a half more weeks.

Two and a half weeks until she betrayed another into slavery, as well as herself.

CHAPTER TEN

*R*ahab greeted the new arrivals to the Scarlet Cord. "I'm so happy you have come. Welcome to our home. This is a place of healing." The woman looked from Neena's bandaged face to Kochi's vulnerable one. "All kinds of healing."

Asha finally felt she could breathe easy. They had snuck out in the middle of the night like thieves. Now as the sun rose over the small collection of mud dwellings, across from lush green fields and resort-worthy palm trees, Asha felt the peace sink into her soul. Getting outside the city, back to where all that surrounded them was natural and good, took away some of the tension Asha had felt building in her since the moment after the first rescue, that night she thought she had seen Ahmad.

Had it really been him? How would he have known she would be there that night? It was impossible. Even if Rashid had come to betray them, he had not known of her rescue that night. No one had known except the believers involved, and Kochi, the rescued girl, and she certainly had little reason to give away such important information.

"I am Rahab, a woman once trafficked into the red-light district, now freed." She smiled softly. "From the district, and from the fear and pain of my memories."

Kochi, the newest arrival, looked at the swell beneath Rahab's sari. Rahab noticed and her smile increased. "Yes, I am with child." Her gaze drifted to a man working in the field behind the main building. "God sent me a man who looked beyond my past and saw me. By his love I came to see an even greater love, one that has given me healing from all my past, forgiveness for those who hurt me, and hope for my future."

"You mean the love of Jesus," Shazari said.

"I do." Rahab led the way to the main building. "Please come in and enjoy some tea before we get you settled. We have several other rescued women here right now. I hope you do not mind sharing your room with more than one person."

Shazari chuckled and gestured toward where Neena remained lying across the back seat of the vehicle. "This child and I shared a one-room hut with our husband for years. These large rooms with no holes dripping rain will be a luxury for us, no matter how many people occupy them."

Stacy alighted from the driver's side and opened the back door. "Let's get her inside. She is still heavily sedated. I did that to help with the pain, and hopefully give her body more chance to heal as she rests."

A group of women congregated at the entrance to the building as they carried Neena inside. Whispers followed them.

"What do you think happened to her?"

"She was probably beaten."

"No, those bandages only cover her face and neck. If she'd been beaten, it would be her whole body."

"I bet it was acid."

"God help her if it was."

Asha felt tears sting her eyes as they gently settled Neena onto a bed in one of the rooms. Shazari wanted to stay with her, so Asha chose the room next door, motioning for Kochi to join her. "We'll stay here."

Kochi hesitantly entered. "Thank you for bringing me here," she said softly. "I have prayed so long to be free. Now it is hard to believe I really am."

Asha smiled. "That is why we brought you here, away from the city. This is a good place to learn how to be free in your heart, not just your body."

"And I want to learn of this Jesus who loves, as well."

Again, tears came. "Kochi," Asha said, "there is nothing I would enjoy sharing with you more."

Stacy got Neena settled into her room and gave explicit instructions for her care before she drove the vehicle back to the compound.

The following morning, when Stacy pulled into the driveway of the Scarlet Cord site again, several occupants peeked out their windows in surprise.

"Why would she return so quickly?" Shazari puzzled.

"Oh, I forgot!" Asha exited the building to welcome the new arrival. "We had another rescue scheduled for last night. It slipped my mind with everything else that happened. Lord willing, there should have been two women rescued this time."

The small group gathered outside the door as the car stopped and Stacy once again stepped into view. In her usual straightforward manner, she skipped pleasantries and got right to the point. "Only one made it. Pastor Hamal's wife told me to tell you the other girl never showed up. I guess she couldn't get away."

Another door opened and Asha felt her eyebrows go up. A stunning beauty stood before them. Her eyes were rimmed with coal-black liner, her lips deep red. Bracelets lined her arms and a jewel decorated her forehead. She had a well-curved body, topped by a heart-shaped face with high cheekbones and perfectly proportioned features. Her gold sari suggested wealth and position.

"W-welcome," Asha began, suddenly at a loss. She was used to seeing victimized, traumatized girls in need of a good bath and much comfort. This woman, standing tall, eyebrows arched as she observed them all, seemed neither victimized nor in need of comfort.

The others must have felt the same way for they subtly retreated in silence, almost as if backing up in the presence of a queen. Only Rahab seemed able to see a person in need behind all the glitter, and she walked forward with grace and her ever-present aura of peace. "Welcome to the Scarlet Cord," she said, her voice full of dignity. "We praise the Creator God for giving you freedom from slavery and sending you here to us."

Silent, the woman looked over Rahab's cotton sari down to her well-worn sandals. Her gaze traveled over the others, all clothed simply, all without makeup or other adornments, ending finally with Asha, who had the sudden urge to curl her toes away from the scrutiny of her own feet, which were bare.

"I am Amrita."

They all nodded, but no one spoke. Finally, Rahab approached and took the woman's arm. "Please come in. We were just about to have our morning tea. Come and let's all introduce ourselves."

Settled onto mismatched chairs and wicker couches, in a room which had previously seemed more than adequate, Asha looked at the new arrival over the rim of the teacup she had lifted to her lips.

Neena, with Shazari's help, shuffled out to join them, still weak from the sedative.

"Neena!" Asha made room on the couch. "I'm so happy to see you up. How are you feeling?"

"It hurts," Neena admitted. "Every place the acid touched, it felt like someone had lit a fire on my skin, but now it is not as bad as at first. I am thankful it was not worse."

"What happened?"

Heads turned toward the new voice. Amrita sat ramrod straight on the edge of a wicker chair, as if it would taint her to sit any farther on it.

"Acid," one of the girls answered.

The woman's face hardened. "You should have kept your customers happy. How will you make money now that you are ruined?"

Asha felt her own gasp join several others. Neena whimpered and turned the bandaged side of her face away.

"We speak of what is good here." Asha looked to see that it was Rahab who gave the gentle reprimand. "In this place, we think and speak and focus on what is true and lovely and good."

"What is true is often not what is lovely and good," came Amrita's retort. "What is true is that we make our living off our beauty. The more beautiful we are, the more comfortably we live."

"But that life is over. Here we—"

"For you it may be," the woman interrupted, rising and facing them all. "I may as well say this up front. I have no intention of becoming one of your little converts and being happy wearing old, faded clothes and no makeup and doing whatever it is you do around here . . ."

"They sew, and make money from what they sew." Kochi reiterated what she had learned upon arrival, options which before had seemed like heaven compared to life in the red-light district. "And they are going to start a farm, where some of us can go and help grow food, or take care of chickens, or—"

"I will do nothing so degrading and low as caring for chickens." Amrita's sneer kept them all in silence, waiting for whatever she would say next. "I escaped because I was tired of making money for the madam rather than myself. However, I am still young and very beautiful, and I can make enough money from my beauty to live in comfort—not like you are living here."

"We have everything we need here," Rahab said. "God provides."

"You don't have everything I need." The woman looked around the room with disdain. "I will stay here only long enough for my madam to give up looking for me. Then I'm going back to start my own business. I will be the one in charge. And I will be rich."

Even Rahab had nothing to say to that. She held her hand to her growing belly and sank into the nearest chair.

Amrita set down her teacup. "Where is my room?" she asked regally.

Asha lifted her own teacup to her mouth again, mostly to hide her face. What had they gotten themselves into?

CHAPTER ELEVEN

Dapika wrenched free, but the man with hate in his eyes grabbed her arm again. "Stupid child!" He swung a hard arm and backhanded her. "I told you to say one week from Tuesday!"

"I thought you said two weeks from Tuesday!" Dapika cowered and acted like the slap had badly hurt. She knew he had said one week, but had chosen to give herself seven more days with her mother. The good feeling of outsmarting the deceiver was worth the surface pain he inflicted. "Don't hit me again!" she wailed, using a childish voice and covering her face with her hands.

He released his grip and she scurried out of the taxi and bolted toward the front door of the building. Her mother would be inside, waiting for her. Dapika would tell her that all went well. That two weeks from Tuesday she would do a job for the man, then she would be free.

And each day until then, she would pretend it was true.

Stacy pulled Asha aside after tea. "I have something we need to talk about, alone."

"No kidding." Asha walked with her through the hallway toward the rooms. "What are we going to do about this woman? How are we going to train and help the other girls, especially Neena, with her presiding over them all, making them feel frumpy and plain and—"

"Wow, she got to you already, didn't she?"

Asha looked down at her own second-hand shalwar kameez and bare feet. "I have always felt so free here, to just be me, that I didn't have anything to prove. I don't want that feeling to leave this place because she's in it."

"Well, people come here because they are in need. Maybe her need just comes in a different package."

"A very trumped up, painted sort of package."

Stacy leveled a knowing look at Asha. "Feeling threatened by her?"

Asha slowed her steps. "You know, I am. And to be honest, a little jealous. I've tried to stop spending money on new clothes or makeup since I began working with these girls, and I've missed getting to dress up and look nice."

"Why don't you anymore?"

"I guess, for one, I feel guilty spending money on such frivolous stuff when there are so many needs, and for another, I didn't want anything that reminded them of their past life, or that made them feel their worth was in their looks."

"Well, those are all good reasons, but you're a woman about to be married, and I don't think there's anything wrong with wanting to look good in general. I know for certain there's nothing wrong with wanting to look good for your husband."

"I probably have been going kind of overboard." Asha blushed with a self-conscious shrug. "I tend to do that when I decide to change something."

"Well, don't let the new girl intimidate you." Stacy continued walking and Asha matched her steps. "They all have hidden wounds, and some are better at hiding them than others. Some hide them by becoming hard and cynical, or by acting better than the rest." Stacy sighed. "Sonagachi is such a terrible place. I've heard there are parts of it where the women don't even get to sleep at night; they only get to take naps when there's no . . . work."

Asha shivered. "I've heard that too, but I was hoping—"

They heard a sound and both turned to see Kochi behind them. Her eyes were moist. "Unfortunately, that is another one of those things that is not lovely or good . . . but is true."

She passed between them and moved on to her room. Asha was wiping a tear away when Stacy spoke again. "That reminds me—the minute I got back to the compound, Milo came hurrying up and said he had an important message for you. He was very insistent."

Asha forced herself to stop envisioning Kochi's world and instead think of Milo, which made her smile. "He's such a little man now. I love how he's always finding ways to help."

"Well, this one is pretty important. He said some girl, a young girl about his age, came to the compound and insisted on seeing you."

"On seeing me?"

"She called you by name."

Asha pulled them farther into the hallway. "What did she want?"

"Milo said she told him she had overheard a woman talking about your rescues in the sari shop and—"

"Oh no! It was such a great setup. Now it's compromised!"

"Hold on. Before you jump to conclusions, let me finish. She said some guy was trying to use her to stop the work you do."

Ahmad. Just the possibility had Asha rubbing her arms at the sudden chill that overtook her.

Stacy continued. "But she says she wants for her and her mother to escape this guy and get away, and the only person she trusts is you. She said she and her mother can get away two weeks from Tuesday—"

"Today's Friday, so that would be two and a half weeks from now," Asha calculated.

"—and she said she and her mother were coming to the sari shop at nine o'clock that night."

"Well, if she's planned to escape him then he must not know about the sari shop." *If Ahmad is behind this girl's plan, he couldn't have been the guy at the tailor shop that first night. What a relief!*

"I guess not. But she said she wouldn't go with anyone else but you. She didn't trust anyone else."

"That makes sense. So many of them who have tried to escape get double-crossed and end up paying dearly for it. I don't blame her for only trusting the one name she knows."

Stacy checked her watch. "I've got to get going. So what are you going to do?"

"Well, I guess I'm going to plan to be back in the city by two weeks from Tuesday so I can rescue a little girl and her mom. Did you get her name?"

"I think it was Dapika."

"Dapika. I'll go write that down. Hopefully by then Neena and my mother will be settled, and who knows, maybe our newest arrival will have toned down a little by then."

Stacy laughed. "If I believed in luck, I'd wish you some."

Asha smiled. "We're going to need more than that."

"You're right." Stacy waved on her way back toward the front door. "I'll be praying for you."

"Bye!" Asha waved back. As she heard Stacy's car pulling away, she wished she had thought to ask if Mark had gone to the village yet and if Rashid had joined him. Was Mark missing her as much as she missed him already? Maybe she would dress up the next time she saw him. Maybe they could even plan some time together—a real date in the city.

Sighing, Asha stared at the pictures of rescued girls along the hallway wall as she thought through all that would need to be done in the next two weeks. Help Neena's wounds to heal. Find the right work for her and Shazari at the Scarlet Cord. Do the same for Kochi. And . . .

Turning with a resigned sigh, Asha took determined steps back toward the main room. She needed to let Amrita know she could stay, but only if she was willing to pitch in and help. A vision of her face as she mentioned chickens made Asha wish the farm was up and running, but then she caught herself. That was petty.

Entering the main room, Asha heard Amrita telling the others what kind of room she required for her stay. She felt herself gritting her teeth.

All pettiness aside, maybe a little floor cleaning would be a good way for Amrita to start her life there at the Scarlet Cord. And while she cleaned—if Asha could get her to do it—Asha would need to do some praying herself.

"I don't know about you, but I've had enough of village life for awhile," Mark joked as they jostled over the dirt roads in the Land Rover. He looked over at Rashid, then remembered Rashid had lived in a village his entire life. He winced. "I'm sorry. That was a thoughtless thing to say."

Rashid just shrugged and smiled. "That second village would make anyone want to get back to the city. All those people catching malaria."

"I know. I need to remember as soon as we get back to the compound to send a bunch of our medication to treat malaria, as well as the pills we take to keep from getting it."

"You shouldn't have given yours away, you know."

Now it was Mark's turn to shrug. "It may keep one or two of those kids from catching it."

Rashid shook his head. He looked straight ahead, his face solemn. "I wish you had been my brother."

Mark looked over, then brought his eyes back to the road when they hit a deep pothole. "That's about the nicest thing anybody's ever said to me," he said seriously. "Thank you." Then he smiled. "But you know, we actually are brothers now."

Rashid's face lit up. "That's right. At every village we stopped at, you told about Jesus, and what He did for us. I had heard this from Shazari and from Neena as we rode the bus to Kolkata. My heart wanted to believe it then, but I was afraid. When you spoke at the village where people were dying of malaria, my fear of dying without God was bigger than my fear of asking God's forgiveness."

"And when you did, God accepted you as His child, and we are now brothers in God's family."

Rashid's laugh held genuine joy. "Though we do not look like brothers."

Mark caught a glance of his blond hair in the rearview mirror. "That is very true. But just the same, I am honored to be your brother."

"The honor is mine." Rashid looked out the window. "No one should be honored to be brother to me."

"The Bible says when God accepts us, He makes us new creatures. The old is passed away and all things become new. You aren't your past, Rashid. Not anymore."

"Praise God." Rashid's voice was quiet. Then he raised his voice. "I wish to start a new life. I want to remain here in India, to get honest work, to become a man worthy to be a husband and father."

Mark felt his lips spreading into a grin. "Got anybody in mind you'd like to be a husband to?"

Rashid was silent so long, Mark almost apologized for his teasing comment. Then Rashid spoke. "You are my brother. I will tell you my secret. My heart walks with Neena. My soul longs for her gentleness and goodness."

"Does she know how you feel?"

Rashid's face turned to stone. "She must never know. After what my brother did to her, every time my eyes see her face, I feel the pain of all the suffering my family caused her. Pain I caused her by not rescuing her sooner. Not being smart enough to keep her safe from Ahmad."

"You can't blame yourself for what Ahmad has done. It wasn't your fault. You were trying to help them and do the right thing."

"Perhaps you are right that I should not blame myself. But I can never allow myself to show my love for Neena after what has happened. She surely hates me as much as she hates my brother."

"Hmm, I think I'll start praying about that."

"Praying about it?"

"Yes. Now that God is your Father, you can talk to Him about anything that bothers you or that you care about and He will listen and help."

"I am not worthy to ask for anything from Him."

Mark swerved around a herd of goats. "No one is. That's why grace is so amazing."

"I would learn more of this grace."

"Sure, but first let me ask you this: If you could have the life you really wanted, what would it look like?"

A cow that had been meandering alongside the road suddenly decided to cross, and Rashid grabbed hold of the dashboard when Mark slammed on the brakes to avoid hitting the lumbering animal. He looked out over the fields. "I would be a farmer. I would live on a farm, with Neena as my wife, raising our children to follow God and do good to others. We would help people in need." He turned to look at Mark. "My biggest dream would be to help rescue people who have been sold, to make up for all those years I was silent as my brother sold others."

Mark's eyebrows came together. "Are you thinking this as a way to somehow earn forgiveness or something?"

"No. I know God has forgiven me. But I spent so much of my life doing nothing, I want to spend the rest of it doing good, helping others. I think this is what God wants also."

"Wow." Mark thought for a moment. "Hey, Rashid, before we go pick up Neena and Asha's mother, I have a place I'd like you to see. Would you mind if we stopped there first?"

Rashid looked over the area Mark and Asha had chosen as the second site for the Scarlet Cord work. His eyes feasted on the acres of land as if looking at a precious treasure. "You will use this place for rescued women and children?"

"Yes. They can farm and raise chickens and whatever else we can think of. It helps restore their dignity, having a way to bring in an income. And it helps sustain the work. We have so many who are ready to be rescued, if we just had a place for them to live until we could find out if their families would accept them back home, or they could get jobs in outlying areas. So most of the people who live here would be temporary, except for one couple we've been praying for—one couple who would live here permanently and run the farm and oversee the others."

Rashid looked at Mark as if he were offering him a trip to the moon and back. "This is my dream, right before my eyes." He grasped Mark's arm. "Would you consider letting a man alone run the farm? I would offer myself for this wonderful job. I would work very hard."

Mark smiled. "Sorry, but that just wouldn't work. We couldn't have a single man in charge of all those women."

"Of course not." Rashid's face fell. He turned away, then turned back in surprise when Mark laughed. His eyebrows rose in question until Mark spoke with a smile.

"There's no avoiding it, Rashid. I think if you want your dream, you've got to go for all of it. You're going to have to ask Neena to marry you."

CHAPTER TWELVE

*C*arefully, slowly to keep from tearing any fragile skin, Asha removed the last of Neena's bandages. She forced her face to remain impassive, but Neena was perceptive. She noticed Asha was holding back tears.

"It is very bad, isn't it?"

Asha's voice was a whisper. "I just hate that anyone could do such a thing to you."

"Let me see."

"Maybe you should wait."

"No, I will see now." Neena rose from the bed and crossed to where a small mirror hung over a set of drawers. When her face came into view, for several minutes, she simply stared.

Asha felt like her insides were tearing apart as she waited. She tried to see through Neena's eyes. Now that the swelling had gone down, the left side of her face looked as beautiful as it always had. The right side, from one patch on her forehead to the lines of burned scarring down her cheek all the way down to the large area that was burned on her neck, the skin was sections of red or white or brown. Part of her right ear was gone.

Neena tucked her hair behind her right ear. Her gaze was direct, but Asha felt her own tears fall when two tears slipped from Neena's eyes to travel down the rivulets of skin and scar along her cheek.

"Neena, I'm so sorry."

"I do not mind so much for myself," Neena whispered to the mirror. "Beauty has always done me harm rather than good." Her gaze dropped. "But I do grieve the death of my hopes for the future."

Asha remembered the day they had washed saris along the riverbank in Neena's village. The day Neena had told her she had always dreamed of a man looking at her with love, touching her face with gentleness.

"Before, I could not dream of love because I was married to a man who did not care for me. Now, all such dreams have been destroyed again. No man could ever love this face. No man would ever want to touch me. He would not . . ."

He? Asha nearly voiced the question, but her heart already knew. Of course Neena cared for Rashid. He had rescued her from Ahmad and taken care of her. He had brought her here and tried to keep her safe.

If only he had succeeded.

Asha felt the familiar fear she was coming to recognize whenever Rashid was mentioned. Was he as good as Neena and her mother seemed to think? Or was he really like his brother, who would enjoy the ultimate betrayal of having them trust him, only to be deceived in the end?

She needed to find out, but how? She certainly did not want him at the Scarlet Cord. Maybe she could call Mark once his cell phone got back in range and ask about them all meeting on the compound. All the missionaries could get together and interrogate—no, interview him. Find out what his intentions were.

Her mind was mentally listing her questions when Neena's sudden sobbing brought her back to the present. "Oh Asha, I had just begun to hope again."

Rising, forgetting Rashid and even herself, Asha went toward her friend, arms outstretched, and cried with her.

"One more stop, then we're on our way to the Scarlet Cord and the women we love." Mark felt in high spirits. He had major hopes for this next stop. And the idea of keeping a secret of this magnitude, one that would mean this much to Asha, filled his blood with excitement.

"What is this place?" Rashid asked when they pulled up to a house only a few miles from the second site.

"I think it just might be my new home," Mark said, his usually staid voice eager. "I was going to build a house for Asha and me, but with all the workers needed to get the farm ready, there just wasn't time to do both. So we were going to live on the farm, or back at the compound if a couple was living on the farm . . ." He grinned at Rashid's embarrassment and turned off the ignition, hopping from the car and taking large strides up the driveway. "But then I heard about this place going up for sale."

"It looks pretty basic," Rashid commented as they approached the mud dwelling. "Not a home one would expect for Americans."

"Exactly," Mark said. "I don't want a house that makes people feel uncomfortable. I want one that looks normal to the Indian people we want to welcome to our home."

"But what about your future wife? She did not grow up here. She is used to living in America, where everyone is rich and lives in comfort."

"Come and see," was all Mark said. "From what I've heard of this place, I think it may be perfect."

He pulled out a key and inserted it into the front door lock. Opening the door, both men stepped inside what looked like a typical mud home with a room for eating and visiting, and an open doorway leading toward a mud-walled hallway. "The people who lived here before were Westerners. They made some additions. Let's go back here."

Mark led the way down the hallway. Behind the area seen from the front was a whole section made from concrete. Two nice rooms with ceiling fans branched out from the hallway. In the back was a kitchen, complete with oven and refrigerator. There was even a bathroom with an American-style toilet and shower.

"I've heard of those toilets where one sits rather than squats," Rashid commented, "but I have never seen one before." He pushed the lever and jumped back when the toilet flushed.

Mark laughed and moved on to a doorway on the side of the kitchen. "Let's see where this goes."

"There is more?" Rashid's voice was baffled, as if he found it inconceivable anyone would have use for more space than what he had already seen.

Mark led the way down a flight of concrete stairs and opened another door that revealed an unfinished basement. "We could turn this into an office, or a den—hey, maybe I could build a ping-pong table!"

"Ping-pong? Is this a food?"

"It's a game. You'd like it. I'll build a table, then have you and Neena come over and we can play pairs."

Rashid frowned. "You assume too much."

"You're right. I'll have to ask Asha if she'd rather have an office."

Rashid began to retaliate when he saw Mark's grin. "You are joking about a very serious matter," Rashid said.

Mark immediately sobered. "I shouldn't tease. It always bothers me when my dad does that; he jokes at the worst times." Mark put a hand on Rashid's shoulder. "I'm sorry. But I really think you should tell Neena how you feel and take a chance that maybe she feels the same way." He gave Rashid's shoulder a squeeze. "Faint heart never won fair lady."

In Bengali, the phrase was confusing enough that Rashid just shrugged and started back up the stairs. "Americans," he muttered.

Mark caught up with him. "This place is great. I couldn't have put together anything better if I'd planned and built it myself. Indian from the front, American in the back. The best of both worlds."

As he started up the Land Rover, he turned to Rashid. "Don't tell Asha, okay? I want to surprise her."

Rashid directed a level gaze toward Mark. "Do you need worry about me having any kind of interaction with your future wife?"

Mark grimaced. "Yeah, we all need to have a talk one of these days. But anyway, she wanted to spend our first night at our own home, but had to give up that dream since we weren't going to have a home. Now I'm going to go ahead and get this place and get it ready, and then surprise her after the wedding by taking her to a home she didn't expect to have. Great, huh?"

Rashid wiped the sweat from his brow. "I am happy for you."

Mark smiled, then grimaced. "I feel so good about this, it almost made me forget about the throbbing headache I've had since I woke up this morning. Man, and my muscles ache too. Must be all this driving around goats and cows and car-sized potholes."

He backed out of the drive, and turned the Land Rover back onto the main road. "I don't know about you, but I need a shower, a decent night's sleep, and a cup of *chai* tea. Let's get going. In a few hours we can be sitting enjoying a nice conversation with your woman and mine."

Rashid just looked out the window. He did not bother shaking his head. Mark would not see it anyway; he was busy thinking of the woman he had already won.

CHAPTER THIRTEEN

"*I* can't believe you brought him here."

Asha's quick joy at Mark's return from his village trip was snuffed out like a candle in a storm wind the moment Rashid also exited the Land Rover.

She stood woodenly as Rashid greeted her, then watched him walk toward the Scarlet Cord's main building where Neena and Shazari enjoyed tea with Rahab and the others.

The sounds of their warm welcome scorched Asha more than the tropical sun above. She bit down her anger and turned to retrace her steps behind the building where she had been hanging wet laundry on a clothesline.

Mark followed. "I thought by now you would have realized he's not a threat. And you know it would have wasted hours to take him back to the compound, then come back here. That just wouldn't be reasonable."

He sighed. She looked back over her shoulder, taking in the dust on his arms from driving hours over dirt roads, and the dust now sprinkling his blond hair where he'd just run his hand through it.

Seeing Amrita's face in the window across the yard behind Mark, Asha turned her back to both of them. "What if he's part of Ahmad's plan? Now he knows where to find all of us!"

Mark reached down to lift a freshly washed sari and pin it up, but then dropped the cloth and put a hand against the clothesline pole.

"Mark, what if he tells Ahmad where the Scarlet Cord is? Everything we're trying to do here would be compromised."

He leaned his head onto the hand wrapped around the pole. A drop of sweat ran a path through the dirt on his face. "Why would he do that? It wouldn't make sense. Why risk his life and break all his family ties to protect these women, only to betray them?"

"Yes, he stood up for Neena and my mother." Asha gave a sharp flap of her hands and heard the crisp snap of material cracking against air. Water droplets escaped in every direction. She draped the material over the line, talking around the clothespins in her mouth. "What if it's all Ahmad's elaborate plan to get revenge? If Rashid's such a great guy, why didn't he stand up for me all those years ago?"

Mark shifted, turned, and slid to sit on the ground, his back against the pole. "He was just a kid then. Kids don't question the older family members." Asha heard him sigh. "In a way, he was just as much a victim as you were in all of that. You can't judge him for something that happened so long ago. I've spent the past four days with him, and I've come to truly respect him."

"Respect him? Really?"

He looked up at her through the bed-sheets wafting between them. "Really." He rose with a little moan. "Man, I ache all over." He stood but remained with his back against the pole. "You yourself said it was God who designed your past, not man. So why is it so hard to trust that a man like Rashid can change?"

Asha hung the last sheet, her head hanging low at his words. "You're right." She trapped the cloth with the last clothespin and turned toward him. "It's not so much that I'm really afraid he'll betray our location. I guess I just haven't really forgiven him."

They walked back toward the front entrance. Asha noticed she had to slow her steps to match Mark's.

"I don't understand it," she admitted. "I forgave my father. Why am I having such a hard time forgiving Rashid?"

Mark held the front door open for her. "Maybe it's because he's here, in front of your face."

Asha looked up sharply and Mark half-chuckled. "Not literally. Literally, I hear him over in the main room still enjoying his tea time with friends."

The word "friends" made her wince. Asha certainly had been nowhere near friendly to him, despite his sacrifice for her family.

Guilt flashed through her. She avoided the main room, heading instead for the kitchen.

Mark's voice was quiet behind her. "If it's hard for you to forgive Rashid, can you imagine how hard it is for these girls, who have hundreds of memories of being abused and victimized—and by men who took pleasure in causing them pain? A one-time choice to forgive is just the beginning."

Asha froze, one hand still on an open cupboard. She had been trying to encourage the rescued girls to return to the red-light district and reach out to those still there, certain it would help them heal to help others.

"It's no wonder some of them are so resistant to the idea of going back. Going back brings it all to life again."

Asha turned to face Mark. "Rani felt like that. She would not even talk about that area and point-blank refused to ever go anywhere near it again."

She waited for Mark to respond. When he said nothing, she stopped analyzing and focused on him. Her voice softened. "You look really tired."

He offered her a weary smile. "I am. A short trip like this isn't usually a problem. I don't know why, but I feel just beat."

"You're pale under that dust, too." Asha stepped closer and put a hand on his arm. It was clammy to the touch. "Are you okay?"

"Probably just too much sun out in the villages." He rolled his shoulders back. "A good cool shower should fix me up just fine." He peeked around the corner to the main room. "If you don't mind, I think I'll skip the socializing today."

"How about I fix you some tea and a snack, and set it in your room?" She smiled. "I know how you hate having to come up with small talk."

"Especially when I feel like I've been run over by a truck." He dropped a heavy hand to her shoulder. "Thanks."

The hand slid away and Asha turned to her task, not noticing Amrita's entrance to the kitchen, her eyes following Mark as he left toward his room, then her footsteps following as well.

Asha smiled down at the small tropical flowers she had used to decorate the tray holding Mark's tea and flat *roti* bread. Not that he would care about the garnish, but she wanted to do something to make it special, to speak love. She had changed her clothes and even added a touch of lip gloss, though he may not notice with as tired as he seemed.

Words. Words would matter more to him. She would have to tell him how she talked with the Lord as she'd fixed his snack, asking Him to help her see the right way. How He'd reminded her of the verse in the Bible about how if you have something against someone, or if they sinned against you, you should go to that person privately and address it.

One of the things Rahab had been teaching at the Scarlet Cord was that the girls did not have to remain victims the rest of their lives; that they could face their past in order to move on to their future, not hiding the past away in a secret place where it would corrode and eat away at them, devouring any possible happiness.

"Guess I needed that instruction, too," Asha said to herself as she lifted the tray and started toward Mark's room. If he had finished showering, maybe they could talk. She wanted to ask him to be with her when she faced Rashid. It would be appropriate, and it would help her have courage to keep from running away, pretending the problem wasn't there, and as Rahab said, letting it eat away at her from the inside out.

Of course, she and Mark would have to find a public place to talk. Asha smiled as she neared the guest room where Mark always stayed. One of their boundaries was to not be alone in each other's personal rooms.

She balanced the tray on her left hand and reached to knock on the door with her right, then hesitated. What if he had finished his shower and fallen asleep? She had talked to God a rather long time in the kitchen.

Asha lowered her right hand to balance the tottering tray in her left. She did not want to wake him if he was resting. He had seemed so weary.

Balancing the tray again, she reached out her free hand toward the doorknob. Maybe she could just open the door a crack, and if he were sleeping, she could lay the tray on his bedside table for when he woke up.

As quietly as possible, she turned the knob. The door inched forward . . .

Mark dried off as much as possible with the humidity-soaked towel, but just the small chore of dressing had him sweating again.

What was wrong with him? Why was he so tired?

He would have to tell Asha he needed to skip the tea and just get some rest. Maybe he'd caught some bug in the village and it would go away in twenty-four hours. Rashid's admonition about him giving away his anti-malaria pills came to mind. What were the symptoms of malaria? Mark tried to think, but his mind felt foggy.

Rest. A good nap would surely help.

He was halfway across the room, and only the whiff of strong perfume as she rose from his bed caught his attention.

His eyes felt glazed as he took in the excess makeup, the dangling earrings and bangles, the curved lips of a woman too much at ease in a man's room.

Even his voice sounded groggy. "Who are you? What are you doing in my room?"

"I'm Amrita." She approached with steady forward steps and ran a confident hand up his muscled forearm. "You must be worn out," she purred. "You've been working so hard. Lie down and rest."

Why was she here? Mark's mind felt as sluggish as his movements. Yes, he definitely needed some rest.

He did not resist when the stranger led him to his bed and pulled the covers back. He had no need of covers. He was drenched in sweat already without them.

He practically fell onto the bed, then remembered someone else was there and struggled into a sitting position. His head felt too heavy to hold it up. He felt a hard thump as it fell back against the concrete wall.

His nerves switched focus from his aching head to the feel of long fingernails trailing up and down his arm.

Was she sitting on his bed? He had to get up. Tell her she needed to leave.

But his body refused his command. His muscles lay heavy and unresponsive.

"To be so exhausted, and then to come home to someone arguing with you and accusing you of things, instead of someone ready to serve you and please you, someone who admires you."

He was conscious she was speaking words, but was too busy trying to figure out why his body was rebelling against him to consider them. He heard a creak. Was that the doorknob? Had she left?

His eyes opened to mere slits, but it was enough to see her still there, still talking. Her voice slipped in and out of his awareness like satin running over skin. Was she asking questions? If he could focus enough to answer them, would she leave?

He ignored the raging in his head and forced a focus on her words.

"Why don't you marry an Indian woman, who knows the Indian way? You don't have to explain everything to her all the time. She just obeys and doesn't ask questions."

She was running those fingernails down the veins in his hand toward his fingertips. Very slow, calculated movements.

"I'm going to marry . . . Asha." Did this girl not know that? Who was she anyway? And why did his head hurt so much?

She put a cool hand against his forehead. "You're warm. Here, let me help you."

He felt the bed shift as she scooted forward. He wanted to get up, get out, but his body refused to move. Why wouldn't she just leave?

Asha held a hand tight against her mouth to keep her gasp from escaping, then she had to release her grip to grab the tray to keep it from falling to the floor.

Her eyes went wide as they watched through the tiny opening. Asha felt the tray shaking in her hands.

Amrita, beautiful, regal Amrita was sitting on Mark's bed. In Mark's room. And he was not resisting.

When her long, slender fingers reached up and unbuttoned the top button of Mark's shirt, Asha nearly lost her grip on the tray. The desire to slap the silken tone right off Amrita's mouth so consumed Asha, she forced herself to remain where she was. If there was an explanation, she would feel terrible for charging in and expressing the jealous wrath she felt coursing through her as Amrita's deft hands released the second button on Mark's shirt.

Why was he just sitting there?

Standing just outside the door, breathing hard, trying to get a grip on her emotions, Asha's mind asked a score of questions while still trying to hear the conversation going on inside.

"Going to marry . . . Asha."

He was only whispering now. His voice was weak. What was going on here?

Asha heard Amrita's low laugh. "But your wedding is two months away. You're a strong man. In the meantime, I could provide you with whatever you need. Whatever you want . . ."

Her voice was full of meaning. Asha felt a pain start near her heart and spread through her entire body. Was this the ultimate betrayal happening right in front of her?

"Have to go." Mark did not even open his eyes. "You have to go. Not God's way."

"Nobody would know."

"I would know. God would know." His voice ended in a groan.

Asha felt her eyes fill with tears. Was Amrita such a difficult temptation to resist?

"All right." Amrita rose to her feet, somehow doing so looking beautiful and seductive. "But I'll be just down the hall if you change your mind."

Though Mark still lay with his head back and eyes closed, Asha watched Amrita walk, her hips swaying—slithering, Asha thought—toward the door. Toward her.

She opened the door wide. Asha still stood there, clinging to her tray, trying to cling to her dignity and not begin crying in front of this woman.

Instead of being ashamed, one corner of Amrita's mouth lifted in a smirk. Her expression was . . . competitive. Victorious?

She faced Asha, chin high, and shrugged casually. "In the Bible story today, didn't even Abraham have a mistress on the side? Do you really expect your man to be stronger than he was?"

Amrita slipped past her, brushing her shoulder as she went by.

Asha stood watching her retreat until she was out of sight. Her mind felt numb. Her emotions were so overloaded she could not even define them.

Eventually, she turned to see Mark still lying, eyes still closed, head back, the two top buttons of his shirt open.

She approached with hesitant steps. "Mark?"

He lifted his head for a moment. "Asha. Feel terrible."

Was he talking about feeling terrible physically, or feeling terrible because of what had just happened?

She asked him. Not getting a response, she tried asking a different way.

After the third or fourth question, tears were pooling in her eyes. "Mark, what is going on? If you feel . . ." she choked over the word, "attracted to her, we need to talk about this."

"Not now. Too complicated."

He rolled into a sitting position and held his head in his hands.

She set the tray down on his bedside table and, ignoring their rules, sat beside him. "Yes, now. We need to deal with this. My parents have bought plane tickets to come out here." She shook her head as he pushed himself to his feet and crossed the room. "I don't even know why I said that. That's not the point."

She followed his slow walk down the hallway. "Mark?"

"Rashid?"

Rashid appeared nearly instantly. Asha, by force of habit, stepped back when he approached Mark. Mark said something, but his voice was so low Asha could not decipher the words.

"We're leaving now." Rashid looked once at Asha. He turned to where Neena stood in the main room. Asha saw the look pass between them and the pain sank sharp again.

As Mark stumbled from the building without one look back, Rashid turned once more to Asha. "I will contact you," was all he said.

Contact her? Why would Rashid need to contact her? Why wasn't Mark promising to contact her? To answer her questions? To give some sort of explanation for what she had just seen?

Asha heard the Land Rover roar to life. She rushed back into Mark's room to look out the window as the dust flew from the dried ground behind the men as they drove away.

She drifted back from the window, sinking to sit on Mark's bed, in Mark's room.

Without Mark.

What was happening?

CHAPTER FOURTEEN

Enough. She was going to find Amrita, and have it out with her, once and for all.

Several hours had passed since Mark's departure, enough for the numbness to wear off, and, like the prickling pain of exercising a foot that had fallen asleep, the emotions that flooded to fill the space were far from pleasant.

In fact, by the time Asha had replayed the scene in her mind a hundred times, all the hurt and confusion faded and anger greedily filled the spaces.

By evening, after several snide, knowing glances from Amrita, Asha was ready to explode. She might as well do it in proximity to the woman causing all the problems.

She stormed down the hallway, stopping short of Amrita's door at the sound of an argument inside.

"How could you do that? Especially to her—she's the one who helped rescue us!"

"She's a fool!" Asha jerked back at the disdain in Amrita's voice. Was she talking about her?

"I admit she doesn't know our culture very well, but she's trying. She—"

"She's come here and taken over everything, and she thinks she's the only one who can do anything, as if one rescue or two makes her an expert on what our lives are like. She doesn't know *anything* about what we've been through."

Asha edged closer, telling herself that one of these days she would really have to break this habit of eavesdropping. So far it had only proven to be a misery-creating activity.

The soft voice—Kochi's?—continued. "So you did it to get back at her?"

"Ha! I wasn't even thinking of her. I was thinking of myself."

"Yourself? I don't understand. Did you really think he would marry you?"

"No, but I have to say I didn't expect him to be quite so difficult to seduce."

Asha gasped, then clamped a hand over her mouth. A hinge creaked behind her, and Asha turned guiltily to see Rahab exit her room, her stomach extending into the hallway many inches in front of her. "My belly arrives before I do," she said, smiling.

Her smile fell into concern, then confusion when Asha silently waved her hands toward herself. Sensing the desire for silence, Rahab quietly huffed her way across the hallway to where Asha stood.

"What's—"

"Shh. Please." Asha held several fingers to her mouth. "I'll explain later. But I need to hear what they're saying."

"Asha." Rahab's voice was a gentle rebuke. "You shouldn't be—"

Asha ushered Rahab back through the hallway and into the kitchen. Even there she spoke quietly. "She was in the room with Mark. Alone. With the door closed. And now she and Kochi are arguing. Something about Amrita seducing him!"

Rahab grasped Asha's trembling hands in her own. Asha looked down and noticed Rahab's hands were swollen. She looked farther down. Her feet were too. Guilt washed over her at unloading her own burdens on Rahab when she had her own struggles.

"Why aren't you in bed? Resting?"

Rahab's smile was loving. "We will speak of me later. Right now we need to find out about the thing that is hurting your heart." She squeezed Asha's hands. "It seems you have developed some conclusions but have not checked them with any facts. Is that correct?"

"I know the fact that she and Mark were in the same room, and—"

"Yes," Rahab gently interrupted, "but did you ask Mark why? Did you express your concerns and fears?"

"I tried, but he left. He wouldn't even talk to me. He said he felt terrible, but—"

"Did you ask Amrita?"

"No, but—"

Rahab's softly shaking head stopped Asha's words again. "You are allowing your feelings to lead the way before wisdom." She smiled. "And just as my belly leads the way before the rest of me, it makes it easy to bump into things and be hurt."

Rahab patted Asha's hand. "Let's go find out the truth."

Now it was Asha's turn to shake her head. "If I'm there, she won't tell you. I know she won't."

Rahab considered for a moment, then nodded. "Perhaps you are right. Wait in the hallway and I will try to—as you Americans say—get to the bottom of this."

Asha followed Rahab, stopping to stand just outside Amrita's door. Rahab entered and respectfully began questioning Amrita. When Kochi exited the room, both she and Asha jolted in surprise as they suddenly faced one another. Kochi's face paled. "He didn't do anything wrong," she whispered quickly, sneaking to Asha's side like a co-conspirator. "I had no idea she was going to try to get pregnant, and—"

"Pregnant?" Asha squeaked out.

"Shh!" Kochi seemed nearly as anxious as Asha felt.

They both leaned toward the door when Amrita's voice rose. "She has everything, and she doesn't even see it!" Something slammed onto a desk or the floor. "Why shouldn't I give him the opportunity to marry a woman who would treat him with respect? She pouts when he doesn't do things her way, while the rest of us would be happy to have any American husband, even if he were unkind, or even unfaithful. To have one who smiles at her like he does . . . and still not—"

Asha heard Amrita's voice break, and something within her twisted in pain.

"I would give my life to be loved by a man like that," Amrita was saying, her voice now broken. "I knew he wouldn't marry someone like me, but I thought maybe if—if I could get pregnant . . . I knew he was a man of honor and he would feel responsible to take care of me and the baby. I had to take the chance of some kind of future. Having a man sending money to take care of his child would be about as good as I could ever hope for."

Asha slid to the floor, still listening as Amrita began crying. "Can you blame me for hating her? She has everything I will never have. No one took her purity from her. Beat her whenever she tried to express an opinion. Kept her chained—sold her—"

Tears slipped silently from Asha's eyes as Amrita cried loudly within the room. "She doesn't even know what she has! If he married me, I would gladly be his slave. I would wait on him and cook for him and do anything for him." Her voice hardened. "She will argue with him and complain about him not helping her enough and be sad that he's not more romantic like those stupid movies they make in her country."

Asha had put her head down on her arms. She looked up to see Kochi watching her, anxiety lacing her gaze. Gulping down more tears, Asha stood and, abandoning all pretense at dignity, floundered through the hallway toward her own room, tears marring her vision, her hands blindly reaching out until they found her own doorway.

Once inside, she willed herself to stop crying. Then she reached for the Bible resting on her bedside table. She had just read it that afternoon, but her anger toward Mark had kept any of the words from sinking in.

After long minutes standing in silence, she sat woodenly on the bed, then dropped from the bed onto her knees, her face pressing down to the woven rug beneath her as she sobbed.

She had thought it was time to face Rashid. Then she thought it was time to face Amrita. Now she knew the truth.

First, she needed to face herself.

CHAPTER FIFTEEN

"It's your turn." Kochi grasped the broom Amrita held out, but only to keep it from falling to the floor.

Amrita's eyebrows were arched high. "I refuse to do such menial labor."

Kochi pushed the broom back toward Amrita. "I have no problem doing my share of the work to earn the right to stay in this place." She forced the broom back into Amrita's unwilling hands. "But I did not get rescued from the red-light district only to become your personal slave. Sweep the floor, Amrita. Do your part."

Amrita looked over the broom as if it were covered with spiders. "Well, I hear a rescue was scheduled for last night. If it was successful, there should be a new girl or two I can convince to take on this low-status chore."

"That may be." Kochi crossed her arms. "But in the meantime, you get to sweep the kitchen yourself." She turned to go, then stopped. "Wait, I thought Asha did all the rescues. But she's here."

Amrita's laugh was mirthless. "She wasn't even in Kolkata when I was brought here. She's not the only person in the world capable of getting someone out of Sonagachi."

A bell rang from the nearby room and Amrita's lips curved. "Ah, tea time. Looks like I won't have time to sweep the kitchen after all." She rested the broom against the closest wall. "Not like it matters. What difference does it make if the place is clean? Everyone in it is poor. Just look at you."

Kochi dropped her gaze. "I'd rather be poor forever than be back in Sonagachi for an hour." She turned toward the main room. "If you hate it here so much, why don't you leave?"

Amrita dropped into a cushioned wicker chair. "I have no place else to go. Not until I can go back and start my own business."

Kochi's eyes glistened. "You would do to others what was done to us?"

"No!" For a moment, Amrita's eyes blazed fire. "No, but I would have my independence. Be on my own. Making my own money. Living my own life."

Kochi shook her head. Her voice was low and soft. "What good is independence without hope?"

For a moment, Amrita's jaw clenched. Then Kochi saw Amrita's lip tremble until she bit it into stillness. "I want—"

Asha and Rahab entered the room with trays of tea and snacks. Kochi looked over to see Amrita was now biting both lips closed, her eyes shuttered of all feeling. "What do you want, Amrita?"

A quick look up showed Asha and Rahab's eyes on them both. A cell phone beeped. Amrita turned away. "Nothing."

Asha flipped her phone open and her pulse sped. She pushed the button to reveal the text message from Mark, then frowned.

"What is it?" Rahab set the tea tray on the coffee table in front of Amrita and Kochi. "Is there news from Mark?"

"It's a text message from his number, but it doesn't make any sense."

Asha handed the phone to Rahab, who smiled and said, "This is Bengali. It must be from Rashid."

"But Bengali is squiggly letters, not English letters," Asha commented, "and why would Rashid be texting me instead of Mark?"

Rahab nodded. "Indeed, but our 'squiggly letters,' as you call them, are not on phones, so we text using the closest equivalent to the Bengali sounds using your English letters."

A look over Rahab's shoulder at the phone again only deepened Asha's frown. "I still have no idea what that says."

"It is difficult. He shortened the words, just like you do in English texting."

Asha waited several seconds, fidgeting, before saying, "So what does it say?"

"It says, 'Mark very sick. Malaria. Doctor coming.'"

Immediately Asha lurched to her feet. "Oh no! That was why he was . . ." She dropped her head. "Oh no."

"Ah." Amrita also stood. "That explains why he was so immune."

"Immune?" Kochi looked from her to Asha. "He's not immune. He got sick."

"No, not immune to sickness." Amrita looked across at Asha. "Immune to me."

Asha was gritting her teeth, clamping down on the sharp response ready to be spewed in Amrita's direction. She forced her focus back on Rahab. "Did he say anything else?"

"Nothing else."

"I have to go to him." She started toward her room, then pivoted back to Rahab. "They have the Land Rover. I don't have a car. Could your husband take me on his motorcycle?"

Rahab grunted with the effort of rising from the chair. "He is not here."

"Where is he? When will he be back?"

"He is visiting, or perhaps at the market. He is just gone. I do not know when he will return."

Asha was twisting the fingers of her left hand with her right for a full minute before she caught herself and forced her hands to her sides. Helpless again. Life in India could be so frustrating sometimes. "What am I going to do?"

"Hello? Anyone there? We've got no time to waste!"

Asha jumped as John Stephen's booming voice burst through the building from the front door. "Mr. Stephens! What are you doing here?"

He looked at the hand Asha held to her heart. "Didn't you hear our car pull into the driveway?"

"No, I was preoccupied."

"Well, get un-preoccupied. My son is a two-hour drive away and I'm leaving in three minutes. If you want to come, be outside in two and a half."

That curt statement finished, Mark's father left the building as quickly as he had entered it. Asha ran to her room to gather a few things, not staying to greet the two new girls Eleanor graciously introduced to Rahab and the others.

"The rescue was successful last night," Asha heard Eleanor's gentle voice say. "It seems the sari shop idea is a very good and safe method. These new girls need to be welcomed and helped, but as you may know, Mark is sick and we'd like to go directly there to help him and be with him. Would you mind very much if we left right away?"

Asha exited her room to see Rahab put a loving hand on each girl's shoulder. "You are welcome here," she said. "Let me show you to your room and explain about the Scarlet Cord— how we got started and what we do here." She turned to Asha. "Go," she said. "Go to the man you love. Make it right."

A shuffling noise from the hallway came closer until Shazari and Neena appeared in the main room. "We're coming with you," Shazari huffed. Neena looked around, her hands gripping a small bag, her eyes shifting from Shazari to Asha to Eleanor.

"You'll need a chaperone." Shazari scowled.

Asha did not bother mentioning that Mark's father and grandmother would be there, and Rashid. With quick goodbyes the group headed outside, where John Stephens waited with the Land Rover running.

Within seconds they were on the road, Eleanor in the front passenger seat, Asha and Neena behind her, Shazari sitting in the back. Asha leaned forward and spoke loudly to be heard over the roar of the wind coming through the open windows. "*Didi-Ma*, I'm so sorry to ask, because I know it must bring back painful memories, but do you think . . ." She swallowed, trying to speak without her voice breaking. "Do you think it might be more than malaria?"

"You mean dengue fever?" John Stephens glanced at Asha through the rear-view mirror. His face was more serious than Asha had ever seen it. Fear crept up her spine, wrapped around it, and clenched her heart.

"Yes," she said weakly.

"Mark's mother died of dengue fever because we were in the village when she caught it. We were very far away from any medical care, and by the time we got her to a doctor, it was too late."

Asha looked in the rear-view mirror and saw the worry lines across John Stephen's forehead. "Have you seen him? Does he look like it's just malaria?"

Eleanor turned to look back at Asha and the others. "Rashid called us just as we were nearing the Scarlet Cord, so we decided to drop the newly rescued girls off, and hopefully pick you up, then all go together to the second site. So no, we have not seen him yet. However, Doctor Andersen went directly there on his motorbike, so he should know something by the time we get there. Malaria can be dangerous, but we will pray, knowing God's grace will be sufficient."

Shazari tapped Asha's shoulder. Asha turned to see a grim face. "Once you get malaria, even if you recover, it never fully goes away. It remains in your body and can flare up at any time. Even if he does survive, he will always be at risk."

Neena touched her hand, eyes full of compassion. "We will pray."

Asha nodded. She bowed her head. Neena prayed aloud, but even after she finished, Asha continued her own prayer every

minute of the ride that stretched into the longest two hours of
her life.

CHAPTER SIXTEEN

As they pulled into the driveway, Asha leapt from the vehicle before John Stephens had it in park. Rushing toward the building, which she vaguely noticed had been much improved, she pleaded with God for mercy. Opening the door, she stopped to reign in her emotions.

Mark was sick. He needed her to be strong for him.

But he was the strong one. The stable one. Asha felt tears sting her eyes. She had taken so much for granted.

"Well, are you going in or not?" John Stephen's voice from behind pushed Asha into action. The entire group filed down the hallway toward the closed doorway at the end. Rashid stood beside the door, his face grave.

"Rashid." Asha forgot to care whether it was appropriate to use his name or not. "Why didn't you come get me right away?"

The man's eyes had brightened at the sight of Neena, but they dimmed again when Asha spoke. Not looking at her, he said, "I am sorry. I do not know how to drive."

"Oh." Tears were threatening again. Now she had shamed him. "I didn't think of that." She hung her head. "I didn't think of so many things. How could I have been so stupid to not see that he was sick?" Thinking back over the entire scene now, it was completely obvious. Guilt burned across her neck and cheeks. "May I see him, please?"

With a nod, Rashid held open the door. "He's been asking for you."

Asha put both hands to her heart, trying to keep the feelings contained there, held tight in a safe place. She did not succeed. As she approached where Mark lay, pale, weak, bathed in sweat, the emotions flooded from her heart and seemed to fill the room. Asha tried to swallow down the metallic taste of fear, but it remained.

"I suppose since you're getting married, you should get to talk with him first." John Stephen's words were nearly as reluctant as his steps as Eleanor led him from the room. "But I'm coming back in five minutes. Got that?"

Asha nodded, her eyes still on Mark. The door closed behind her. Now alone, Asha sat on the side of Mark's bed and took his limp hand in her own. "Mark, I'm here."

Chills shook his body. His eyes opened to slits, and in them she saw recognition. "I'm so sorry," she said, not even noticing how emotion altered her voice. "I should have seen that you were sick. I was so jealous of Amrita, so threatened by her being in your room, I wasn't thinking of you. I was only thinking of me and how I felt and—"

"Rambling . . ." His one labored word stopped her. She leaned forward to hear him. "Must be nervous." One corner of his mouth tipped into that half-smile she loved so much. "Is okay . . ." He drifted off and Asha held his hand up to her cheek, her tears running down through his fingers.

Eleanor and John Stephens wandered to see the new chicken coop, quietly discussing Mark's condition and the best way to treat it. Neena directed Shazari toward a shaded area under a tree near the larger of the two buildings.

When Rashid followed, at a distance, Neena sensed his presence and trembled. Shazari looked from his hesitant approach to Neena's youthful blush. "It wasn't Asha who needed a chaperone," Shazari said, her words blunt, her voice coarse. She gestured a flat palm toward Neena. "I knew you would want to come out here to be near this man." Her hand swiveled to Rashid and Neena felt her face flood with a heat that had nothing to do with the noonday sun. Shazari spoke toward Rashid. "And I knew you would want to be near this woman. I am no fool. I have eyes in my head and can see what is in front of me." She glared. "And I won't stand for it."

Neena's voice was horrified. "You are shaming me!"

"Shaming you?" Shazari flung her arm in Rashid's direction. "I am protecting you. From a man who has no money and no job. What kind of a husband would he make? How could he take care of you?"

"Please," Neena pleaded. She turned her face away. "Please do not speak this way. He would never want me for a wife. I am destroyed. Worthless. Ugly."

She heard the pain in her own voice. Felt the shame fill every crevice of her heart. When Rashid spoke quietly to Shazari, she did not dare listen, did not dare risk hearing him laugh at Shazari's idea that he might consider her for a wife. It would be too painful to bear.

Suddenly all was silent. Neena slid cautious eyes upward, expecting to see Rashid walking away and Shazari crossing her arms in anger. Instead, her eyes widened. Shazari was nowhere to be seen. Rashid stood three feet away. His eyes were on her.

They held no disdain.

Turning away from what must be her own imagination, Neena choked out, "Forgive Shazari, please. She does not see as she should."

"No, Neena." He had never said her name before. The sound increased her pain. Her name from his lips was beauty itself. "No, she sees the truth. It is you who do not see."

She heard him take a step closer and turned her head farther away.

"Do you not know my love for you?"

A gasp, small and shallow, did little to fill her lungs. Neena kept her face turned away. It could not be true. He could not have said it.

"I have loved you for your beauty." She winced but he continued. "And also for your compassion. For your heart and your gentleness. I have loved your loyalty to Shazari, and your concern for those you care about."

He stepped closer, but she crept away. "No." She heard unshed tears in her own voice. "Please, you must not say these things to me."

"I know." Rashid's voice was raw. She now had her face nearly against the tree to keep it from his sight. "I know I should not speak of my heart. I have no right to tell you of my love. No right to ask you to be my wife."

She gasped at his words. Heard him take another step, but this time it was away from her. "It was my brother who hurt you. My relation who made you suffer so. Every time I see your face . . ." His voice broke. She heard his voice fade and knew he had turned away. "I know you can never love me. I failed to protect you. You must hate me."

Neena turned in awe and disbelief. "How can I hate you? You are a good man, who chose to do the right thing even when it cost you everything! How can I not love—"

Her eyes went down the moment he turned back to face her. She put a hand against the right side of her face and turned so only the left side was in his view. "I know that no man will ever love me. My face—"

"Your face is beautiful." In two steps he was in front of her. "Neena, look at me."

She could not. And he could not touch her, not even with one finger to lift her face to look on his. "Please, Neena." His voice was hoarse with feeling. "Look at me."

With excruciating slowness, Neena moved her head until she faced him, her hand still covering the right side of her face.

"You are beautiful."

She winced again and began to turn away.

"No. Look at me. Do not cover your face with your hand. Do not turn away from me in shame."

She obeyed, her eyes wide, her hands trembling at her sides.

"I have an opportunity." Rashid's eyes lit up and Neena's own could not help but respond. "A couple is needed to oversee the work here, to run the farm and be caretaker to the girls who would live and work here until they could find permanent homes."

He looked down at her and Neena wanted to run away, to flee the small flicker of hope that flamed to life within her.

"I want to stay here, to be a farmer, to make a difference." He took a half step closer. Neena placed a hand to her face again.

"I want you to be my wife, to serve here with me." His own head dipped down. "Only I am too unworthy to ask you. After what my brother did to you. After failing to keep you safe, I could never hope . . ." He turned then, and Neena felt her heart breaking. "Tell Shazari she need not fear. I will not speak of this again."

CHAPTER SEVENTEEN

Asha pestered Dr. Andersen for answers he could not give. He had given Mark the medication he needed, and now they had to wait to see how his body would respond to it.

That was it. Just waiting. Mark was suffering, his body shivering with chills even as his skin burned with fever, and all they could do was wait? Asha kicked a hardened clump of dirt and watched it explode from the force, particles scattering in every direction. She hated waiting.

Mark's father and grandmother had returned to Mark's room, and Asha reluctantly left. She'd much rather have stayed by Mark's side, but they deserved their time with him as much as she did. After all, she wasn't his wife yet.

She meandered out back, again absently noting several improvements. The chicken coop had been rebuilt. Asha approached and pulled on the door. It was stuck.

She pulled harder. Just as it released and fell open, there was a simultaneous volley of sounds from several directions.

"I have to speak with you!" a male voice said from behind.

"I need to talk to you!" a female voice came from the side.

"Squawk!" A chicken escaped from the coop, flapping its wings wildly and causing Asha to shriek in surprise.

The shrill sounds brought Shazari running from around the front hut. "What is happening?"

Asha turned, her heart racing. She glared down at the hen, now pecking around her feet and clucking with indignation. "A chicken?"

"I have to say this," the male voice stated again. "I wanted to wait until I could do it with Mark, but I cannot bear the weight any longer."

Asha stepped away from the chicken, as it was pecking dangerously near her bare toes. She looked at Rashid. "What?"

"Rashid, I love you!"

Rashid and Asha both turned to Neena. "What?"

"Where did that hen come from?"

Rashid, Asha and Neena all turned to Shazari. "What?"

"Well, somebody must have brought it." Shazari folded her arms and scowled.

Rashid looked from woman to woman. "I cannot speak everything at once." He looked back at Neena. "Your words fill me with both hope and pain, but I must do this first." He turned to Shazari. "I stole your child from you." He turned to Asha. "I stole you from your mother, from your family." His head lowered. "I did not want to, but I will not make excuses for my sin. All through the past twenty years, I have tried to forget what I did, cover it by doing good." He lifted pain-filled eyes to Asha. "But the day you returned to our village, the shame returned with you. I could not hide from it or escape it. And I knew that nothing I could ever do, not even a lifetime of good, could take the bad away."

Asha watched Neena unconsciously stepping toward him as he spoke, his pain reflected in her own eyes.

Shazari stepped forward. "Ahmad meant it for evil. God meant it for good. In my eyes, you carry no blame."

"Blame or no blame, I beg your forgiveness."

Asha bit her lip. She knew Rashid was lowering himself beyond the bounds of his culture, humbling himself before a woman. Even apologizing at all was a major step; most people would just give a gift to try to restore the friendship. He really had been changed by the gospel.

Shazari looked from Rashid to Neena, then back to Rashid. "You have my full forgiveness. And my blessing, if you still want it."

"I want it." It was Neena who answered rather than Rashid.

Asha's eyes went wide. The chicken squawked again.

Rashid's eyes filled with emotion, but then he turned from Neena to Asha. "Mark told me the Bible says that sins are ultimately against God. God forgave all my sins when I received Jesus as my Savior. But we should also make it right with the person we sinned against. This I have feared doing, but I must not cower away any longer. To be a man with a future, I must face my past."

Neena gasped. "You have believed in Jesus?"

At his nod, a smile burst through that transformed Neena's face and made it beautiful again.

He took one longing look back at Neena, then stepped toward Asha. "I hate what I did to you. I hate myself for doing it. I know it is impossible that you could ever forgive me, but to obey God I must ask for your forgiveness."

Asha felt her eyes glaze over with tears. "I forgive you. Will you forgive me?"

Rashid's eyebrows came together. "Forgive you? You have every right to despise me." He gestured toward Neena. "You have every right to despise me. I should be despised."

"I do not despise you." Neena's voice was soft.

"Neither do I." Asha's voice was less loving but no less sincere. "I ask your forgiveness for my lack of obedience to God in not forgiving you before now. And for not bringing it up. I was not a good example of how a Christian should act. Will you forgive me?"

The hen pecked at one of Asha's painted toenails. "Ouch!"

She hopped up and down, muttering at the animal, barely hearing Rashid say he forgave her. However, when Neena again stepped forward, Asha stopped hopping and watched with interest.

"Is it possible that you truly meant what you said before? That you care for me?"

"More than my life," he said simply. "If I had known what that man was planning, I would gladly have stepped in the pathway so the acid would have fallen on me and not you. Every day I see my failure and am disgusted with myself."

"I thought you saw my ugliness and were disgusted with me."

Asha put fingers to her lips as Rashid's eyes traveled over Neena's face. Anyone could see the love there. He reached up a tentative, shaking hand, and so very hesitantly ran a finger down her creviced cheek. "Never."

The chicken approached again. Asha started shooing it back toward the coop, but Shazari stopped her with a vise grip on her arm. "Shh. This is important."

Wincing, Asha whispered, "Shouldn't we give them some privacy?"

A mischievous smile, something Asha had never seen on Shazari's face, suddenly made her look years younger. "There are advantages to being the chaperone."

Neena took her hand away from her face, revealing every scar. "I have loved you since the day you first led us from the village."

"Truly?" His own face beamed into a smile, but it fell again. "But I am much older than you. Surely you would want a younger husband."

Neena laughed. The sound was so surprising, he stepped back.

"I want no husband other than you, if God wills it."

"Then we shall ask Him together."

Asha rubbed the spot where Shazari had grabbed her arm. The chicken was pecking around her feet again. She kicked at it. "Why don't you go bother someone else?"

Rashid smiled. Asha did not know if she had ever seen that expression on his face before. He even smiled down on the hen as he picked it up, holding it forward as it flapped and protested. He tried tossing the animal back into the coop and shutting the door, only to have the hen escape again before he could get it closed.

Shazari scowled. "Stupid chicken. Don't you know this is an important moment?"

Asha giggled. "Maybe she wants to call herself a chaperone so she can stay and listen in."

"Hhmph!" Shazari huffed. "I'm going inside." She looked at Rashid. "If you're engaged, that is."

"Yes." The word came from Neena.

"I haven't asked yet." Rashid was looking frustrated. He reached for the hen again, who scuffled away.

"Well, ask then!"

Rashid gave up on the chicken. He turned his back to the two other women and faced Neena. "I want you to marry me. I want us to give the message of forgiveness and hope to others. If I can be forgiven, anyone can. And if you can love me, anything is possible. We will share that hope with the women who come here."

"Hope. A beautiful word." Neena smiled. "Let's name this place the House of Hope."

CHAPTER EIGHTEEN

Asha felt tears prick her eyes. She wondered how Mark was doing. Turning, she started back toward the larger mud dwelling when Neena called her name and rushed to her, surprising Asha speechless by enveloping her in an American-style hug. "It is true. All of what you said about God's perfect love, the love that casts out fear. I could never fully believe it before, but now I know it is true. I have seen it just now." She looked back at Rashid. "In his eyes."

"You have been given your heart's greatest dream." Asha was fighting tears. "I am so happy for you, my dear friend."

"And it did not happen for my beauty." Neena sighed. "Oh Asha, if God could give a mere man such love, just imagine how much bigger and more amazing His love is." She looked around the second site in awe, as if gazing upon a palace. "Already this place has become a House of Hope."

Rashid approached and Neena's eyes went wide.

"What is it, Neena?" Asha asked.

"I want to talk with him." She looked dazed.

Asha shrugged. "Okay, go ahead."

"No." Neena shook her head. "You don't understand. Remember when you were in our village and I asked you what men and women could possibly have to talk about?"

Asha's mind traveled back to the village, to the day she and Neena washed clothes in the muddy pond and discussed the incomprehensible idea of men and women being friends. "I remember."

Neena's eyes were huge. "I want to talk with him." She gestured toward Rashid, love shining from her eyes. "I want to tell him my hopes and dreams. I want to learn who he is." She hugged Asha again. "I had no idea it could be like this. Oh, it is wonderful—this desire for friendship, this love."

Asha looked up the path to the building that sheltered the man she loved. "Yes, it is."

She left Neena and Rashid and climbed the path. She had to be with him. Even if he was sleeping, she just needed to be near.

Mark had gained enough strength to sit up in bed. Asha spooned a chicken-flavored broth into his mouth. For a moment, she wondered if the broth testified the end of the pecking chicken, and giggled.

"What's funny?"

Mark's voice sounded weak. His head was back against the wall behind the bed—there was no headboard—and his hands lay limp at his sides.

"There's a chicken outside that escaped from the coop. It pecked my toe and I was imagining a little vengeance in the form of chicken broth."

He almost smiled. "Sometimes you scare me."

"Here, take another bite—or sip, whatever you call it." She held the spoon to his lips.

He drank it, then rested his head back again. "Rashid told me he wants to talk with you. I really think you should meet with him. I'll come with you once I'm better. You two should get this resolved."

Asha set down the bowl of broth and rested her hand against his cheek. "He did. I did. It is."

Slowly, as if it took great effort, Mark lifted his eyebrows. "Really?"

"Really, right in the middle of him and Neena getting engaged, and the chicken pecking my toe."

Mark's eyes opened wide. "They got engaged?"

"Mm-hmm. It was very romantic."

"You were there?" He looked sideways at her. "Or were you eavesdropping?"

She chuckled. "There are advantages to being the chaperone," she quoted her mother.

"So they're going to be our second site couple."

"Yes. Well, sort of. Your dad said you tend to put people into leadership positions too quickly. Rashid is just a brand-new believer and has never been in charge of anything in his life. He needs to be discipled and trained."

Mark frowned. "That's true. I do tend to do that. So what did my dad decide?"

She leaned forward. "Well, fortunately for you, Pastor Hamal and his wife just this week told your dad they would come live here and run the farm for a year while we get the ministry on its feet. So your dad said the Hamals could mentor and disciple both Rashid and Neena, and everybody could live here on the farm so they get on-site training. When the year is over, the Hamals will go back to their church in the city and Rashid and Neena, if they're ready, can be in charge."

She smiled dreamily. "And this site is now officially called the House of Hope."

"Wow, a lot seems to be happening while I'm just lying here in bed."

He started to rise but Asha's firm hands pushed him back. "Don't even think of getting up. Doctor Andersen says rest is the best thing for you."

"How can I rest with all that hammering those guys are doing all day long around here?"

"You have a point there." Her own head was throbbing with the constant work being done on the area. "Maybe we should take you back to the Scarlet Cord. It's quiet there." *Well, except for Amrita's high-maintenance demands.*

Asha cringed at the catty thought. At least that one hadn't come out of her mouth. Maybe she was improving.

"I like that idea." Mark's voice was slowing. His eyes drifted closed. "Silence. You fussing over me. And maybe some better food than just chicken broth—no offense to your chicken."

"He's not my chicken."

"I know. He belongs to one of the workers—and actually he's a she, being a hen. The guy brought her in to keep her contained since he doesn't have a coop of his own."

"Well, that idea didn't work, but I guess I'm glad he—she—didn't end up in the broth then."

Suddenly, Mark grasped Asha's hand with surprising strength. "Need to tell you something."

She leaned closer, sensing the seriousness in his voice. "What?"

His voice strained. "If we're going to be working in this ministry together, with women of the night, there's something you need to get clear."

She laid a hand on his chest. "Maybe you should rest now and we'll talk about it later."

He shook his head. "No, now. Before we go back. You can ask me questions. You can bring up any subject. I will keep no secrets from you."

Asha's face pulled tight in confusion. "I don't understand."

His eyes opened. They were blood-shot, but his gaze was clear and focused on her. "You can question any action I do, but never doubt my faithfulness or commitment to you. You don't ever need to be jealous or feel threatened by any woman who crosses our path. Ever."

Asha covered her mouth with her hand. "Mark, I—"

"I mean it." He pulled her hand down from her mouth. He reached up to rest his own hand against the curve of her face. She leaned into it. "You are the woman God chose for me. No one else is you, so no one else can compare. Got it?"

Asha thought of Amrita. Her curves and her makeup and her sneaky ways.

"Got it?" Mark's hand tugged on her chin, gently pulling and pushing it, making her face nod in affirmation. "Good."

She smiled down at his beloved face. "I'll try," she promised.

"We need to have that settled before we get married. I can't be any help in this work if you're always worried about every beautiful woman that passes by."

Her mouth tipped wryly. "Well, not *every* beautiful woman . . ."

He struggled to sit up, and she reached forward to help him. Once settled, he pulled at her shoulders until their faces were close. "I'll say it again. If it's you God told me to love, then nobody else can fill that spot but you." His eyes bore into hers. "You are the woman I want for life. To have children with. To grow old with. To—"

Asha's heart was filling with joy until she saw him hesitate and frown. "What is it?"

His mouth dragged downward. "I just realized . . . I got malaria."

Asha nodded. "I know. We've been worried about you for days."

"No, I mean, I just realized what that might mean. For us. For the future."

"What do you mean?"

"Asha." He looked her in the eye. "What if it flares up often enough that I can't stay here? What if I have to go back to America for treatment? What if . . ." He sucked in a breath. "What if I could no longer live in India?"

His hands dropped from her shoulders. "I need to rethink this."

Asha felt herself shudder. "What?"

"Everything." He rubbed his forehead. "You. Me. Getting married."

CHAPTER NINETEEN

Asha gripped his shoulders. "What on earth are you talking about?"

"God has called you here to a great work. You shouldn't be married to a man who could jeopardize all of that." He looked out the window. "I've always been healthy, but now I have a virus that will lay dormant in my system for life. It could flare up rarely or often enough that I could not live in this climate."

His eyes reached for her but his arms remained at his sides. "I think we should rethink you marrying me."

Asha stood and walked across the room to look out the open window. The escaped hen still wandered the yard. The workers still hammered. Rashid and Neena walked around the area, Shazari following a short distance behind.

Turning back to where Mark's despondent form lay the full length and beyond the Indian-sized bed, Asha put both hands on her hips, put her tongue between her teeth and made a childish sound. "*Ttthhhhpppp!*"

He looked up in surprise. "Was that supposed to mean something?"

"It sure was." She marched over to the bed and sat on the edge, shaking a finger sternly in his direction. "If you can give me a speech about not feeling threatened by beautiful and tempting women because God wants you to marry me and therefore they are not a threat, then listen up, mister. It's your turn to hear my speech."

She stood and leaned over him. "If God wants me to marry you, then that's all there is to it. It doesn't matter where we live. Nobody is sure of living in any certain place for any certain time anyway. You are not in charge of that. If God keeps us in India, we'll serve Him here. If we can't stay here, it's because He has a plan for us somewhere else."

She sat again, her tone softening and her hand gently tweaking his nose. "So no more thinking that way, okay? I'm marrying you whether you like it or not."

His eyes were closed, but his lips curved upward. "I like it."

"Well, then. This conversation is over and you need to rest."

He sighed. "Can't. Hammering."

"Oh, right. Well, try to rest and I'll go make arrangements for getting us all back to the Scarlet Cord as soon as possible."

She rose to leave but his hand held hers firm. "I'm going to like being married to you," he said.

Her smile was tender, then fun. "Just don't expect me to catch and kill any chickens, okay?"

She saw a hint of his former grin, and her heart soared.

"Deal."

Dapika stoked the fire, her back turned as it had been the entire time the angry man talked with her mother, reminding her of their agreement.

"She must do exactly as I say. Don't forget," he said. Dapika inched closer to the fire as he talked. Better to be burned than to be any nearer the coldness in his eyes and voice.

The child turned her head just enough to watch her mother kowtow and appease the man with words and smiles, even after his open threat of what would happen to them were Dapika not to show up at the appointed place at the exact time.

Sickened by the mixture of pity and shame she felt for her mother, Dapika turned back toward the cooking fire and away from their conversation. When the door closed, signaling the man's exit, her stomach finally uncoiled its tight knot.

She added a few vegetables to their meager stew and tried to pretend an enthusiasm at her mother's words of joy. "Just think, one more week and you will be free!" The woman joined Dapika at the fire. She stirred their supper and smiled into the distance. "You will be able to get a job somewhere. Be independent. Have a life beyond this terrible place."

A warm and loving hand on Dapika's shoulders caused her to cringe. The hand pulled away and the voice became very soft. "Will you be ashamed of your mother then? Will you stay away? Never visit? Never want anyone to know who your mother is?"

Dapika rushed to her. "No, Mother, never! No matter what, I will always love you. I know you do not want this life." The child looked up. "I would save you if I could."

The woman ran a hand through the child's hair. "It is enough that you will be spared." She sighed, and smiled. "Though I will miss you more than I can say, I cannot wait for these last days to end and your freedom day to come."

Dapika returned to the fire. She leaned toward its heat so if her mother saw her tears, she would think they were from the rising smoke.

Her freedom day. If only it were true. But Dapika knew that the days were passing quickly, and the day coming held anything but freedom for her.

"You're feeling better; I can tell." Asha's voice was cheerful as she set the tray on Mark's bedside table.

"I am. Last night was the first night in a week where I didn't have the fever, chills, and sweating routine. I slept well. Think I'm on my way out of this thing." He stood shakily and wandered into the hallway. "And not soon enough either. I'm getting awfully tired of being in bed all day long."

"Aw, even with all this pampering you're getting?"

He grinned and pulled her toward him. "Well, I don't mind the extra attention from you, but I have to say being brought cups of tea and snacks by every female at the Scarlet Cord is starting to get old."

She nestled in his arms, enjoying the rare moment of privacy. He rested his chin onto the part in her hair, running a hand through the silky strands. "Besides, I have to be totally well by the wedding. If I'm going to be Rashid's best man, I definitely need to be able to stand up without help."

"You're going to be the best man? I'm Neena's maid of honor!" She bounced in his arms. "I'm so excited. We can walk down the aisle together, if they do that sort of thing." She grinned again. "And I have the best wedding present for them."

"Oh? Do tell."

"Nope. It's a secret."

He pursed his lips. "I thought we weren't keeping secrets."

"We aren't married yet. Not to mention, it was you who promised to never have secrets. I never promised that."

"Hmm, guess I'd better put that in our vows somewhere."

She laughed. "Who says you get to write the vows?"

"Would you rather have my dad write them? He's an ordained minister."

Asha imagined all the fun John Stephens could fit into that project. "No thanks. How about *we* write our vows, as in you and me?"

"Okay, *we* get to write our vows. I think you should put something in yours about cooking chickens."

"Or not." Asha grinned. She hugged him tight. "Maybe we should have the preacher write the vows."

Mark hummed an Indian love song as he tapped his pen to a blank notebook, trying to think of what he could give Rashid for a wedding present.

Surprise spread across his face when a soft voice called his name. He looked up then stood up.

Just below his chin stood Amrita, her painted, full lips spread wide, her face lifted toward his, heavy-lidded eyes looking at him with expectation.

"Amrita." Mark tried to keep his voice neutral. "Did you need something?"

Bright red lips curved. "Your door was open," she purred. Long fingernails ran up his arm. He backed away. She chuckled. "I thought maybe it was an invitation?"

Mark took another step back. He looked toward the door and noted that it was now closed.

"Last time I came in here, you were sick and our conversation was rather one-sided." She stepped forward. "I thought perhaps now that you're feeling better, we could continue our . . . talk?"

"Excuse me. I need to go check on something." He took two solid steps toward the door when she grabbed his arm with both hands.

She was stronger than she looked.

"Before you go . . ." She held tight to his hand and slipped closer. "There's something I needed to talk to you about."

Mark swallowed. "Why don't we talk about it out in the living room?"

She tapped his chin with one crimson fingernail. "Scared?"

He nodded. Several choice Bible passages came to mind referring to this exact kind of situation. None of them encouraged naivety at such a moment.

She smiled and slipped her body up next to his. "Smart man," she murmured.

The door opened. Mark walked out with a steady, purposeful pace. Amrita followed more slowly, noting Asha and Rahab's presence in the hallway. Rahab's mouth had dropped open. Asha's was in a tight thin line.

Amrita gave the smile she used whenever she won. "Seems this just keeps happening, doesn't it?" She turned from their stunned faces and sauntered down the hallway, being sure to allow her hips to sway more than usual.

Rahab turned to Asha. "What did you say?"

Asha was muttering to herself, her eyes closed, her fists clenched. "I am quoting that verse about how being quick to get angry . . . oh, I don't remember exactly what it says but I remember it's something not good; it doesn't please God. Maybe I'll go look it up and memorize it, word for word, before I go and—very calmly with God's help—ask Mark what that was all about."

Rahab's one hand set protectively on her belly. Her other hand grasped Asha's shoulder. "I am truly proud of you, my friend."

"Don't be proud yet," Asha said with a grimace. "Wait to see if I actually have the self-control to apply the verse after I memorize it."

Rahab chuckled. "God will give it to you."

A sigh brought Asha's shoulders up and down. "I suppose in this line of work I should expect things like this to happen sometimes. I've either got to decide I trust Mark to handle temptation, or I'll spend the rest of my life half-sick that someone prettier or smarter or more . . . well, more like Amrita is going to come along."

"I know of what you speak," Rahab said. "I have learned to pray that God will give my husband the strength to resist temptation rather than trying to always keep him from it. Such is an impossible and very stressful task. God is much better equipped to handle it than I."

Asha pulled Rahab into as much of a hug as possible with the unborn baby filling the space between them. "I am so glad to have a friend like you."

"And I, you. Now, go memorize that verse, then talk with the man you love."

"That woman." Mark shook his head. "She's a Proverbs five woman."

Asha's brow furrowed. "The only woman I remember is the Proverbs thirty-one woman."

Mark rose from the couch and stretched his shoulder muscles. "The Proverbs five woman is the one God says to avoid. To keep from even walking near her house." He let out a breath. "I wish I could avoid her place, or at least that she'd stop invading mine."

Asha rose and stood to face him. "I guess you got an opportunity to test out that promise you made me already, huh?"

"That no matter who came my way, you were the only one for me?"

"Mm-hmm."

He looked around and since no one was in sight, put an arm across her shoulders and gave them a squeeze. "Well, then, who knows? Maybe that whole scene was for your sake, so you'd know what I said was true. Even Amrita with all her paint and sparkles doesn't compare to you."

Asha frowned, thinking of Amrita's beautiful face and curvaceous body. "Oh, she compares alright."

He tipped her chin up with his hand. "But she's not you. And that's the thing." He grinned. "I said it before, but you're not getting it. It's really very simple. You're the one for me; anyone who isn't you, isn't. That's all there is to it."

Asha wrapped her arms around his waist. "You're amazing, you know that?"

Mark pulled back and looked deeply into her eyes. "Listen, I'm going to tell you this once and I want you to never forget it. I prayed long and hard before I asked you to marry me. I believe God wants me to marry you. That is what is going to hold our marriage together. I know it may not sound as romantic as me talking about feelings, but feelings change and go through stages, and life out here is hard. Feelings aren't something to base a whole lifetime commitment on. God is." He took both her hands in his. "The biggest reason I am marrying you is because I believe it is God's will. That means you never have to compete with any other woman, and you never have to feel insecure in my commitment to you."

Asha felt tears prick her eyes. She threw her arms around his neck and pulled him close. "I love you, Mark."

She felt his smile as his cheek curved against her skin. "I love you, too. Always."

CHAPTER TWENTY

Asha was pacing back and forth in front of the wicker couch when Mark entered.

He let out a low, appreciative sound. "Wow, you look great." She did not pause. "At least I think you look great; it's hard to tell when you're moving past me so quickly."

She did not seem to hear him. On her next lap past him, he snuck a hand out and wrapped it around her waist, stopping her mid-stride.

"Oh, Mark!" She looked up into his face. "I didn't know you'd come in." She stepped back and looked him over. "Wow, you look great."

"That's what I just said to you."

She cocked her head to one side. "You did? When?"

"Just now." He chuckled. "What are you stressing about?"

"Me? Stressing?" Her voice was high-pitched. "What makes you think I'm stressing?"

"Asha . . ." Mark pulled her into a quick embrace, knowing the rest of the ladies were already at the House of Hope setting up for the wedding. "Tell me what's going on."

"It was supposed to be a surprise, though I guess it wouldn't hurt to tell you. But you won't tell Rashid? Or Neena?"

He laughed out loud. "They're both at the House of Hope. How would I tell them if I wanted to? Be reasonable, woman."

"*Ew*, there's that reasonable word again."

He grinned down at her. "You know, in just a little over a month, it will be our turn to do this."

His lips dropped down to cover hers. For one brief, heady moment, she allowed her arms to creep up his shoulders and wrap around his neck. He pulled her in close.

By the time he released her, she felt like a piece of chocolate left out in the tropical sun. "You just did that to get me to tell you my secret, didn't you?" She could not keep the smile from her voice.

"Nope." His own lips curved up in response. "But that's a good idea. Maybe I'll try it." He kissed her again. "Did it work?"

"Would've worked the first time." She sank into the nearest chair. "Gracious, you make my knees go weak."

He took a step toward her, then stopped and instead backed away, crossing the room and taking a seat on the couch opposite. "So what's the big secret?"

"I wanted to do something really special for Neena and Rashid's wedding today . . ."

"Yeah. And?"

"Well, I thought of getting them something to decorate their new home, but I didn't know if you could put nails into a mud wall to hang something with, and—"

Mark checked his watch. "You do know we have to leave in ten minutes, right?"

She crinkled her nose at him. "Okay, fine, I'll get to the point. I sent plane tickets to Neena and Rashid's parents so they could come to the wedding."

Mark stood immediately. "Really? Asha, what a great idea!" Then his eyebrows came together. "But wait, do the parents even know each other? With them not arranging the match, there's bound to be some tension there."

"I hope not." Asha bit her lip. "Just the process of getting them out of Bangladesh was a major upheaval—passports and visas and then trying to figure out which route they needed to take to get from the airport—I should have told you about it, since you likely would have thought of all that stuff. I never seem to think about the details ahead of time."

She sighed. "You'd think I'd learn. But at this rate, it might not happen anyway. The paperwork only got finished at the last minute. They were supposed to get a taxi ride here from the airport and we would take them from here to the House of Hope." She bit her lip again. "I'm worried they might have been delayed somehow. You know how things are around here. The flight could have been late, or—"

Mark reached out for both her hands. "You're right. In India, one can't make expectations too high on anything regarding transportation."

"I just wish they had a cell phone so we could make other arrangements if they were delayed. What if they get here after we leave? They'll miss it! And what if—"

"Hey, it's going to be okay. We'll all adapt and even if—"

"Hello? Anyone there?"

Asha turned, her eyes brightened. "I was going to suggest we pray together, but I think God may have just answered my prayer before I even said it!"

It started out as a perfect moment. Asha was thrilled at the joy in both Rashid and Neena's eyes when their parents exited the Land Rover with Mark and her.

Then everything went bad, fast. Seeing Neena's face, her mother shrieked. She began wailing about her beautiful daughter. "What has happened to you? You are ruined! Oh, my beautiful daughter, your beauty is gone. Who will want you now?"

Mark leaned toward Asha. "You didn't tell them about the acid attack, did you?"

"I didn't even think of it. I was so excited about having them come to the wedding, I just—oh, Mark, this is terrible."

He frowned. "And I think it's about to get worse."

Asha's heart sank. Rashid's parents had quickly joined their son, and their conversation did not seem to be pleasant either.

Neena's father asked questions while her mother continued her weeping tirade, then suddenly he turned toward Rashid's parents and shouted, "It was your son who did this to my daughter? How dare you show your face in my presence? How dare you even think of an alliance between our families?"

"Oh, what have I done now?" Asha wanted to run and hide. "I thought this was such a good idea!"

John and Eleanor Stephens, along with the Bengali pastor, his wife, and all the girls from the Scarlet Cord, had exited the House of Hope and were staring in amazement.

Neena tried to speak, but her mother threw her arms around her and continued mourning Neena's loss of beauty. Rashid tried to speak but could not be heard over his own parents' defense to Neena's father.

John Stephens stepped forward and let out a shrill whistle. All noise immediately stopped. He said the Bengali version of, "All right, everybody calm down. You came out here for a wedding, not a shouting match."

Several started voicing objections, but he held up his hands. "Okay, here's what we're going to do. All the wedding guests, why don't you come stand over here?"

Dutifully, the unaffected parties collected into a huddle near the building, all eyes on John Stephens.

"Neena and Rashid, come over here please."

Asha's fingers were twisting as she watched Neena walk to stand on one side of John, parents in tow. Rashid, his parents following him, approached to stand on the other side.

"Now." John's voice was stern. "I think we should let Neena start." He turned to the young woman. "Don't cry, sweetie. Go ahead and tell your story."

Neena looked around. Everyone was staring. Her eyes went wide and her mouth clamped shut.

"Go," Mark whispered to Asha from behind. "She needs a friend."

Asha shot a look of love back in his direction, then walked away from the group to stand before Neena. "My dear friend." She lifted the white veil that had become jarred by the mother's frantic flailing and readjusted it, dropping the sheer, misty lace over Neena's features. "There, now pretend no one is looking at you and speak your heart. You are beautiful, you know. All of us know that. Especially Rashid."

Neena's eyes shone with unshed tears. She turned to speak with her parents. Her soft voice carried across the air between her parents and Rashid's. She told the story of Ahmad's threats and Rashid's act of courage in taking them away from the village. She spoke of the acid attack, of her certainty that she was ugly and unlovable.

Her mother began crying again, but her father shushed her. "I want to hear the rest of this." His eyes had lost their glare. He waited, indicating that Neena continue.

However, it was Rashid who spoke next. Stepping forward, Rashid opened his heart and risked lifetime shame by revealing it through his words to the entire crowd. He told them of his love for Neena, his desire to marry and serve alongside her.

"To me, she is the most beautiful woman in the world."

A collective sigh came from the crowd of girls near the building.

Neena's mother walked over to Rashid. "You are willing to marry my daughter, even though she is ruined?"

Asha winced.

The woman's eyes narrowed in suspicion when Rashid answered in the affirmative. "What is it you want? How much of a dowry?" She turned accusing eyes to Asha. "Why did you bring us here? What is it you really want?"

Asha backed away. "I only wanted you to enjoy this beautiful moment with your children." She gestured toward both sets of parents. "I wanted Rashid and Neena to have your presence on the happiest day of their lives." She swallowed a choking cry.

Rashid's parents walked to face Neena's. "We could never ask a dowry from you for your daughter. It is our eternal shame that our own son caused this," the father said with head hung low. "We have not seen Ahmad since his evil was exposed to the village, but we have felt the shame every day since." He looked at Neena. "And now it is multiplied."

Neena's father considered the words for several seconds. Asha waited, her breath caught in suspense. When the father reached out to touch Neena's scarred face through the veil, Asha forced herself to let air out of her lungs.

"My daughter, is it true? This man sees the beauty of your heart? The worth I have always seen in you?"

Neena nodded, teardrops escaping and trailing down her cheeks. "Yes, Daddy."

"And you love him?"

"Yes."

"And he will care for you?"

"In ways I never dreamed."

Neena's father touched his daughter's veil. "This is what I wanted for you all your life. You know how I sorrowed over having to marry you to a man who did not care for you, but we had no choice then." His voice was husky with feeling. "If this man loves you, sees the beauty I see, he is the one I choose for you."

He turned to Rashid. "I have no dowry to give. We are—"

Rashid bowed. "None is asked for or wanted." He turned to Neena and even Neena's mother gasped at the love in his eyes. "She is all I want."

"I bet for a minute there you were wondering if this wedding was going to happen at all." Mark's voice was light and at ease.

Asha laughed in exasperated relief. "For more than a minute." She looked to where Rashid and Neena, newly married, received congratulations from the group. Nearby, the two sets of parents had started a cautious but friendly conversation. "I'm so relieved it worked out."

"More than that." Mark led her around behind the chicken coop so they could speak in private. "Guess what? Not only are Neena's parents happy because Neena is going to be married despite being ruined—not that I think she is!" he quickly clarified at the look on Asha's face. "But Rashid's parents were talking about how they couldn't bear living with the shame in the village anymore. They were thinking about moving to the capital city to try to find work, but as you and I know, that's not so easy to do. They'd likely end up begging, or doing really hard manual labor for very little money."

"But . . ." Asha leaned forward. "I'm assuming this story has a happy ending?"

Mark grinned. Looking around to be sure no one was in sight, he cupped Asha's face and kissed her. "It does. Rashid asked permission, then invited his parents to move here, to the House of Hope, helping them set up the farm."

"Really?"

He smiled with satisfaction. "It would be great all around. For Rashid, he'd rescue his parents from shame in their village. For the parents, they would be with family, and have the opportunity to hear the Good News. And for the House of Hope, having two generations living here would not only add credibility, but I think the girls would enjoy having an older couple as parent figures."

Asha smiled through tears. "So God made this a beautiful day after all."

"Yep. It was a great wedding." He snuck in one more quick kiss. "But I have to say I'm still looking forward to the wedding to come."

"Mark." Now it was Asha's turn to look around and make sure they were alone. She reached up, pulled his head down, and kissed him slow and long. "Neena is happy and loved. I'm not scared of Rashid anymore. Next week I get to rescue a young girl and her mother, and then in less than a month I get to marry you."

She snuggled against him with a sigh. "My life is perfect."

Part Two

For I know the thoughts

That I think toward you, says the Lord,

Thoughts of peace and not of evil,

To give you a future and a hope.

Jeremiah 29:11

CHAPTER TWENTY-ONE

It was sometime past midnight when Mark awoke. He rolled over and started to close his eyes again when he noticed a faint light coming through underneath the door of his room.

Who would still be up at this hour? Maybe Rahab had gone into labor, or someone had escaped and needed help.

Knowing he would not be able to rest until he knew if there was a need, Mark slipped on his worn t-shirt and a pair of jeans, leaving his feet bare as he quietly turned the knob and squinted toward the light.

Even from the back, he could tell it was Asha. She sat hunched over an open Bible spread across the large desk in the living room.

He watched as she slid the Bible across the desk, mumbling. She picked up a pen and started writing furiously in a notebook. When she dropped the pen, then dropped her head into her hands, Mark knew there was a need after all.

He purposefully shuffled his feet as he approached from behind.

"Hey," he whispered. "You okay? Need a hot cup of tea?"

"Hi." He heard weariness in her voice. "In this heat?"

He shrugged as he passed her desk. "It's what my mom used to fix for me whenever I couldn't sleep. Just a habit now I guess."

He looked back to see her features soften. She slid from the barstool and followed him into the kitchen.

The night sounds came through the screened open windows. Mark opened the refrigerator and pulled out a boxed carton of milk. Suddenly he felt Asha reach from behind and wrap her arms tightly around him. She buried her face deep into the crevice of his back between his shoulder blades.

"So you couldn't sleep either?" he whispered as he poured sugar into a pot of heating water, adding milk then two herbal tea bags.

Asha sighed again, this time with a sound of frustration. "I haven't even tried sleeping yet." She dropped her arms. "You'll be shocked to know I just finished going through that self-defense DVD you gave me. Twice."

Mark followed her back to the dimly lit desk. "Seriously?" He sat across from her, watching as she blew into her teacup. "I am shocked. You must not be feeling okay."

She responded to his grin with a small smile, absently stirring her tea while her eyes drifted to the Bible that remained open on the desk. "This next rescue has me nervous. I figured learning a few defense moves might make me feel more prepared."

"Don't they all make you nervous?" He leaned back in his chair, enjoying relaxing, talking. Was this what everyday married life would be like? He liked it.

"Yes, but this one feels different. Maybe it was the verses I was reading today. The reminder that evil has been around for a long time, and sometimes . . . well, sometime it feels like God isn't paying attention."

"What do you mean?" He leaned forward.

She set aside her steaming tea and reached for the Bible. "It's here, in Habakkuk. The guy says, 'Oh, Lord, how long shall I cry, and You will not hear? Even cry out to You, 'Violence!' and You will not save.'"

Mark heard Asha's voice waver. He angled the Bible toward himself and continued reading. "Why do You show me iniquity, and cause me to see trouble? For plundering and violence are before me; there is strife, and contention arises. Therefore the law is powerless, and justice never goes forth."

He closed the Bible and walked around the back of her stool. When he put warm hands on her shoulders, she stiffened in surprise. "Relax," he whispered. "Just let it all go for a minute."

She let her head fall back against his broad chest and sighed. "I wish God would just fix it. Stop the bad people. Rescue the victims. Make the evil go away."

He placed a soft kiss down on the part in her hair. "I do too. But that's something we'll have to wait for." His hands stilled on her shoulders. He released her and reached down around her to open the Bible to Isaiah chapter 11. "But someday . . ."

He leaned down, almost into an embrace around her, and read aloud, "The wolf also shall dwell with the lamb, the leopard shall lie down with the young goat, the calf and the young lion and the fatling together; and a little child shall lead them."

Asha sighed again. "No more violence."

"Wait, there's more." He continued reading, "They shall not hurt nor destroy in all My holy mountain, for the earth shall be full of the knowledge of the Lord as the waters cover the sea." He ran his finger across the words. "And my favorite part a little ways down: 'And His resting place shall be glorious.'"

"Hmm. Glorious. Rest." She leaned back against the strength of his hard chest.

He wrapped his arms around her and said a soft prayer.

Then his arms grasped her shoulders and gave them a quick squeeze. "And now, my love, you should get some glorious rest yourself. Tomorrow it's back to the compound to get ready for the big rescue."

She stood and stretched like a cat and he loved it. "Oh, I should get the DVD out."

He grinned. "Did you actually learn any of the moves?"

"Oh, you might just be surprised." Her face suddenly went serious. "Mark, there's something I've been hesitating telling you, because I'm afraid you'll overreact, and—"

"Me? Overreact? When do I ever overreact?"

"Whenever I mention putting myself in danger."

He crossed his arms. "Maybe you should re-phrase that into something like the times when you used to run headlong toward danger without thinking through any of the ramifications."

She ejected the disc. "Well, I'll give you that, but this is something I really wanted to keep a secret till the whole thing was over, but I am actually nervous about it and thought maybe if I told you, you'd have some logical reason for it that would make me feel better, but then again you might freak out and—"

A finger to her lips stopped her words. "You really are nervous. I'm intrigued. Why don't you tell me what's bothering you? Maybe I can help."

She started twisting her fingers and he had the sudden urge to sit on the couch and pull her into his lap while she told her story. Instead, he motioned her toward the couch and he sat on the chair opposite. This waiting to be married was hard stuff.

"Well, that first rescue, when I picked up Kochi at the sari shop, you remember?"

He nodded.

"As we were leaving, I looked around and saw a man who looked just like—well, I mean, I couldn't be sure of course, but he really looked so similar, and—"

"Asha . . ."

She bit her lip, closed her eyes, and said in a rush, "He looked just like Ahmad."

Mark was out of his chair and next to her on the couch before she had even opened her eyes. "What? Why didn't you tell me?"

"Well, at the time I had no idea he was even in town, and when I found out, I mean, how would he know to be right there, and—"

"You can't go to the sari shop to get that girl and her mother. It's not safe. If he knows that's where you rescue girls—"

"See, I knew you'd overreact."

"Asha." He held both of her hands in a tight grip. "Be reasonable. If he—"

"I'm actually trying to be reasonable," she said, then smiled. "I know it's hard to believe."

He could not help but smile back.

"Here's the thing. None of the rescues since then have had a hint of a problem. And, the little girl I'm rescuing said some bad guy wanted to stop us—and I was figuring that must be Ahmad trying to thwart what we do, or get back at us, or whatever—and so if she said she'd meet us at the sari shop to escape him, then that would mean he doesn't know about the sari shop rescues, right?"

His mind processed the information. "That seems . . ."

"Reasonable?"

"Actually, yes." He stood and reached for her. "But I still think you should send someone else."

"I can't." She shook her head against his chest where he held her. "She said I was the only person she would trust. So I just have to go."

He let out a low sound, almost like a growl. "I wish I could go with you. It's not fair that I'm white and have to stay home whenever you're out rescuing people."

She chuckled. "You just want to be involved."

"If you are, definitely." He wrapped her tight in his arms, wishing he could always keep her this secure. Protected. "I don't like you out there without me. I like us working together, serving together." He touched a finger to the tip of her upturned nose. "Someday growing old together."

She snuggled into his embrace. "I like the sound of that. Not the growing old part—the together part."

He rested his chin atop her head and sighed. "Me too. But for now, you should get to bed." He reluctantly pulled away.

"And I should get going too. We're breaking our rules, you know."

Asha smiled up at him. "Well, tonight was kind of an exception."

His eyes darkened. "In that case . . ." His hand trailed down one strand of hair that had come loose from her ponytail. His fingers curved from it down the line of her chin, pulling it up toward him. His kiss was sweet, gentle.

Sooner than he wanted to, Mark backed away.

"Goodnight, Mark," she whispered.

He watched until she disappeared around the corner into the hallway, stood staring at the spot she had left empty until he heard her bedroom door close with a soft click.

"Goodnight, my love."

CHAPTER TWENTY-TWO

$\mathcal{A}$drenaline raced through her body as Asha stepped down from the rickshaw. This was it. She had covered both face and form with her heavy black *burkah*. The veil obstructed her sight, adding to the darkness of the night street. She winced as she unwittingly stepped into a puddle of mud near the edge of the road. Asha tried to ignore the feeling and rejected the desire to stop and wipe the splattered mud from her foot and leg. She pretended to be a woman comfortable in her clothing, stepping with a contrived air of confidence the last few feet toward the light of the tailor shop.

Once safely inside, she breathed out a sigh of relief. Paul, the Christian Bengali worker, gave a nod in greeting and Asha grinned beneath her veil. This was such a great setup. Lord willing, it would remain the perfect method of rescuing women and girls for a long time to come.

Paul went through the motions of writing down a few instructions, just for show in case someone watched from the street. Then he directed Asha toward the measuring room.

Inside the small room, Asha removed the head covering and smiled. "Is she here?"

"*Heh.*" The man tossed his head to the side. Yes. "But the mother is not."

"Oh no. Did the girl say what happened?"

"She would speak to no one."

"I'll try talking with her. Thank you." Asha kneeled before the secret panel and gave a soft knock. A slow push and the panel opened to reveal Dapika, huddled within herself, her head down into her knees, arms up and over her head.

Asha looked back at the Bengali man. "I'll wait in here with her until the auto comes."

Paul looked with compassion on the girl. "*Heh*," he said again.

Bending over, Asha crept inside the small opening. A feeling of claustrophobia threatened to overtake as Paul closed the panel, enveloping them in thick darkness.

She could see nothing. Though she was sitting up against Dapika, there being no room to sit apart, she could not even see the shoulder right under her chin. "Dapika? You were brave to come here. We'll get you out. Was your mother unable to escape?"

There was no response.

"We'll get you out," Asha repeated. "And with God's help, later we'll try to get your mom out, too."

She could tell the child was afraid, could feel her trembling. She put a hand on each of her shoulders in the tight space where they hid and began speaking in English, hoping her tone would calm the girl. "Don't worry," she said, knowing she was speaking to her own fears as well. This was the part she hated, the waiting. The darkness. "We've already done several rescues this way. A friend will come with an auto, and we will go to a safe place. And Mark will be there."

She breathed hard, her lips curving upward even as her heart hammered against her chest. "Mark is wonderful. You'll love him. Don't be afraid of his yellow hair or white skin. His heart is Bengali." She could hear the love in her voice as she whispered, "I'm going to marry him. He is my best friend. And we will love as God meant a man and woman to love. We will show that a marriage can be happy, and good, and . . . and . . ."

Her voice caught. "And so far away from the life you have always known."

"Dapika . . ." She switched to Bengali. "We will show you hope."

The sound of footsteps approached. Asha's grip on Dapika's shoulders tightened. "They're here." She smiled in the darkness. "It's time to go."

The panel door opened with a creak and Asha cried out. Fear shot her legs forward to push herself away, toward the back of the tiny enclosure.

But there was nowhere to go.

It was not a friend's face that appeared as the panel opened.

It was Ahmad's.

Ahmad's presence filled the opening, the light behind shrouding him in an eerie, frightening glow.

He said only one word, his voice low and deep. One word that had Asha trembling and cowering behind her own frail hands.

"Revenge."

CHAPTER TWENTY-THREE

Ahmad instructed the man with him to tie Dapika's hands together. He held the remaining length of rope up to Asha. "We won't need this with you, will we?" He smiled with sheer delight. "You will follow wherever I lead this child. If you try to flee, she will die." He leaned in close and she smelled the alcohol on his breath. "But she will not die until after we make her suffer in your place. Do you understand?"

Mutely, helpless tears raging up into her eyes, Asha nodded.

She was trapped. He knew she would not save herself if it meant the child's destruction.

Ahmad had won.

He jerked the rope and Dapika's arms went forward. Her body followed, out of the paneled hiding place and into the small measuring room.

Asha, too, stepped out. She wanted to open the door to the sari shop. What had happened to the Christian men, their partners? Had they been hurt?

"They're not there." Ahmad answered her unspoken question. He nodded in the direction of her gaze. "They escaped to go get help." He chuckled. "Exactly as I hoped they would."

Asha wanted to ask what he was planning. What more he wanted to complete his vengeance. Who else he wanted to hurt.

But the gleam in his eye that begged her to ask kept her mouth clamped shut. She would not give him the satisfaction.

Instead, she prayed.

They were forced into a rickshaw with the man holding the rope. Ahmad rode in a rickshaw ahead of them. Asha remained silent, but her heart screamed. As they rode from the tailor shop onto the main road, she tried to keep aware of which direction they were going while silently praying, pleading, begging God for help.

It barely registered that Dapika had not made a sound since their capture. Asha took her eyes from the road for a moment to the girl squeezed tight beside her. On Asha's other side sat Ahmad's accomplice, the rope in his hand. It draped over Asha's lap to where it knotted around Dapika's wrists.

The man gave the rope a little twitch and it rose and fell on Asha's legs. He laughed.

After a glare in his direction, then another toward Ahmad in the rickshaw ahead, Asha turned again to Dapika. "Are you all right?" she whispered.

Dapika kept her head turned away. "Hate me," she said. "Hate me. I did this to you."

A weight sunk deep between Asha's shoulders. She stopped watching their turns, stopped trying to discern any recognizable streets. "Since the beginning? It was all Ahmad's plan from the first day you came?"

Her head still turned away, Dapika nodded. "I'm sorry. He said he would kill my mother if I didn't do it."

Asha grabbed the child's hands, wrapped her fingers around the ropes. "This is not your fault," she said fiercely. "You were trapped." She looked up at the back of Ahmad's head. "Just as we both are now."

Dapika's eyes lifted with impossible hope. "You don't hate me?"

Asha shook her head and put an arm around the girl's shoulders. With a sob, the child buried her head against Asha. "He said once he got you, he would let me go free. I knew he wouldn't. But I had to save my mother."

The rickshaw stopped at a corner. Ahmad dismounted and motioned they do the same. Asha's mind ran fast.

If they yelled, would someone help them? If she jerked the rope, would it surprise the man enough into letting it go? Even if he did, could they outrun Ahmad?

Ahmad summoned an auto. Once they all climbed in, the small vehicle sped forward. No, she could not even attempt to get them both to safety on their own. She had heard enough stories from the women at the Scarlet Cord to know that trying would only cause greater suffering when they were caught again.

Their only hope was being rescued.

As the minutes passed and the auto continued driving, that hope stretched farther and farther away.

"He got her! He got them both!"

Mark and Rashid stood from their wicker chairs as the two Bengali men raced into the building.

Mark recognized the men and his heart started pounding. "What happened? Why aren't you at the sari shop? Where is Asha?"

Both men spoke rapidly in Bengali. One reached and grabbed the other's arm. At that, the second man stopped and the first started over. "We were there. Everything was going perfect. She came and went inside the measuring room. She hid behind the panel with the little girl. I don't know how he knew it was her. She was completely covered!"

"Who?" Mark tried to listen above the sound of blood rushing through his ears.

"Ahmad."

"Ahmad?" both Mark and Rashid shouted. "Dear God, help us," Rashid said.

Mark started pacing. "How do you know it was Ahmad?"

"He said so." The first man sat. The second stood like a statue, his only movement a nervous clasping of his hands. "He came in and said his name was Ahmad, and he was here to get the girls—both of them."

The second man bent his head. "He laughed. We tried to keep him out, but he pulled out a gun and laughed. Said we were stupid and helpless."

The first man continued. "He went into the measuring room, so we escaped while we could and came right here to tell you what happened."

Rashid nodded, but Mark stopped pacing to shout, "You escaped and came here? Why didn't someone think to stay nearby and watch where they went? Who knows where he took her!"

Rashid's quiet voice filled the air, low and purposefully calm. "Ahmad is very smart. He found where we were so he could attack Neena. I should have suspected he would not be satisfied with hurting her . . . and me." Rashid lowered his gaze. "If he planned to capture Asha, he has a complete plan for her." He looked at Mark. "And you."

Mark's hands clenched into fists. He bit his lips closed and left the building, heading outside around the back. He found the clothesline pole and stormed toward it, slamming his fist into the metal, welcoming the pain that shot up his arm.

She was gone. His worst fear, that she would be taken, was staring him in the face.

Asha's face came to mind. Laughing. Eyes bright with love as she promised to wear the *burkah*. To keep safe.

His beautiful, fearless Asha. She would not be fearless anymore.

He flexed aching fingers and thought of her afraid. Of Ahmad's hands touching her. Slamming his other fist into the pole, he leaned his head onto his fist and tried to think. He needed to think.

No. He needed to go. Every second he remained was one second more she was in danger, being taken farther away from him. He took off at a run, rounding the building, not wasting precious time telling the men inside—the men who had allowed the woman he loved to be taken—where he was going or why.

Rushing from the compound, he hailed the nearest taxi. His instructions were simple. "Drive me to the nearest place where I can buy a gun."

CHAPTER TWENTY-FOUR

The auto stopped and Asha had no time to take in their surroundings before the man shoved them out onto the sidewalk.

People passed by. No one seemed to notice the ropes around Dapika's hands.

Asha wanted to cry out, "Somebody help us! We need help!" One look around, however, silenced any hope of such an action being effective for good.

Across the street, a line of shops had closed for the night. The one shop still lit, a very small *dokan* with snacks and trinkets for sale, had only one customer. When the person left, the man behind the counter stepped from the shop and reached up to what looked like a small garage door. He pulled it down. It covered and closed the shop like a shell of armor. Stepping on the handle of the door, now down near his feet, he snapped the door into place against the floor, then turned away and started down the road.

The facing street now abandoned and dark, Asha turned to the side of the street where they now stood.

To her right, she looked down a narrow alleyway, concrete walls covered in graffiti, one wall decorated with a line of women. Their saris touched every hue of color. Some of the women stood alert, surveying the men who passed by, beckoning those who looked like good prospects. Others sat, slouched over, weary with the day and the night and the endless waiting in line.

The line that led to nowhere.

A stray dog scavenged behind a man who walked purposefully through the throng of night shoppers. A woman called out to him. Several approached. He continued on. Asha wondered where he was going, and why a man would choose this route if he had no interest in the market of flesh sold there.

Nearby, men squatted around a tray cluttered with empty shot glasses. They smoked and drank. One man counted money. Another looked to a woman behind him, then turned to his friend and said something that made them both laugh. Asha felt the bile rising in her throat.

A sound of false laughter pierced the night. Asha looked down at Dapika. Her young eyes, dark brown under lifted eyelids and falling bangs, surveyed the scene as she had. The eyes held too much awareness, too much knowledge, too little hope for a future any different than the one they saw.

Asha was praying ceaselessly now. Her stomach churned. She wanted to run, scream, fight. Claw her way back into freedom. The risk didn't matter. She would do whatever it took to get away.

Ahmad had planned well. She could do none of those things, knowing the consequences that would face the young life at her side.

Defeat washed through her. As Dapika was led by rope toward the alleyway, Asha followed, wondering if her eyes were as dead and hopeless already as those of the women they passed.

A drizzling rain dribbled down their faces and bodies; it, like others, touching the women without asking permission. The women ignored the rain, endured it as they did the touches. Somewhere a baby cried.

One woman stood and walked down the hallway. Wet footprints followed behind her. The imprint of her bare feet made a path toward somewhere, as if she had a place to go.

They were led up a flight of concrete stairs with no railing, each stepping over the body of a sleeping child sprawled across a step, his arms and legs dangling down onto the step below. The man with Ahmad did not bother to lift his feet enough to miss the boy and his foot brushed a layer of grime across the boy's chest. The child did not budge.

Once on the second level, they were led down another outdoor hallway, and then inside a building.

The hallway inside was normal sized for a regular house, inadequately small for the traffic coming and going through the building. Asha followed Dapika, her skin crawling each time a passing man's arm would brush against her in the hallway. The doors to the rooms . . . There were no doors to the rooms. Only sheets hanging over the doorways.

She kept seeing children. Running through the hallway. Playing in a corner. Some standing still and staring, eyes as lifeless as the women in line behind them.

One young girl walked toward them. Her face was aware, almost angry. Asha waited until their eyes met, then willed herself to smile through her own fear. The girl's responding smile shocked her. She was transformed.

Asha felt her own lips lifting into a real smile, until a man behind them noticed the girl's beauty as well, made a comment, and the girl's features fell back into those of an aged and angry woman. She turned away. Asha had to continue on.

She was glad when the men shoved Dapika and her into a room at the end of the hall, one with a door. She was even glad when a lock sounded and she was trapped inside. She wanted to be trapped in alone. She did not want to see any more, hear any more, know any more.

Dapika sat on the edge of an uncovered mattress laid out over a flimsy spring bed in the corner. Asha joined her, too full of fear and weak of heart to give any words of hope.

God . . . God, she prayed, her spirit groaning as she curled up into the corner farthest away from the locked door. She pulled her knees to her chest and wrapped her arms around them. *Please rescue us both before they make us part of this.*

Mark stood at the counter, asking questions and surveying several different weapons. He had never purchased a gun in his life, knew nothing about them really.

"Look, I'm wasting time here." He looked the shopkeeper in the eye. "Give me a gun that will kill someone."

"At point-blank range or from a distance?"

Mark's eyebrows closed together. His face went hard. "Point-blank. I'll be looking him in the eye when I shoot him."

The shopkeeper took a short step back. "Okay." He reached down into the glass case and pulled out a pistol and ammunition. "Here. A weapon to kill."

Mark paid the man and picked up the gun. He looked it over. Nodding once, he positioned it in his belt and left the store.

It was time to go after Ahmad.

Rashid had watched out the window earlier as Mark ran from his sight toward the gate at the entrance to the compound. He leaned against the windowsill, head bowed. Ahmad was a snake. He had always bested Rashid, had always been smarter.

Wise as serpents . . . wise as serpents . . . What was it Mark had quoted from the Bible? Something about being as wise as a serpent but harmless as a bird?

"Lord God," he prayed quietly. "I have never been able to even understand Ahmad's plans. I cannot anticipate what he will do. I need help. My brother is evil, evil as a snake. So I need You to make me as wise as a serpent as well."

He turned from the windowsill. The two men stood in the center of the room.

One stepped forward. "There were three of us," the man said quietly. "My brother and I in the sari shop." He gestured toward the second man. "And Kolol in the tailor shop."

"Where is your brother?"

The man gave a slight smile. "Paul hid nearby to watch where they went and hopefully follow."

Rashid dropped his head back. Relief flooded his soul. "Thank You," he said skyward.

Then he sat and asked the two men to join him. "Please tell me everything, from the first moment until now. I need every detail."

Eleanor Stephens found Mark packing a small duffle bag, his face hardened into stone. She saw the gun and gasped.

"Mark, what are you doing?"

"I'm going after her, Grams. I have to."

"But the gun . . ."

Mark stuffed an extra shirt into the bag and zipped it tight. "Ahmad has trafficked children since Asha was a baby. He has destroyed families without regretting it. And look what he did to Neena!"

"I know, dear, but—"

"He's got Asha, and you know he doesn't plan to just hold her hostage. He's a trafficker, Grandma!" He turned bloodshot eyes to her. "Do you know what that means? For Asha? For my . . . my wife?"

Would she ever be his wife now? Would he even be able to find her?

Eleanor put a trembling hand on Mark's arm. "I know," she whispered. "I know. But you are not the one to bring vengeance on Ahmad. Vengeance belongs to the Lord."

"She's right, Son." John Stephens entered the room, his face devoid of its usual smile. He took the bag from Mark's hands and placed it back on the bed. "Let's take some time and make a plan for rescuing her, and the little girl. Rashid told me—"

"There isn't time!" Mark's voice rose. He picked the bag off the bed and shouldered it. "He may be selling her right now! Don't you understand? I have to do this."

John Stephens stood between Mark and the door. "Son, ever since you became an adult, I have admired your choices. For the first time since you became a man, I am asking you to obey me. Don't go do this on your own. It's not wise."

Mark did not raise his face to look his father in the eye. He passed around him and moved toward the door. "I'm sorry, Dad, but this is going to be the first time as an adult that I deliberately disobey you."

His mouth tightened into a thin line. "I have to find her. I have to get her out of his hands."

At the door he stopped just long enough to say, "And if he tries to stop me . . . I will kill him."

CHAPTER TWENTY-FIVE

A bare light bulb hung from a beam in the unfinished ceiling, sending out lines of garish light. Moths flitted and hovered around the light, bumping against it, seeking entrance, not gaining any. Twigs from an abandoned bird's nest sent strings of shadows down around the beam near the light, like nightmares on a wall.

Looking out the one window, lined with heavy metal bars, Asha saw several boys flying makeshift kites from a rooftop across the street. Were they brothel children? What kind of men would they grow up to be?

"How does anybody endure a life like this?" Asha spoke to herself as the sun rose to conquer the darkness of their first night in Ahmad's captivity. At her words, young Dapika opened her eyes and shifted.

She shrugged, but it was a slow and laborious shrug, as if her shoulders were weighted down with a burden too great to lift blithely. "Life is difficult, full of pain and sadness and hardship. If we endure and accept, maybe next life it will be better. Maybe next life we will be born men, and get to be in control of our own destinies."

"You think if you are good in this life you might be born a man in the next?"

"Of course." Dapika shrugged again. "We must have been bad in our past life, for in this life we were born women. This is our punishment."

Dapika's young eyes flashed up, then down. "I like the story you told me last night about Jesus and the children. It was not just boy children, was it? There were girls, too. And Jesus did not send them away."

Precious child. Asha's heart was breaking. She pulled the girl into her lap, as if she were a much younger child, which in heart and soul she still was. "No, Jesus did not send the girls away. Jesus loves girls and boys. He says you are important. I know you are a Hindu, and you think girls are less than boys. But in my Holy Book, about the God who created all things, it says boys and girls were made just as God wanted them to be."

"You say the big God made me to be a girl? On purpose?"

"Yes."

The child sat up and looked into Asha's eyes. "Why would He do such a cruel thing to me? And if He made me, why did He make me to be here? In this life?"

Asha felt her throat coat with unshed tears. "I don't know. I don't know why you are in this terrible life." She reached up and tucked a strand of hair behind the girl's ear. "But I do know that God hates it, just as you do."

"I do not believe you, *Didi.*" The child shook her head. "If God were real, if He really cared, there would not be places like this."

The girl snuggled into Asha's arms like a toddler and drifted off to sleep again. Asha wrapped her in a mother's embrace as tears slipped down her cheeks. *God, what are we doing here? Why have You allowed this?*

After several minutes of Asha praying silent, desperate prayers, Dapika stretched and yawned, then sat up.

"Remember when they took us away, *Didi*?"

Asha nodded. Her skin crawled just thinking of it.

"I wish they had taken us in a car. I've never been in a car. Only autos and rickshaws. I've always wanted to ride in a car."

Coughing as she tried to swallow a nearly hysterical laugh, Asha clasped her hands and kept her voice nonchalant. "Really?" Here they were, trapped, waiting for Ahmad to come back and sell them, and the girl was talking about nothing.

Maybe that answered her earlier question, Asha realized. Maybe the way to survive in a life like this was to not think about anything that mattered. Keep focused on nothing.

Asha tried. "Tell me more."

"My mother has ridden in a car once. A police car. The police came and arrested some of the women in our building. They took them, and my mother was one of them, to the police station. They told all the women they must not do these things any more. They do not understand that none of them want to stand on the line. They have to because of the madam. They do not ask my mother if she is free to come and go out of her own room. If she is locked inside and cannot get out."

The girl rose to stand on the dirty mattress and look out the barred window. "So the madam comes and pays money to the police and they send the women away. They say they are letting them go, but they are not letting them go. They are sending them back to be slaves to the madam. I wish they would keep my mother in the prison. She would have a better life there."

Dapika continued chattering about life in Sonagachi as openly and randomly as any child would speak of a parent's occupation, only Dapika's words had Asha huddled into the corner of the room, wanting to put her hands over her ears to shut them out.

"When my mother has the men coming, she tells me to go outside and play. Or in the night, she tells me to go up on the roof. Sometimes I play, but I get bored, so I fall asleep. In the morning the birds hop around me on the roof. They chirp so loud. I think they are asking me why I am there instead of in bed." She turned from the window. "I've never ridden in a car before," she said, retreating to her first subject. "When they took me in the auto to your compound, it was the farthest I had ever been. I never go anywhere outside Sonagachi. It is the whole world for me. Now I have been far, but still not in a real car. I do not think this is fair. Do you not agree?"

Asha could not speak, could not bring herself to voice agreement about the unfairness of life in terms of getting to ride in a car or not. She only nodded mutely, but it was enough for Dapika.

Finally, the child's energy wore down. She flopped down on the bed and put her head on Asha's lap. "Riding in a car is not really so important," she said softly. "But if I think about it many times, it helps me not to think about what is real. Sometimes I think about becoming a bird. How I would fly away from places like this. I would fly far, where they could never find me again."

She pulled Asha's hand into her own. "It helps to pretend. My mother used to tell stories, but now she just stares and cries. It makes me sad, so I pretend and I fly away from her sadness." Bored, the child pulled on each of Asha's individual fingers. "Do you know any more stories, *Didi*? Would you tell me a story? Something that is better to think about than what is real?"

"Yes, I will tell you a story." Or two, or twenty. As many as it took to keep Dapika from talking more about the red-light district, and Asha from giving in to panic. "I have the best kind of stories to tell you." She tried to keep her voice light, free from the despair that had begun clutching at her. "They are stories that are good, but they are also stories that are real. I will tell you more stories about Jesus."

Asha looked heavenward. "And maybe, as we talk, He will send someone to help us fly away from here."

Mark turned in a slow circle. His gaze swept from the tattered ceiling, its drooping bars threatening to fall right into the tailor shop, down the paneled walls, to end at the concrete floor beneath his feet.

Nothing. No clue. No sign that anything unusual had even happened.

His teeth were grinding against each other. Mark forced his jaw to relax and tried to force his mind to focus. He needed to think of an excuse to go into the inner room and investigate the secret panel where Asha and the girl had hidden. Maybe she had suspected something and left him a hidden note. An address. Anything.

"I'm surprised you're open today," he said. His voice sounded casual, but he noticed his fists were clenched and hid them in his pockets.

"We are always open on this day, sir," the employee responded.

"So everything's been normal around here. No . . . strange events?"

Uncertainty covered the man's facial features. "I'm not sure what you mean . . ."

"Your new nighttime employees, they are doing a good job?" Mark's jaw clenched along with his fists. Had they been doing a good job, they never would have run when Asha needed them, fleeing the danger on the pretext of getting help.

"Yes, sir. They are fine." The man's feet shuffled as he hovered near Mark's elbow. "Their shift ended this morning. Did you have an order they were supposed to fill?"

"No. No, I was just curious." So the men must have returned before the end of their shift. At least they had not botched that up.

"Were you wanting a new shirt, sir? We have very nice cloth over here." The employee's eyes, darting from the bolt of cloth to Mark, showed curiosity. And perhaps a little suspicion?

Mark should take things slow. Act like he wanted a shirt so he could go be measured. Leave no room for any potential damage to their cover for future rescues.

But every minute in the shop was time lost, time he should be using to search for Asha. What good would any of this setup do anyway if he didn't find her soon?

His voice low, removing his tight fists, he stated plainly, "I need to go into your measuring room and look at something."

"Uh . . ."

Mark pulled out some money and tossed it toward the man. "Now."

Not waiting for an invitation or even permission, Mark crossed the small shop, yanked open the door and looked around impatiently until his eyes adjusted to the lack of light.

No shred of paper on the floor. No small note tucked into a crack in the wall.

He opened the secret panel and crouched down to fit inside. He barely fit even on his knees. His eyes and hands searched the floor, the shelves of saris, even the walls.

Nothing. Sharp pains shot up his jaw. He told himself to stop clenching it, but the seconds kept ticking away in his mind, every moment closer to ending his small window of time to find her. Mark was no fool. He knew the statistics. If he didn't find Asha in the first few days . . .

A creaking sound brought Mark's head up. He turned to see the panel door closing, him still inside.

"Wait. I'm still in here."

"I know."

The voice was tense. High-pitched with strain. It had none of the deference of the shop worker's, nor the youth.

Senses on full alert, Mark watched the panel door swing until two dark fingers reached around to stop it from closing fully. "Listen well, for I will only give my message once."

Mark's knees hurt from kneeling on the hard concrete floor. He remained still.

"You are looking for the woman and girl who were taken from here last night."

It was no question, so Mark gave no answer. He remained silent, slowly reaching into his backpack for the gun. Sweat broke out on the back of his neck as his fingers found the cold metal.

"I have information. But you must pay."

Mark's hand reached further, his fingers slid down until he gripped the gun. He had not loaded it yet, but maybe—

"There is a man who saw what happened and knows where the women were taken. He will meet you, if you will pay."

In one swift collection of moves, Mark dropped the backpack, shoved the panel door forward and barged back into the measuring room. His left hand gripped the man's neck, thrusting him against the wall, his right hand holding the gun to the man's cheek.

Thou shalt not kill.

Vengeance belongs to the Lord.

Mark ignored the verses whispered softly to his spirit. His voice was full of death as he ground out, "Where are they? Where did he take them?"

Wild, frightened eyes looked at Mark. "It was not just one. There are three men. And I'm not the one who knows! If you kill me, you will never find out where they went!"

Mark dug the point of his gun into the man's face. "Tell me what you know."

"I'm just the messenger." He whimpered and Mark eased up, but only a little. "The man said he would meet you at the Plaza Hotel this evening at six. You are to get a room so you can talk privately. Room 222. He will come and meet you there. You must be there at six o'clock."

The thunder of Mark's heartbeat had slowed. He pulled back and the man slumped to the floor.

"What is his name?"

The man rubbed his neck where Mark's hand had just been, and a blazing heat ran through Mark. Was it leftover adrenaline, or the searing of his conscience?

Mark looked away.

"I don't know. I have told you everything I know."

Mark reached out a hand to help the man up, but he scrambled away from the outstretched palm. Again, Mark felt the hot wash of shame. He pulled several bills from his wallet. "I'm sorry. Please take this for your trouble."

One hand reached toward the money, but hesitantly, like a small mouse wanting a crumb but fearing a trap. With a sudden flash of movement, the hand snatched the money and the man ran.

Mark followed at a much slower pace. His mind half-registered the tailor shop employee hunched over a sewing machine, making a feverish attempt to look busy and uninterested. He vaguely looked around one more time as he stepped onto the street, not expecting to find any clues but checking just in case.

Signaling to an auto, Mark gave him the name of the hotel. It was only four o'clock, but he had no desire to return to the compound—to the pleading of his grandmother, the disappointment of his father.

The auto sped out onto the main street. Mark gripped the side edge of the window until his knuckles turned white. This was his only chance, his only lead.

He was not going to miss it.

CHAPTER TWENTY-SIX

$\mathcal{A}$ new man entered the room, his hands wringing either with anticipation or anxiety. It looked like the latter.

Asha mentally named him Tense Man. His eyes constantly darted back and forth, and he kept mentioning the risk, the possibility of being caught, the horrors of prison, until finally Ahmad told him to either give his news and shut up or he would shoot him.

"I found him. The white man with yellow hair."

With a gasp, Asha sat up straight. She and Dapika had huddled into the corner of the bed when Ahmad and his hired thug entered that afternoon. Asha had named the thug Bulky Man for his wide girth and slow responses.

Ahmad sent Bulky Man to go get lunch, then he sat in the one chair available, leaned it back onto two legs and looked over at Asha. She kept her gaze away, but could feel his smile. Every few minutes he would chuckle, verbalizing his delight. Every time, Asha pulled Dapika closer, bit down on the angry words she knew would only please him to hear, and continued her unceasing prayer.

The tightening fear in her chest released a little when Bulky Man returned with a meager lunch for each of them. When Tense Man showed up, somehow Asha felt even better. A full room was better, anything was better than being alone with Ahmad.

Until the men started talking about Mark.

Now Ahmad looked over at her with a smile. She had removed her arms from their protective embrace around Dapika and nearly rushed to Tense Man to plead with him for information.

One look at Ahmad told her he was waiting for her to do just that. Using all her willpower, Asha bit her lips until they bled. She would not let him play games with her. A game with him could have only one winner.

Each muscle had to be forced into submission before Asha could will her body back into its slouch in the corner of the bed. Her head turned away from the men, as if she were indifferent to their conversation. But her ears, and her heart, strained to listen as the man spoke.

"He came to the tailor shop, just like you said he would."

"Did you deliver the message?"

"He has a gun."

Asha's eyes went wide. Mark had a gun? Or were they speaking of someone else?

Ahmad's voice slipped across Asha's senses like the caress of a python, ready to begin an embrace of death. "He will come. I know he will." She looked up just as his eyes turned to her, his mouth curving around the lush taste of victory in his words. "I have his most precious possession."

Mark paced from one end of the room to the other. Where was she? Would the man have enough information for him to find her that night? Would Mark actually follow through with his words to his father and kill Ahmad if he tried to stop him?

It had been a bad idea to come early. There was nothing to do in the hotel room but wait. Wait and fear and wonder what was happening to the woman he loved right at that moment. Were they hurting her? Was she afraid? Would they—

Mark slammed a hand down on the makeshift desk in the room. The gun on top of the desk bounced slightly from the force and the bullets he had laid out started to roll.

He picked them up and methodically, bullet by bullet, he loaded the weapon.

Thou shalt not kill.

Mark sat on the bed and put his head in his hands. "God, I . . ."

For the wrath of man does not produce the righteousness of God.

"I know." He spoke toward the ceiling. "But didn't You call men to protect their families? Their wives? Doesn't Ahmad need to be punished for the evil he has done? Not just to Asha, but to all those children and their families?" He ran shaky hands through his hair. "It's been twenty years since he started trafficking people, God. Twenty! Isn't it justice to stop him for good from ever doing this again? Isn't it right?"

Vengeance belongs to the Lord.

Mark felt his eyes sting with unshed tears. "My whole life, for as long as I can remember, I've trusted You. I've been faithful. I've tried to live the way You wanted." He ran his hands down his face and again looked upward. "But this is too much to ask of me. I'm only a man! He's taken the person I love most in the world."

He heard his own voice, brittle and sharp, like broken shards of glass. The words coming through his throat slashed and brought pain. "I've always held lightly to things, even my own life. But now there is something—someone—I want to hold tightly to. Why would You give her to me, give me this new desire to protect her, to keep her safe, if You were only going to take her away?"

He looked across the room at the small wall clock. The glass was cracked, but the clock still worked, still ticked away second after long second. Only four-thirty. Mark watched the small black line jolt moment by moment until it had made a full circle around the clock. One minute. Two minutes.

He looked at the gun in his hand, looked again at the clock, paced. He opened the one small window and leaned out, forced himself to breathe in and count to ten, then breathe out. He watched a street kid run down an outside concrete stairway that stretched from somewhere to his left down to the road below, and thought about the house he had bought for them, the home he would surprise her with on their honeymoon.

If they had one.

Shutting the window, he crossed the room, opened the door and peered into the hallway. Looked back at the clock. Four-forty. Of course the man would not be there yet.

Five minutes later Mark had run out of things to keep his mind off Asha. He sat at the desk and stared at his gun, picturing her afraid as they took her away, in pain as Ahmad struck her, pleading with tears as he sold her to the highest bidder, calling to God—or to him—to come save her when . . .

He couldn't stand it. Mark put his head in his hands, and for the first time in his adult life, he sobbed.

"I've decided to tell you my entire, amazingly well-thought-out plan."

Asha pretended to ignore Ahmad as Bulky Man untied Dapika from the leg of the bed and yanked her toward the door. Where were they going? She kept her eyes on Dapika as she followed the girl into the hallway and down toward the road in the exact reverse path they had taken before.

Her ears, however, were tuning out all the extra noises, focused solely on whatever Ahmad would choose to say. It may be the truth; it may not. But any information might help her think of some chink in his plan, something that would give her an opportunity for escape.

"I was going to keep it all a surprise," he said as he walked directly behind her, "and enjoy watching your dread and fear as you wondered what would happen next."

He passed by her with the gleeful grin of a child, an evil child, and said, "But I've decided I'll enjoy the even greater fear you'll have knowing what is coming." He gestured toward Bulky

Man and Tense Man, who led the way. "And these idiots are worthless to talk to. No, you are the only one who will fully appreciate the genius of it all."

Asha wanted to stop listening. She wanted to not care. But her body strained to keep up with him. Not to miss one word.

Once on the sidewalk of the busy road, Ahmad gestured for Tense Man to signal a taxi. When a yellow taxi car pulled up, Asha heard Dapika suck in a breath. "A car," she whispered. "A real car."

With no tenderness, the men pushed Asha and Dapika into the waiting taxi. Asha was glad for Dapika's fascinated distraction. She looked down at the fingers twisting in her lap and listened to Ahmad, who this time was sitting too close next to her in the back seat.

His voice was low, for her ears only. "First, we will trap your fiancé. I have a wonderful, foolproof plan for that. It includes your little friend here."

Asha clasped her hands together and squeezed so tight her arms started shaking. Ahmad let out a sound somewhere between a chuckle and a hiss.

"Don't worry, the one you love will not be killed. Oh no, I will make sure he is not killed." When Ahmad touched a strand of Asha's hair, she flinched away. "I want him to live a long life, every day knowing that the woman he wants is alive somewhere in the world, but he can never find her." He played with her hair and Asha's whole body began to tremble. "I got my revenge on Rashid by destroying Neena's beauty. And I will get my revenge on your Mark by taking you from him forever."

His voice took on a sing-song quality, as if he were telling a bedtime story to children. "And you," he said softly, "on you my ultimate revenge will be played out. This girl, who we will use to trap Mark, will be sold first. I will get a high price for her innocence, and you will live knowing you failed to rescue her."

His arm dropped to play with the edge of her sleeve. Asha gripped her knees with her hands, trying to physically stop her body from shaking.

"Last and best of all, you will be sold. A trafficked woman. Ironic, don't you think, that you will end up becoming one of the very women you tried so hard to save?"

He barked an order to the driver, then dropped his voice to the lullaby tone again. "It is an added bonus that you are beautiful, and pure. I actually have a bidding war going on for you. There are several buyers interested. I will wait and tease them a little. We have time. With Mark in prison, there will be no need to rush you across the border. I can afford to wait as your price goes up."

"Prison?" She had tried so hard to keep silent, but the word burst out.

His soft chuckle merged into a hard laugh. "Oh yes. It is a beautiful plan. Tonight at six-fifteen, your Mark will be arrested for child trafficking. Someone is going to call in and tip the police off, and they will arrive at room 222 to find a foreigner with a young Bengali girl."

He lifted his hand to her hair again, tightened his fingers, and gave one short tug. It hurt, but Asha closed her eyes, blocking the tears from release so Ahmad could not enjoy watching them fall.

"Even though I have not been in the city long, I have developed some beneficial connections. Like one certain police officer who will be happy to bring the young Bengali girl back to me once she is out of the clutches of the white man." He laughed again, and Asha heard madness in it.

She felt sick.

"Ah, we're here. How nice."

The car stopped and Ahmad politely paid the taxi driver and thanked him for the ride to the bus station.

Asha knew she should be looking around, discerning facts about their location, thinking about escape. But her mind kept rewinding and replaying Ahmad's words. Ahmad's plan that was, indeed, a horrifying sort of genius. A plan that would, as he wanted, cause the greatest pain.

Oh, God, help us! Help Mark!

They walked in an arc around the seemingly abandoned bus station. Behind it, across a small, narrow bridge, four long buildings stood parallel to each other. Each was only one story high, but had multiple doors on one side like a hotel.

There were no people in sight.

"We will not be interrupted here," Ahmad said, using a key on a rusted-over doorknob toward the end of the second building. Looking around from that spot, Asha saw that again, Ahmad had thought carefully, choosing a room far enough down that only the other buildings could be seen. Even if anyone did pass by the area, no one would see this room. There was no chance of alerting someone through an open window.

Asha could not stop thinking about Mark. Praying for him.

Her shoulders slumped as they entered the room and the dank smells of mold, sweat and alcohol gave little welcome. Her shoulders slumped further when Dapika slipped a hand into hers, tears in her eyes. "Now I have ridden in a car," she said. Her face dropped down. "Now I have nothing left to dream about."

Ahmad produced a scrap piece of paper from somewhere. He ordered Asha to sit on the bed and placed the paper and a pen on the bedside table.

"Write," he demanded.

Asha looked at the paper, her mind still full of Mark. "Write what?"

"A note to your beloved, of course. Your own words will be the ones used to trap him."

CHAPTER TWENTY-SEVEN

Asha held the pen and saw that her hand was shaking.

"Write exactly what I say, but in English," Ahmad ordered, lighting a cigarette and quickly filling the small room with smoke. Dapika coughed. "And if you obey, I will give you the reward of getting to continue writing to him. A chance to say goodbye. Must be the romantic in me." He laughed wildly at his own joke, then immediately sobered and leaned toward Asha with a frightening fierceness. She pulled away.

"Write this. Now. Dear Mark, Ahmad is very smart." He smiled as he paced the room, dictating, puffing smoke.

Asha wrote slowly, but her mind was running at a frantic pace. If Ahmad was going to let her write a full note to Mark after his dictation, then she could warn him about the trap! She wrote Ahmad's next words, "You will never win Ahmad's game. But he will give you three choices, and you can try to play."

Her brows furrowed with confusion. What was he talking about?

Ahmad had his back turned and something woke up in Asha's mind. Ahmad would never give her the opportunity to warn Mark. He was playing with her.

She continued writing the translation of what Ahmad said, but at the end of each sentence, she inserted several words of her own. His three choices were her undoing. A tear slipped down her cheek and landed on the paper, making a small round mark and blurring one of the words.

Dapika moved to sit by her side. "He is very evil. His choices are terrible, but he will not even allow those. You know that, don't you?"

Asha nodded. She knew.

"Will the foreigner know that?"

Another tear dropped to her cheek. This time Asha wiped it away. "I'm not sure."

Ahmad turned and looked over the paper. "Now, in the bottom empty space, you may write to him. Whatever you wish."

Once more he smiled and turned away.

Asha looked down at the small inch of white left on the paper. It might be her last words to the man she had planned to grow old with. What could she say?

> *Mark, I love you so much. I already miss you, and I know the hole in my heart will only get bigger over time. I will never stop trying to escape and return to you. And I promise I will never stop loving you. Ever. No matter what happens, I am always and forever yours. I will pray for you every day. I will pray God somehow makes a way for me to come back to you.*

There was no more room, but it did not matter, for Asha's tears kept her from seeing the paper any longer.

Ahmad approached and looked over the words at the bottom. "I'm sure this is very sentimental," he said, his tone slippery and snide. "Or maybe it isn't." He held the paper up. "You are a smart woman. You would love to have the chance to warn him of my plan, wouldn't you?"

Asha stared at the floor, willing her face not to betray her.

"I've got an idea." Ahmad laughed. He reached up and tore the paper down the middle. "I'll keep my part of the note, and you keep yours. A memento to remember the occasion."

He let Asha's part of the note float to the floor and remain there, like an abandoned hope.

She looked from the corner of her eye to see him step on the paper and use his foot to grind it until it tore. She closed her eyes against the sight. Felt her heart tearing.

When Ahmad was finished with her, would there be anything left?

Dapika whined when Ahmad grabbed her by the arm and forced her to her feet. "You are coming with me. I have a job for you to do."

He looked over to where Bulky Man and Tense Man stood near the door. "Stay here with her." He pointed with his chin at Asha. "Don't let her try anything, but do not touch her. Not one touch. She must remain pure or I don't get my high price, and you don't get paid. Do you understand?"

The men nodded wordlessly and Ahmad dragged a struggling Dapika to the door. Asha remained frozen on the bed, hands twisted into a knot on her lap.

"Oh, I almost forgot, one more souvenir for you." He reached into a pocket.

Ahmad pulled out a worn piece of material that Asha recognized as her baby blanket, her one keepsake of her village family. Last summer she had given it to her biological mother. Seeing it now, Asha could not keep from crying out.

Watching her, beaming at the devastation in her eyes, Ahmad slowly and calculatingly tore the blanket in two. Already worn, it tore away easily, but the sound wrenched through her. He approached and gently laid one piece on Asha's lap.

"The other half is a present for someone else," he said, his voice low and dark.

Asha waited until he pulled Dapika through the doorway, reminding the men to lock the door behind him. She waited until she heard the sound of a vehicle pulling away. She waited until the sounds had died away to silence, until only her own ragged breathing could be heard.

Then she lifted the shred of blanket and buried her face in it, giving in to the tears.

Mark woke to the sound of hard knocking on the door. He sat up groggily. Where was he?

Another loud knock. He looked around. Saw the clock on the wall. Six p.m. Awareness flooded in and Mark shot off the bed. "I'm coming!" How could he have fallen asleep?

Rushing to the door, he remembered that he had not slept at all the night before, but even so, with something this important he should have stayed alert and very aware.

With one hard pull the door opened. Mark frowned at the young girl standing there. She had not been the one knocking so forcefully earlier. He stuck his head into the hallway and looked to the left, then the right.

"Where is the man who promised to meet me here with information?" he asked in Bengali.

The girl looked up at his hair and gulped. With obvious effort, she said words in English he could tell she had memorized and did not understand.

"I-am-your-"

She hesitated, swallowed, and started again.

"I-am-your-conso-la-tion-prize."

Something inside Mark churned. This was not right.

He ushered the little girl into his room. "What are you doing here? Who sent you here?"

"She did," the girl said in Bengali, holding out a torn shred of paper covered in a handwriting as familiar to him as his own.

His heart immediately raced. Asha. Just thinking the name had his throat tight and his eyes burning.

He read the English words aloud.

> *Dear Mark,*
> *Ahmad is very smart. You will never win Ahmad's game.*
> *But he will give you three choices, and you can try to play.*

His face hardened. He looked at the girl. She motioned for him to continue.

> Here are Ahmad's three options for you:
> 1. Trade the child back for me. Mark, escape with the girl!
> 2. Meet me one last time before I'm taken away and sold forever. It's a trap!
> 3. Come to the bus station, and if you kill Ahmad you can rescue me. Run! Run!
> Write your answer and give it to the child. Then wait until someone comes to pick her up at 6:15. Don't wait, Mark. Go now. I love you.

His mind analyzed, processed. She was warning him. Ahmad had set this meeting up to trap him. But if he stayed, maybe he could defeat whoever came and find out where they were keeping Asha. He could try to—

Something tugged on his sleeve. He looked down into the huge, fear-filled eyes of the girl. Everything in his own flesh urged him to stay. A still small voice communicated something else, through the trusting eyes of a child.

"Okay." He choked over the words. "Let's go."

He started toward the door when the sound of quick footsteps coming down the hallway stopped him. He turned. "The window."

Running ahead of him, the girl reached the window just as someone began banging on the door. "Open up! Police!"

By the time he reached the window, she had slipped through it and was hanging from it over the stairway. He plucked her hands from the edge and lowered her so her drop was only a few feet. Then he maneuvered his body through the small opening, dropping to the stairs and falling down them, rolling away so he would not harm the child.

He heard the sound of a door being busted in above them. Picking up the waif of a girl, he ran, rounding the corner just as the voices came to the open window.

Practically throwing the child into an auto, he jumped in after her while simultaneously yelling, "Go as fast as you can! That way!"

He pointed and the man sped off. Mark looked back to see several men in police uniforms at the window of room 222. One tried to squeeze through the window, then they all retreated.

Mark turned back and settled into his seat. "By the time the men get out of the hotel and into their vehicle, we'll be long gone."

Gone. He with a rescued person, but not the one he wanted.

It was then that the child pulled something out of her torn dress pocket. She handed Mark half of Asha's baby blanket. He remembered it; it was one of her most precious possessions.

Ahmad's revenge was complete.

Mark closed his eyes tight against the pain and told the driver the address back to the missionary compound.

CHAPTER TWENTY-EIGHT

Asha wanted to scream. Her fear had been diluted, then overtaken altogether by a completely different feeling. She was downright annoyed.

It was enough that Ahmad had taken her and was going to sell her. But to add the insult of sitting in front of her, blowing smoke in her face as he gloated over how easy it had been to manipulate Mark into coming to the hotel room, how much fun it was going to be to hear about him going to jail, was just too much.

She started imagining shoving the cigarette down his throat and watching him choke on it when a loud knock at the door brought her to attention.

Ahmad's lazy smile spread. He slowly rose and walked toward the doorway. The knocking had not stopped. It was louder, more forceful, urgent.

"Now we will hear how the man you love was defeated," Ahmad said with a happy sigh. He opened the door.

Asha craned her neck to see around him. A man in a police uniform, sweat dripping down his face, shifted his weight from one foot to the other. His eyes were panicked. "He got away!"

Quickly, Ahmad shoved the man backward. He stepped outside and shut the door behind him.

Asha ran to it and put her ear up against the door. Ahmad was yelling. The man responded, something about the girl being gone too. She heard the sound of a hard punch.

"You fool! How could you let them get away?"

The door opened and Asha stumbled back against Bulky Man, who had joined her at the door to listen. Ahmad pushed them both aside, marching around the room, mumbling to himself. "It was so perfect. Foolproof. He must be smarter, or the others more foolish than I thought."

He walked outside again and kicked the policeman where he lay on the ground. "Get out of here before someone sees you." Ahmad spit on him, then returned inside and slammed the door shut.

Asha's heart raced. Had her warning worked? Had they really gotten away—both of them? *Oh, thank You, God!*

"This changes everything. He's ruined my plan!"

"You promised we'd get our share of the money from selling the little girl. I'm still expecting that money." Bulky Man had his thick arms crossed in front of his chest.

"I can't be expected to pay money I don't have," Ahmad hissed between his teeth. "You'll get your money when I've sold her." He pointed at Asha. "Her price will be more than enough to make all of us happy."

"But if we wait on the bidding war, the fiancé might find out where she is, especially now that he's got the girl!" Tense Man was wringing his hands, his eyes shifting around the room.

"Shut up!" Ahmad silenced the man with a hard slap. The snapping sound of flesh on flesh made Asha wince.

"The girl is young and stupid. She was never taught to think." He rubbed a hand across his chin. "But you have a point about the foreigner. Our time may have to be cut short."

"The only bus that comes to this station is in the middle of the night." Bulky Man shifted forward, arms still crossed.

"Yes, of course." Ahmad stopped his march around the small room, still rubbing his chin. "The special bus, utilized by criminals of all kinds. I've heard of it."

Suddenly he had his gun in his hand and was pointing it toward Asha. She sucked in a breath. He spoke, his words hard and fast. "Stay right here. I'm going to make arrangements." He looked at the two men. "We leave tonight. We'll take her across the border and find someplace to stay so we can continue the bidding war. Maybe we'll even take her to the places so they can see in person what they are bartering for. If we play our cards just right, we may get enough to make up for the loss of the girl."

"You'd better."

Ahmad walked over and this time gave Bulky Man's face a hard smack. His face barely registered the impact, but Asha saw Ahmad rub his hand. As Ahmad turned away, Asha's eyes went wide. Bulky Man walked behind him, hands outstretched to cup an empty space right behind Ahmad's neck. He rounded his hands and shook them, as if he were choking Ahmad.

By the time Ahmad turned around, his arms were crossed again. Asha tried to still her heart's suddenly frantic pace.

"Get everything ready for us to leave at midnight," Ahmad ordered the man. "I'll be back later with the tickets."

Silence reigned after the door shut behind him. Asha watched Bulky Man and Tense Man whisper their hatred for Ahmad. Could she use their anger somehow?

Now that Dapika was safe, she could try to escape. But how? She had so little time. Only until midnight. Less really, because as soon as Ahmad returned, he would be sure to keep her confined.

These men, however, were paying less attention to her. *Think. Think!*

How could she get away?

Mark's heart felt as if it had been filled with stone. It sank in his chest as the compound came into view. A deep and heavy hopelessness pushed on his shoulders.

All was lost. He had failed.

The young girl stepped from the auto and looked around in wonder. "I remember this place. He brought me here once."

When Milo emerged from the guard shack, she smiled. "I remember him, too."

"You're the girl from Sonagachi," Milo said, his crutch clacking against the concrete as he approached. "I thought you were captured with *Didi*. What happened?"

Before she or Mark could speak, a door opened across the way. Eleanor Stephens, John Stephens, Rashid and the Christian sari shop workers all funneled out the door and rushed toward him.

Mark swallowed his humiliation. "I've got to go speak with them. I need to apologize, and then ask for their help—and the Lord's—on what to do next."

Dapika backed away at the sight of two more white people. "Can I just stay here and talk to him?" She gestured toward Milo.

"Sure," Mark said absently. He grimaced at the hug from his grandmother—one he didn't deserve—and grimaced again at the tears in his father's eyes as John Stephens' arms wrapped around him too.

As the group walked back toward his grandmother's house, Mark heard Milo say behind him, "How did you get out? Where is Asha *Didi*? Tell me everything!"

CHAPTER TWENTY-NINE

"It's hopeless. I lost. Ahmad played me for a fool and I walked right into his hands." Mark looked down at his feet, then forced himself to look each person in the eye. "I am truly sorry to each of you." He looked at the Christian shop workers. "To you for blaming you for something that was not your fault. I wanted to be angry with someone other than myself, and that was wrong. Please forgive me."

"To you." He looked at his father, his eyes stinging. "For willfully disobeying. You were right and I was wrong. I'm sorry."

When Eleanor Stephens wrapped her arms around him again, shedding tears on his shoulder, his heart clenched. "And to you, Grams, for making you worry so."

He heaved a breath. "I didn't trust God or listen to you. I tried my own way to get Asha back, and I failed. My pride and anger—she's lost to me forever now." He sank onto a chair and put his head in his hands. He did not care if they all saw him weep. What difference did it make? His future had shattered. His heart, too.

"Son, I forgive you." John Stephens put a hand on Mark's shoulder.

"We do, too." Paul, one of the Christian brothers, spoke for his group. "But hope may not be as lost as you think."

Mark lifted bloodshot eyes. "What do you mean?"

Rashid stood and directed Mark's attention to several crude drawings with street names spread out over Eleanor Stephens' dining room table. "While you were out searching, we have been working as well."

Within two seconds Mark was at Rashid's side, looking over the papers. "What do you mean? Have you found something?"

The group filed forward until they circled the table. "We think so," Paul said. "When Ahmad came and forced us at gunpoint to leave the shops, I ran across the street and hid. When he took Asha and Dapika, I followed them as long as I could."

Fire spread through Mark. "Someone stayed and followed?" He lowered his head. "Again, I am sorry."

Paul nodded his acceptance of the apology. "I, too, love someone. I would have felt the same way."

Mark looked over the drawings. "So what have you discovered so far?"

"We think we know which direction they are headed. There is a place across the border, a common stopover for pimps and madams with their newly trafficked victims. A stopping place where people are bought and sold before they are taken to their smaller—and more difficult to trace—intended destinations."

Mark's eyes squeezed shut. If they were headed there, Ahmad would not harm Asha. Not allow her to be abused until they arrived. *Please, God . . .*

Eleanor Stephens raised her small hand and got their attention. "We have much to discuss, but first, could we pray?"

Heads nodded. Mark could not trust himself to speak. Reaching out, he grasped his grandmother's hand. Her voice wavering, Eleanor prayed, followed by Mark's father, followed by Rashid and the others in the group.

Mark was last. His heart had groaned within him at their requests for Asha's safety, for her return, for her soul and spirit to be protected. When it was his turn, he could not speak more than to say a rough "Amen."

He dropped his grandmother's hand, tempted to ask them all to pray again. He had tried in his own strength to help Asha and failed. He knew now that for Asha to be spared, God would have to intervene.

"Now, let's—"

The door to the dining room opened. The group looked up to see Milo rush in, Dapika close behind him. "I think I know where they are!" Milo shouted triumphantly. He reached back and pulled Dapika forward by the hand. "She told me enough. I've heard of this place where they took her. But I don't know how to get there. We need her mother."

"Asha's mother?"

"No." Milo shook his head. "Dapika's mother. We have to go rescue her from Sonagachi right away."

Asha looked over the two men, then the hotel room, with frustration. She had tried asking for food, but the men would not leave the room. She had gone into the bathroom and tried to pry open the window, but it was rusted shut. Shouting would do no good; no one was around to hear.

Time was running out. Darkness had already fallen. It had to be at least eight in the evening. Ahmad would return soon, then midnight would come. After that, her chances of escape would dwindle. Then once he sold her, Asha knew her chances of escape would practically be snuffed out.

God, what should I do?

Tense Man said something that must have irritated Bulky Man, for he lifted a huge fist and shook it in Tense Man's face. Over the past two days, Asha had watched the lumbering man nearly snap several times. Pity the man in front of him when he finally lost his temper.

Or the woman . . .

Asha looked away from the two arguing men and tried to think. Last summer, when they had rescued Rani, Mark's grandmother had mentioned that because Rani had been beaten, her price would be diminished until the bruises faded.

What if Asha could get Bulky Man to lose his temper and hit her? That might stall Ahmad's bidding war until she could think of another plan. Or at least give Mark more time to search for her.

"Hey," Asha called out, inserting derision into her voice. "Why are you letting Ahmad push you around the way he does? You're bigger than he is, and stronger. At least you look like you are. But then again, maybe you're really weak. Too weak to stand up to another man."

Bulky Man stared her down. His fists clenched.

"Don't listen to her. Don't go near her!" Tense Man pulled uselessly on the man's thick arm.

When Bulky Man stopped and stepped back again, Asha forced herself to laugh like Ahmad had earlier. "You can't even stand up to a woman, can you?"

She saw him swallow. Saw his eyes narrow into slits. "Don't push me, woman," he growled.

"Why not? You can't do anything to me. Ahmad told you not to. And you're his little slave, aren't you? His little servant, paid to stand there and not think until he tells you to."

"Shut your mouth."

He walked toward her. Tense Man was wringing his hands. "No, no! We'll never get any of our money if you damage her!"

Asha ignored her racing heart. She tried to still her breathing enough that he would not see the fear pulsing through her. "You hate him," she said, swallowing away the breathlessness in her voice. "But you won't do a thing against him. You won't touch me. You won't lift a finger against me. Ahmad told you not to." Her voice took on the whine of a child chanting victory over the loser in a game. "You can't hit me. He won't let you. You can't hit me. He won't let you."

Over and over she said it, watching as red flushed his face and the veins in his arms began to stand out. "Enough!" he shouted. He barreled toward her until she had backed against the wall. His hand palmed her face and he pushed it back against the solid surface behind her. His fingers dug into her flesh until she saw sparks behind her eyes.

When he started talking, Asha's bravado fled. She had chosen the wrong man to manipulate into action. He stood with his hand on her face, talking, growling out exactly what he would do to her.

It was not a beating he described.

CHAPTER THIRTY

Chest heaving, Asha tried to maneuver her face away, but her efforts only made him laugh. He continued his description, graphic details of how he would make her suffer, and she found her whole body trembling with fear.

"No! You can't!" Tense Man paced behind them. "We won't get any money out of her!"

"Be quiet!" the man yelled, his booming voice immediately silencing the other man. "We'll get enough money out of her." He pushed against her face again. "I'll teach her a lesson, then we'll teach Ahmad a lesson, then we can take her across the border ourselves and sell her." He laughed and Asha's blood chilled at the sound. "Or what's left of her."

God . . . God . . . God . . .

She could think of no other words. His laugh continued to punch through the air. It registered that Tense Man had run from the room, leaving her alone with the monster she had woken inside this man.

God . . .

"I love it that you're scared." The man's voice morphed into a whisper. His fingers squeezed on her face. His other hand touched her and she reacted, lifting her knee and kicking him in the groin.

With a yelp, his hand fell away from her face. He doubled over, shouting curses, and Asha scrambled, arms flailing, over the hotel bed and toward the door.

A heavy arm reached around her middle and threw her entire body back against the wall. She gasped for breath as pain shot through her.

"One hour with me and you will never have the courage to look a man in the eye again!" His voice sent shock waves through her, worse than the pain. He laughed and Asha shut her eyes tight. This was the end. The end of her innocence. The end of her future.

"What is going on here?"

The sound of the door banging against the wall brought Asha's eyes open wide.

Bulky Man's fingers unclenched and she fell back against the bed. His hands went behind his back, but the huge gash where he had just ripped her shalwar kameez in one fierce yank gave silent witness to his intentions.

Inches of bare shoulder were visible, torn threads reaching out between the front and back portions of her top like long, desperate fingers trying to clasp each other again. He had ripped the seam from her neck across her left shoulder.

She hunched over, trying to hide her body, even this small exposed area leaving her vulnerable and ashamed.

Ahmad asked no questions. He gave no reprimand. Very slowly, very deliberately, he pulled his gun from his belt, aimed, and shot.

Asha's scream rent the air. The large man dropped to the floor at her feet. A pool of red blood spread out slowly beneath him. It inched toward her toes. She pulled her legs up onto the bed and cowered into the corner, as far away from the twitching, then lifeless body as she could get.

Asha's eyes were still locked onto the grueling sight when Ahmad's shadow neared. It covered the man, then crept up her legs, up her body as he came closer. She shrunk from his outstretched hand. A hand that had just killed.

She heard him sit in front of her on the bed. Asha could not bear to open her eyes to see what he was doing. Was he playing with her pain? Enjoying her face contorted with fear, her teeth biting down on her lips to keep from crying out?

She huddled back against the headboard, as far away from Ahmad as she could get.

Finally she opened her eyes to see Ahmad tuck the gun again behind his back. Then his hand reached toward her face. She cringed and shuddered, but could not get her eyes to look away from it.

He smoothed down the hair that Bulky Man had mussed. His tone was polite and icy. "Those still living have been reminded how important it is to keep you safe and secure without any . . . unexpected difficulties . . . getting in the way."

He put a long, cold finger under her chin. It lifted her face for his perusal, but she refused to lift her eyes. Asha willed herself not to shudder as he spoke. "It is good that I was alerted in time. You are such a beauty, I should have expected him to be tempted," he said, his whisper deceptively soft. "You know, selling you will be a delight." His finger rubbed across her jawline. "Not only will it complete my revenge on all who have betrayed me, but now that there is one less man to pay, the price you fetch will make me rather rich."

She did look up then, and the hate shining in his eyes filled her body with terror. "And since you so effectively separated me from my brother, and even my parents . . ." His finger brushed up to her cheek and slowly squeezed into a pinch until Asha whimpered. He removed his hand before a bruise developed. "I will be all the more wealthy, for now there is no one to spend the money on but myself."

He leaned in until one knee rested on the bed next to her. Asha had already backed away until there was no place else she could go. His face was inches from hers. His breath pushed against her. She wrapped her arms around herself and tried not to cry.

Ahmad backed into a standing position but Asha remained huddled against the wall. She hid her face in her hands.

"Don't worry," Ahmad said as he walked away, his feet treading through the pooled blood and leaving a trail of red footprints to the door. "You have at least two more hours until the bus leaves." He turned in the open doorway so she could see his emotionless smile through her upheld fingers. "Plenty of time to think about what's coming at the end of the trip."

He opened the door and summoned Tense Man back inside. "Watch her closely. I'll be back."

With one hand on the doorknob, he turned. Slowly, making sure the agony of each second of lost freedom was fully felt, he slid the door shut.

The sound of the lock echoed in the silent room.

Asha curled into a ball on the bed, not bothering to cry. She wrapped her arms around herself, trying to collect all the broken pieces of who she was and hold them together as long as possible.

But the truth, the death, assaulted her mind from every direction. The smell of blood filled her senses.

She covered her face in her hands and burrowed into the mattress.

She had lost. Ahmad had won.

CHAPTER THIRTY-ONE

"*T*hat was the easiest rescue I've ever been part of!"

Mark looked up from the table to see Rashid, Paul and Milo enter the room. Each man was smiling. Behind them, Dapika entered, her hand pulling the arm of a hesitant older woman.

"Come in, Mother. You are safe now."

The woman, looking dazed, followed her daughter, her eyes searching the room.

"God was surely leading the way tonight," Paul said. "We just pushed open the door and marched inside. The madam came out and started yelling, but I pulled out my official card and flashed it at her. It was only a card to rent movies at the video store, but she did not know that."

"'You don't want to get arrested, do you?'—that's what Rashid said and the woman ran into her room and locked the door. It was great! We just walked back to Dapika's mother's room and escorted her right out."

The mother, eyes still wandering the room in what looked like confusion, approached the table where Mark and his family sat. "Thank you for rescuing my daughter. That man lied to me. I will help you any way I can."

Dapika crept up to Milo and spoke in his ear. Milo approached behind Mark and whispered in English, "She is probably—what you say?—on drugs. They give them to her at night. So you must be speaking real slow because she is thinking slow, okay?"

"Okay, thanks," Mark said to Milo. To the mother, he described the area where they thought Ahmad had taken Asha. "Milo says he has heard of a midnight bus, one that drug runners and traffickers like to take."

Dapika's mother nodded. "I have heard of this bus. Some of the women came to Sonagachi on it. Yes, it is in that area. I can tell you where it is."

Mark wanted to drop his head into his hands and thank God. But there was no time. It was already ten o'clock. Instead he gave his thanks silently, even while stating aloud, "Let's go. We can develop our plan on the drive."

John Stephens parked the Land Rover several hundred yards away from the station, ensuring no one could hear their approach. Mark pulled the second vehicle to park behind him. The group gathered into a circle and prayed one last time.

Once finished, Eleanor called Mark over to where she now sat in the front seat of the Land Rover. "Your father and I will remain here, praying." She reached for his hand. "I forgot to tell you earlier, but we had to call Asha's parents in America and tell them what happened."

Mark winced. How awful for her parents. "I guess they're coming out here?"

"That was their first response. But then as we talked, they realized they could do nothing to help out here, and so they decided to stay in North Carolina and start a twenty-four hour prayer chain with the people of their church. I called them again on the way here and they said over a hundred people had gathered at their church to pray. I told her what we were planning, and they said they would tell everyone so they can be praying especially about the next hour."

Mark's voice was husky. "Thanks, Grams. Prayer is what we need most right now."

She nodded. "You know Zechariah 4:6. 'Not by might, nor by power, but by His Spirit.'"

He felt the building tension release a little. "Thanks for the reminder."

She reached to the backseat where a Bible lay. "And on the way here, I found this verse: Psalm 72:4. 'He will bring justice to the poor of the people; He will save the children of the needy, and will break in pieces the oppressor.'" She lightly touched his arm. "God will deal with Ahmad. Don't become like him by seeking revenge."

Mark pulled his grandmother into a tight hug. "All I care about right now is getting Asha safely home."

"We need to go." Rashid's voice behind him was hushed.

Mark turned. "Is everybody ready?"

The men nodded. "Oh, wait." Rashid reached into his pocket and pulled out his wallet. "Here, take this," he said to Milo, who stood at his side leaning on his crutch.

Milo grinned. "Sure!" He snatched the wallet from Rashid's hand. "I'd better go find someplace to spend this!"

He took off at a run but Rashid slowed him with his words. "Don't start running yet. We've got a long way to go."

Mark looked back at his father and grandmother. "Lord willing, we'll be back soon. With Asha."

Both nodded, standing silently as the men, led by one boy with a crutch and one small girl, walked into the darkness of the night toward the bus station.

Tense Man was wringing his hands again. He kept looking at Bulky Man's body and muttering to himself. "He said nobody would get hurt. He said we'd be rich. He never said we'd have to go across the border. Risk getting arrested."

Asha heard noises outside. Rising from the bed, she walked carefully around the body on the floor toward the window next to the door. Peering out, she could not see anyone. But she had definitely heard the sound of a vehicle.

There was another one. Someone was nearby!

Tense Man stood and joined her at the window. "It's eleven-thirty. Almost time. People are coming to take the bus across the border." He looked over at her. "If you're thinking of trying to get one of them to help you escape, don't bother. The midnight bus is for people who will do anything for money, and will do nothing if money is not offered. You have no money, so you have no hope."

"What if I could promise someone money?" Asha stood stock still and tried to speak casually. "What if I could promise you more money than Ahmad promised?"

He sniffed. "If you could show it to me, I'd listen. But you and I both know you have nothing."

Asha tried not to sound too eager. "But I know people who do. People who would pay you to help me get out of here."

"Well . . . what would—"

Ahmad burst into the room, shouting on his cell phone. Tense Man immediately backed away from Asha and their conversation. Asha banged her head against the window.

"No, you said you would give the higher price." Ahmad's voice was filled with rage. "You can't lower her price just because I only have one girl to sell instead of two." He pulled his gun from behind him and threw it on the bed. "No, I'll go to your competitor. They'll pay, and you'll be sorry!"

He slammed the cell phone closed and threw it across the room. "Get everything ready," he spit out toward Tense Man. "It's time to go."

Asha stared at the gun lying on the bed. If Ahmad took just a step or two farther away, she was sure she could get to it before he could.

She held her breath, inching toward the bed half-step by tiny half-step, eyes glued to the weapon.

"I'm going to the bathroom," Ahmad said. "You'd better be ready when I come out."

The moment he closed the bathroom door, Asha dashed toward the bed. Her arm reached out, but Tense Man was faster and grabbed the gun. He held it over his head like a trophy.

Asha saw that his finger was not on the trigger. This was her chance. What were those moves she had learned from Mark's self-defense DVD?

With as much force as she could muster, she kicked him in the shin, put an elbow into his gut, then when he bent over in surprised pain, she reached above his head for the gun.

Now both their hands were around the weapon. They careened back and forth, like a couple doing an odd sort of dance. Tense Man spoke with effort. "He will be back soon. How much are you willing to pay for me to let you out right now?"

Asha stopped her frantic pulling and looked the man in the eye. "How much do you want?"

She saw the bathroom doorknob turn. Her palms were sweating, slipping on the gun. His were, too. With one lunge, he pushed her back and onto the floor. Just as Ahmad opened the door, he swung his arms down and hid the gun behind his back.

"Where's my phone?" Ahmad said crossly. He stepped over the dead body with irritation. "We've got to go now. I want to get on the bus early so we can get a seat in the back and not draw attention."

He found the phone on the floor near the bed and pocketed it. His eyes went to the bed. "Where is my gun?"

"Right here."

Ahmad turned to see his hired thug holding the weapon. "Well, give it to me."

"I don't think so."

Ahmad looked the wiry little man over. "Don't be stupid. We've got to go now."

"Oh, we'll go. But just the girl and I," the man said. Ahmad felt a tremor run through him. The man's voice suddenly sounded very much like his own.

"As you said," the man continued, "if there's one less man to pay, there is more money for whoever is left."

Ahmad felt a line of sweat start at the back of his neck and run down his back. Anger flooded him and filled him with heat. When the man pointed the gun at Ahmad's heart, the anger was replaced with wariness.

As he stared at the gun, his own gun, Ahmad suddenly saw his life with a blinding clarity. He saw babies being taken and sold. Mothers grieving. He saw money passing from his hand to other hands to keep men silent. He saw his brother, his parents, Neena's face in torment as the acid ate away her skin.

Turning slightly, he looked to where Asha stood, her eyes on the gun, her hand to her heart. For one small moment, he wondered if he should call on God for help.

But the moment passed and Ahmad even laughed at himself a little. He would diffuse this situation and find some way to end up on top again. He always did. That's what his life was all about, being on top, having everything he wanted.

Looking back at the man holding the gun, Ahmad schooled his face to look calm and in charge. He spoke with authority, using the tones that always brought about submission from those beneath him. Which was everyone.

"Give me the gun. You know you can't pull this off without me."

The man looked down at the body near his feet. His eyes filled with a dark and lecherous knowledge. Ahmad knew that look. It was his look—the look he had given the other man before killing him.

A strange sensation swept through him. Was this what fear felt like?

When the bullet burst from the gun and found a place within his chest, Ahmad stood in dazed shock for a full three seconds before the impact brought him to his knees. He heard a scream behind him as he fell to the floor.

Lying on his side, he watched in a sick sort of awe as his own blood spread beneath him. He imagined the millions of tiny blood cells enjoying a cold new freedom as they fled his body and slid across the floor.

Darkness began to consume the edges of his vision. He looked up to see Asha, the woman he had stolen, bending over him. She was crying. The man pulled on her arm and ordered her to stand.

"Ahmad." He heard her say his name, but she sounded far away, as if she were calling to him from another world. "Call out to Jesus. Ask Him to forgive you! Don't die without believing in Him!"

Was she telling him to suddenly come to faith? To be forgiven?

A silence, dark and terrifying, closed in on him. He fought it, but it was winning. It flooded through his body, enclosed and engulfed his eyesight, his hearing, his sense of touch. Soon nothing was left but darkness. Darkness and fear.

Was this how his victims felt when he betrayed them?

One flicker of remorse called to him. For one moment he considered humbling himself, asking forgiveness, putting his faith in something other than himself.

No. No, he would triumph. He would overcome. There was no way he was going to prostrate himself before God and ask for help. Not Ahmad.

The darkness took on a red tint. It started in the middle, then spread and grew. A sudden terror like he had never known filled him, surrounded him, swallowed him alive.

"Wait! Wait!" he tried to say. "I'm not ready!"

The darkness, the heat, the eternal despair did not heed his demands.

Ahmad heaved in one last breath, and the release of it carried his final words.

"Too late."

CHAPTER THIRTY-TWO

"I didn't expect there to be so many people here."

Rashid looked over at Mark. "Let's hope your white skin won't draw too much attention from the wrong people. We just walked quite a distance to avoid attention."

"Maybe we should go ahead and split up. I don't like the look of this whole setting."

Milo and the girl, Dapika, had stopped ahead of them. "What is it?" Mark asked when they caught up.

"It is just as her mother said," Milo whispered. "They bring girls to the hotel for the people coming in the middle of the night. That is why there is a bridge." He jutted his chin toward the small, rickety bridge that separated several long buildings from the station itself. "See the man in front of the bridge? He is there to guard it."

"My mother said there would probably be a guard, someone who would not allow you to pass unless you pay."

Rashid's voice was low as he leaned toward Mark. "And like you said earlier, we could possibly pay and get passed through, but you would stand out too much. It would be too risky."

"So we do the plan?" Milo's face was practically lit up with anticipation.

"Looks like we'll have to." Mark looked down at Milo and spoke with the seriousness of a father leading his own son into battle. "Be safe. This isn't a game. These men are deadly. Follow the plan exactly, okay?"

"No problem for Milo. Milo will help save the day for Asha *Didi*."

"I pray it will be so," Mark said softly. He looked over at Rashid and Paul, then down again at Milo. "If you succeed, meet us back at the Land Rover. The officer should be there by the time any of us get back."

"A policeman?"

He looked down to see Dapika shivering. "Not exactly," he said. "This man runs a non-profit organization that works alongside the law. He will not be bribed to do wrong. He is a follower of Jesus and Jesus says we should set the captives free and bring justice for those in need, not help those who do evil."

Dapika's eyes went wide. "I hope you are right," was all she would say.

The guard at the bridge looked around and yawned. He blew his nose out onto the street, then pulled out a cell phone and started dialing.

"Now's the perfect time. Go!"

Mark took Dapika's hand and ran to the left while the two other men ran to the right.

Milo headed straight toward the guard and the bridge. While the man spoke on the phone, Milo approached, leaning on his crutch, and held out his hand.

"*Baksheesh*," he said with a forlorn whine. "*Baksheesh.*"

Dapika giggled at Mark's side. "He's a good beggar, isn't he?"

The man on the phone shook his head at Milo, then gave him a little shove when he wouldn't go away. Suddenly through the darkness, Rashid's voice startled the man into dropping his phone.

"Stop that boy! He has my wallet!"

The man reached down to pick up his phone and Milo scampered deftly across the bridge and to the right. Rashid and

Paul ran up to the bridge. "What are you doing?" Rashid yelled. "Help me catch him!"

Rashid and Paul half-led, half-pushed the man across the bridge in the direction Milo took.

Milo looked back to see if they were following. With a grin, he took a sharp left to run between the first two of the four buildings. The three men followed.

"Our turn." Mark and Dapika ran across the now empty bridge.

"This way." Dapika led Mark to the left and down between the third and fourth buildings.

Suddenly the sound of a shot rang out from one of the buildings. It echoed around them. Mark could not tell where it came from. A scream followed. It was a woman's voice, coming from the building on their left, several doors down.

"Asha!" Had it been her? Mark broke into a run. *God, please don't let me get this close only to lose her forever.* His legs burned as he sprinted the last few yards to the end of the building. No one was there.

"Here!"

He turned to see Dapika standing beside a room three doors back. He had passed it.

"It's this one!"

Running back, he pulled his gun and held it in front of him. He needed a weapon in hand if he would soon be facing whoever made that shot. Hopefully his face would not give away the important fact that the gun was once again empty and completely useless.

At the door to the room, Mark stopped only long enough to tell Dapika, "Step back. When I kick the door in, if you see trouble, go and find the others and get out of here. Understand?"

Dapika gave a wordless nod, eyes wide, and Mark turned to face the door. Holding the gun ready, he lifted his leg and gave the door a strong, hard kick. The rusted doorknob gave way and the door crashed open.

Mark ran in and tried to process, think and respond all at once. His eyes took in the facts. His heart raced with both delight and terror.

She was here. She was alive. But she was being pulled toward the door by a man with a gun. Mark saw him react to his presence by pulling Asha's body in front of his and holding the gun to her side. "I'll kill her."

"Mark!" Her voice made him want to sit down and cry like a baby. "Oh, Mark, thank God."

Mark took a quick look around and his eyes found the two bodies just as his nostrils filled with the scent of fresh blood. He had to force himself to not think about the surety that one of the bodies was Ahmad's. "Let her go."

He heard the steel in his voice. Knew it was also in his eyes. He hoped it would be enough, as there was no steel packed in his gun.

"Mark, he'll take money," Asha said breathlessly, her windpipe blocked by the man's arm around her neck. "You want money, right?" She directed her question back toward the man. "We talked about it. Wouldn't it be easier to sell me to this man than to take me across the border and risk getting arrested?"

"I'll buy her," Mark said immediately. "I'll save you the trip. What price do you want?"

The man's eyes shifted from Asha, to Mark, to the open door. Slowly, he loosened his grip and Asha coughed and bent over, taking in huge gulps of air.

He was still holding the gun to her side, so Mark could not move to her, though every muscle in his body strained to do so. The man's hand around the gun was shaking and Mark fought down fear that he'd accidentally pull the trigger.

"Put the gun down, please, and we can negotiate. I have no desire to kill you. I just want her."

The man eyed Mark warily. Mark lowered his own gun, hoping he was doing the right thing. "See. I'm putting my gun down." He dropped it to the floor. "Now can we talk?"

The man's face filled with suspicion. "I don't trust you." Pushing Asha behind him, he gestured Mark outside the room with his gun. "We'll talk outside. She stays here until I see the money."

Mark took a step back. The man poked his chest with the gun. "Outside!" he ordered.

Very cautiously, slowly enough to check with his peripheral vision if anyone was outside the room or not, Mark backed out the door and into the alleyway. He hated leaving Asha alone in there with two bodies, but the man had offered him the perfect opportunity.

Smiling in triumph, the man followed Mark out the door, closing it behind him. The one moment where his attention was more on the door than on Mark was all that was needed. A wooden crutch swung in the air and knocked the gun from the man's hand.

"Got you!" Milo's shout was triumphant. "I told you I help save the day!"

Rashid and Paul grabbed the man from each side and pinned his arms back. "Are there more inside?" Rashid asked. "Where is Ahmad?"

"He's inside." Mark's voice was grim. "I'm sorry, Rashid. He's dead."

For a moment tears reflected moonlight in Rashid's eyes. "I am sorry as well. I will mourn his loss. The loss of the brother he could have been."

As they pulled the struggling, whining man away, Paul stopped to say, "The bridge guard is tied up nearby. We'll take him and this man back to where your father and grandmother are waiting with the officer." He looked toward the closed door. "Do you need anything more? If not, we will take the children and the men. You can bring her in the other car. She may need some time with only you, without anyone asking questions. But you'll need to be quick. People will be curious about that gunshot."

Mark put a hand to Paul's shoulder and squeezed, unable to voice his gratitude around the hoarseness clogging his throat.

Paul nodded and turned away. "Milo. Dapika. Let's go."

As the group faded into the darkness, the man indignantly protesting, Mark turned back to stare at the door.

Asha was behind it. His Asha.

He rushed forward.

CHAPTER THIRTY-THREE

It had been less than five minutes since she had risked everything by reaching for Ahmad's gun. In those five minutes she had lost her fight for the gun, watched Ahmad die, and been held hostage with the weapon to her own side.

When the door had crashed open seconds ago and the dust settled enough for Mark's face to be revealed, something in Asha unraveled. It was too much to absorb all at once.

After Mark backed away and Tense Man followed out the door, holding a gun to Mark's chest, she wanted to run to the window and make sure Mark was okay. Instead, she heard herself begin sobbing. Instead of moving toward the door, she moved away from it. Away from the bodies. Back into the farthest corner where she wrapped her arms around her legs and cried away the terror of the last few hours.

When the door opened again, she hid her face deeper into her knees. Had he killed Mark too? She could not bear to look up and see who had entered. Could not handle facing one more fear.

Someone knelt on the floor close to her. When a hand touched her arm, she jerked away. Only when his beloved voice called her name did Asha dare look up.

"Is it really you?" Her voice was a child's. "He didn't kill you?" She looked behind him to Ahmad's body. "He killed Ahmad. The bus is leaving soon. They were taking me across the border. There was a bidding war . . . Oh Mark, that big man—Ahmad killed him after he—"

She put her head down in her hands, pressed tight balled fists against her eyes, blocking out the sight. But it remained in her mind. Would she ever be free of the memories from the last terrifying days?

Mark's chest ached. Too many emotions crammed into his heart and fought for space there. Joy at seeing Asha alive. Fear at the gun held to her side. Painful concern when he opened the door to see her huddled in the corner. Agony when he touched her and she pulled away in fear.

"Asha, it's me. It's okay. You're safe now."

She looked up at him. Her eyes were glazed with fear. Her voice trembled with confusion.

Mark felt his insides shredding when she turned toward him and he saw the torn material of her shalwar kameez. Just the thought of someone touching her with violence filled him with a fury he had never known.

It was good that none of the men involved were facing him now. Even without a loaded gun, the temptation to rip someone in pieces would be too strong. The blood and death in the room made it clear that something had gone very wrong with Ahmad's plan. The rip across Asha's shoulders testified to his worst fears. With a small moan, he pulled her to him, covering her shaking form with his arms, feeling her pain as deeply as his own failure to keep her safe.

For a moment she curled up in his arms. He held her, wanting to think of only her, but the death in the room was haunting. It surrounded them both with its smell of blood and anger and defeat. He could feel her trembling.

Mark looked down to see her staring at the two bodies lying near them on the floor. The fear in her eyes was palatable. Her shaking increased.

He pulled back just enough to see her face, cupping her cheeks in his warm hands. "Asha," he said, trying to keep his voice sounding strong and steady for her sake, but even he heard the urgency in it. It was enough. She stopped staring at the two men and looked up into his eyes. "I love you so much. There is so much I want to say to you." He looked back over his shoulder. "But we have to leave this room right away."

He pulled her to her feet and was concerned when she took his offered hand and followed him without question. This wasn't his inquisitive Asha. They stepped over the bodies and he saw her face pale. He reached back to wrap an arm around her waist when she swayed and held a hand to her throat.

What had they done to her?

He tried to keep his thoughts focused on their escape. That was what mattered most right then. He could deal with, or attempt to deal with, any other terrible realities later. Right now he had to get her to safety.

Holding her tight against his side, they ran in the opposite direction of the bridge. Again, Mark expected Asha to ask why they were not heading directly toward the road and freedom, but again, she did not even seem to be aware of what was happening to her.

Once at the edge of the building, Mark scanned the area. The packed dirt around the hotel edged out another several yards. From there all that could be seen were overgrown weeds and neglected bushes, which faded into trees and brush.

Good enough. "We'll go hide out in this mess until things calm down."

He stomped over the weeds, through the bushes, and into the dark hideout the trees provided. Once he was certain they were enclosed enough to not be seen, he led Asha to sit at the base of one of the larger trees. His mind was sprinting back and forth. He wanted to ask her what they did to her, how badly she'd been hurt. Another part of him didn't want to know.

When Asha started trembling, looking back toward the hotel, he stopped thinking and spoke his heart.

Asha looked through a break in the bushes. They could not be seen from their position in the dark woodsy area, but she could see people running down the path between the hotels. They tried opening doors as they passed. Soon someone would get to her room and find those men. The dead men.

She felt herself shaking again, but did not bother trying to keep her body still. What difference would it make? When Mark knelt in front of her, she heard pain in his voice.

"Asha." He touched her cheek. His voice was ragged, but sure. "Asha—it doesn't matter what they've done to you. Not who or how many. I know that, no matter what has been done to your body, you have kept your heart pure for me, as I have kept pure for you."

Asha stopped looking toward the hotel. She stopped thinking of the men lying on the floor in their own blood. Turning to face Mark, she searched his eyes. Saw into his very soul. He meant what he said.

The vision before her blurred as her eyes filled with tears and overflowed. Mark wiped them away tenderly, his voice a balm of healing to her heart.

"Marry me," he said, and she gasped. "Marry me now, before you tell me anything. I want you and me to be joined for life, so you always know I wanted you no matter what."

His tone of loving tenderness crept into her soul and held her, touched her, brought warmth into places of her heart she was certain would remain cold and without hope forever. His words told her this nightmare was really over. Not only over, but even had her worst fears come true, he would still want her as his wife. Asha started sobbing again.

She cried for what might have happened to her and to them. She cried for Rani and all she had suffered. She cried for

Kochi, and Dapika's mother, and for a thousand others who were suffering still.

How could there be such evil in the world?

Mark must have run out of words, for a sudden silence filled the night around them. Asha tried to stop the sobs, but found she could not. Finally, she felt him adjust to sit back against the base of the tree. He pulled her to him and cradled her in his lap. As if she were a child, he rocked her, and sang in a whisper.

"Jesus loves me this I know . . ."

Through the fog of midnight despair, Asha heard his lullaby. It was the song she had sung night after night to the orphans a year ago, the song she had sung to keep herself sane waiting in the darkness for her fate, the song she had questioned was still true.

"Yes, Jesus loves me . . ."

Mark's love washed over her, carrying to her its message of even greater love. God's love. Her heart opened wide to receive it.

"Yes, Jesus loves me . . . for the Bible tells me so."

She had carried the weight of the darkness, and it had nearly consumed her. Now she gave it freely into the only hands strong enough to bear it. Without that burden, she nestled into loving arms, and slept.

Mark felt her body relax against him. He looked down at the curve of her face against his shoulder, the shadow of her eyelashes against her cheek.

They needed to go. Get back to the car and get home where she could really rest, far away from all that happened in this place this night. But for now he just wanted to hold her. To know she was safe and in his arms again. They could wait awhile longer before he woke her and they started back.

As her body settled into sleep against him, Mark again looked down. In the soft set of her lips, no longer trembling, he saw an expression he had feared he'd never see again. Mark let out a breath of wonder. He didn't know how it had happened, but she was at peace. He could see it.

"Thank You, God," he whispered. He let his head fall down to rest against hers. "Thank You."

CHAPTER THIRTY-FOUR

Dust swirled up around the vehicle in an unwelcome embrace. The tires skidded as Mark turned the Land Rover from the road onto the dirt drive. As they pulled up to the Scarlet Cord, a flood of women emerged into the morning sunlight. Neena, Shazari, Amrita, Rahab, plus several newer girls whose names Mark had yet to learn.

He slid wearily from the vehicle and shut the door behind him. Crossing around the back, he opened the door, his eyebrows furrowed with concern at how Asha moved with slow, drugged-like movements.

Neena and Shazari rushed toward Asha, shedding glad tears and praising God for her safe return.

Asha stared numbly at each of them. Their joyful questions quickly faded to an uncomfortable quiet.

"Are you alright?" He thought the question was for Asha, but then Rahab repeated it and Mark realized she was talking to him.

"No. I'm worried about her."

Both watched Asha move in a trancelike state to sit on the front bumper of the Land Rover, staring straight ahead, seemingly oblivious to the women gathered around her.

"I'm so glad you found her in time."

He ran a hand across his eyes. "I'm not sure now it was in time. Last night, when we rescued her, she talked to me; she cried; she slept. But since we left this morning, she hasn't said one word. She kept curled up against the opposite door and stared out the window. She wouldn't answer my questions. I don't think she even heard me."

Mark's insides tied and knotted. "It's like she's in shock, but she wasn't last night. Why would it only kick in today?" He clenched his fists. "I don't know what to do. I don't know what to tell her parents. They were so happy to hear she had been rescued, but were understandably confused when I said she probably wasn't ready to talk to them yet. I don't know how long I can stall them before they'll want some real answers about what happened. Answers I don't have."

Rahab took a step closer to Mark. "I hate to bring this up right now, but I should do a medical examination on her. Perhaps now would be a good time when she is still in shock."

Just the thought brought bile to Mark's throat. He tried to speak over the sandpaper that seemed to be filling his mouth when Asha's voice stopped them all. Everyone immediately quieted and turned to look where she leaned against the vehicle, her eyes still looking forward, her gaze still unfocused.

"What did you say?" Rahab rested a gentle hand on Asha's arm.

"I said you don't need to examine me." Her voice was dull. Toneless. "I was not abused in that way."

Mark felt his chest heaving as he took in a gulping breath. They didn't hurt her. He did not even try to hide the tears that escaped at her words.

A piercing sound filled the air all around them. Mark looked sharply to where Asha stood, but she remained stoic. It came again. Metallic. Harsh. Almost a scream. More than a yell. His gaze swerved toward the sound and his pulse raced. It was Amrita.

"I hate you!" she shrieked, flinging herself forward until she stood inches away from Asha's face. Mark watched a hint of surprise cross her features. Her eyes actually focused on Amrita's red, screaming mouth.

"Amrita, please," Mark said. He moved to intervene, but Rahab held up one firm palm. Her head shook. No.

"Wait," Rahab said.

Wait? *For what?* he wanted to ask. *For someone else to harm her? Destroy her confidence?*

Mark took another step forward. The palm appeared again, this time nearly right up against his chest. Again Rahab shook her head. No.

He stood in helpless pain, watching as Amrita's hands pierced the air between her and Asha, her voice piercing his ears and her face contorted with unrestrained anger.

"Why do you get everything?" she raged. "Even when you get taken, you get rescued before they sell you. No one beats you. No one takes your future away. How dare you stand there as if you've been through something horrible? You have no idea what horrible is! You have no idea what it's like to be treated like we've been treated—for years!" Her voice broke. "And years. But everybody is so concerned about you. Everyone cares about you!"

Mark took an involuntary step forward when Amrita suddenly dropped to her knees, bursting into such mournful sobs it hurt to hear them.

"Why?" she looked up to the sky, as if beseeching heaven itself. "Why do You love her and not me? Why does she have everything, and I have nothing?" She dropped her head into her hands and rocked back and forth like a child. "Why didn't you rescue me before they made me worthless?"

Mark turned to Rahab. Why wasn't she doing something? He noticed her keen eyes alert on Asha, not Amrita. His own gaze followed and widened. Asha was not staring straight ahead any longer. Her eyes were down where Amrita huddled in the dirt, weeping.

Without warning, Asha burst into tears. She dropped to the ground in front of Amrita. Her voice was full of pain. Mark clenched a fist against his chest.

"Amrita, you're right."

The woman lifted incredulous, reddened eyes.

Asha's voice was choked and raw, the same voice he had heard the night before when he found her. "I don't know what you've been through. I suffered nothing compared to what you suffered. I'm so sorry." She let out a sob. "I'm so sorry for all that happened to you. All that was taken away from you."

Amrita stared. Her hands remained in front of her face a few inches away, as if she had forgotten to fully lower them.

"I'm sorry for being proud and thinking I could help when I didn't even understand." Asha's words were difficult to comprehend through the tears. "I resented you and judged you and—and I'm so sorry."

Asha began sobbing again. She stunned Mark by throwing her arms around Amrita and crying with her. "You are not worthless. You never were. God made you in His image and you are beautiful to Him."

Mark turned to Rahab, then to the others, He was not surprised to see that none of their eyes were dry. His own vision blurred.

Rahab moved to stand next to him. "How did you know that would happen?" Mark asked her.

"I didn't." Rahab's smile was full of peace. "But I knew Asha needed something to jolt her from her own bubble of trauma. I assumed Amrita's words would stir up her anger and that would be a start. I did not expect reconciliation."

He shook his head, not certain he could believe what he was seeing. "The Lord works in mysterious ways . . ."

". . . His wonders to perform." Rahab smiled over at him. "This has indeed proved to be a wondrous day."

Mark nodded. Something like a sigh released the tense breath he had been holding. She was going to be all right.

He smiled when Amrita pulled away from Asha and gave her a half-frown. "You are so annoying," she said as Asha wiped her tears. "You never let me have my own way. You won't even let me hate you."

Through tears, Asha laughed. The group around them joined in, and even Amrita's face hinted of a smile. They filed into the building, one gaggle of little girls in adult bodies, chattering about the rescue.

"Amrita," Mark heard Asha say as they neared the entrance. "I really need your advice. I have so much to learn about what women need once they're rescued. I want your help, if you're willing to give it."

"If I help you, does that mean I don't have to sweep the floor anymore?"

They moved inside the building, but Mark heard Asha laugh again.

He remained outside. He looked upward and spoke the same words he had said after Asha's deliverance the night before.

"Thank You, God. Thank You."

CHAPTER THIRTY-FIVE

Asha took a bite of chicken pot pie. "Oh, this is so good. I don't think I'll ever take a plate full of comfort food for granted again."

"Thank you, honey." Eleanor refilled Mark's glass then turned to Asha. "More tea?"

"Oh yes, please. This sweet iced tea makes me think of my mother. I can't wait to see them soon."

"They're still coming the morning of the wedding, right?"

"Yes, ma'am. I missed them already, but after the last few days I am really, really looking forward to having everyone I love near." She looked to where Mark sat next to her. "Especially you."

He put his hand out on the table and she placed her own within it. His hand was large. Strong. Safe. She felt her eyes sting.

"How did the debriefing go, dear?"

Asha held up a finger until she finished chewing and swallowing another bite. "Mmm. It was a very special time. Rashid and Neena were there, and Paul, Silas and Kolol. Mr. Stephens got each person's version of the story, and in hearing them, we all could see so clearly God's hand of protection. We praised Him, and I had the chance to give my personal thanks to each person. Toward the end, even Milo and Dapika came in with Dapika's mother, and I was able to thank them, too."

Mark's grandmother reached across and patted her hand—and Mark's, as hers was still wrapped inside his. Asha looked at her with love. "And I thank you too, future grandmother-in-law," she said softly. "So many people worked to help rescue me. I am so blessed."

"You are a beloved friend." Eleanor Stephens smiled. "And I would love you even if you weren't marrying my grandson." Rising from the table, she picked up her plate, silverware and glass and headed for the kitchen. "But since you are, and rather soon, I think I'll leave you two to wash the dishes while I take a little nap."

"Are you okay?"

Asha dried the last of the dishes and turned with a smile. "For the fifth time today, yes, I'm okay."

He frowned. "I just . . . I just want you to be okay."

The loving concern in his eyes brought tears to Asha's. It was the first time they'd had the chance to be alone since her rescue. *God bless Mrs. Stephens for her thoughtfulness.*

Mark left the kitchen and paced to the living room. When he pivoted and held his arms out, lines still running across his forehead in uncertainty, Asha ran to him. Threw her arms around him and held tight.

His own wrapped around her protectively and pulled her close against his heart. She could feel her own thundering against his. "Mark, I was so afraid they were going to take me away from you forever."

"Don't even talk about it," he said hoarsely, his arms tightening. "I can't even think about the possibility of all that might have happened to you."

"That's the thing." She snuggled into his embrace. "Amrita really made me see that, for these women and girls, it's not just the possibility—it's reality for them. It's memories, for some of them going back as long as they can remember. I don't know how they stand it."

She pulled back enough to look up at him. "I was surprised, and a little worried, when you didn't come to the debriefing."

The lines on his forehead reappeared. "I couldn't go." He removed his arms and turned, leaning his forearms on the nearby windowsill and looking out to where Milo and Dapika played with the other orphans on the playground. "I could not bear hearing over and over again how close you were to being sold. To being hurt. To being—"

His voice broke and Asha hurried around his side. She touched his arm. "The thing I missed most about your not being there was not getting the chance to thank you publicly for what you did for me." When he faced her she put both hands to his strong, solid jaw line. "But now I think I'd rather do it here with just you."

She could feel her eyes welling with tears. Would she ever be able to talk about that time—even think about it—without wanting to cry?

"Mark." Her voice was barely above a whisper. "You rescued me. I had given up hope, and then there you were. I can't even tell you—I—"

Tears choked away the rest of her words. With a little moan, Mark reached out and pulled her into his arms again. He held her tight, as if he would never let her go.

"Asha." He dropped his chin to rest on top of her hair. "I said something back when we hid under the trees outside the hotel. I meant it. We haven't had a chance to really talk since we got back, but I want you to know that I would marry you no matter what. If you want to get married right now, tonight, I'll go find a preacher and promise before witnesses to love and cherish you forever."

Asha fought the urge to sob against his chest. "You'll never know how much what you said then mattered to me." She pulled her head back to look up into his eyes. "I thank you with all my heart." She palmed his cheek. "But I think I'd like to have our wedding when we'd planned it. I want some time to deal with all that happened, to go through it all and be okay. I want my dad to walk me down the aisle, and I want to be able to come to you without anything haunting me. Does that make sense?"

"It doesn't have to," he said tenderly, reaching out to run a hand down her hair. "I want you to have what you need."

"God has given me what I need." She sighed into him. "He's given me you."

"Asha *Didi!* Mark *Dada!*"

Mark and Asha pulled apart at Milo's voice. Mark sighed, then grinned. "You know, I'm looking forward to our honeymoon for multiple reasons, but one of the biggest is being able to have you to myself for longer than five minutes without being interrupted."

She giggled, then put a hand to her mouth and blinked away tears. "It feels good to laugh again. I didn't think—oh good grief, I wish I would stop crying so much!"

Mark touched her cheek gently before leaving her side to answer the door. "Hey, Milo. How are you?"

"No need you making the little talk with me, *Dada.*" Milo strode comfortably into the room.

"What? Oh, you mean small talk."

"That's what I said. Little talk. But we need to have big talking time right now."

"Has something happened?"

John Stephens walked through the door that Mark still held open. "No, it's something that might happen," he interjected, flopping down on the couch. Milo grinned and flopped down beside him.

Asha had turned her back to wipe her tears. "*Didi,* you okay?" Milo asked. "It's a hard thing that happened to you. Milo is happy you are back home."

Home. The word brought tears to her eyes again. "Yes," she tried to say, but her voice squeaked. She nodded instead.

"Is hard coming from that bad place into a happy life. Hard to sit down on all the bad feelings and squish them until they are flat. Good to be around people who are happy, yes?"

"Yes," she said cautiously. "I—I think so."

"Yes," Milo said with confidence. "And you are going to be okay, because you are having Mark *Dada* to be with. But Dapika only has her mother, who is much in trouble because of the drugs."

John Stephens spoke toward Mark's confused face. "Milo suggested that Dapika stay here at the orphanage while her mother goes to the Scarlet Cord."

"Yes, is good idea. Hard for Dapika to see her mother having sad time learning to live without drugs. Dapika already is thinking like person who is free, but the mother has more memories to sit on and squish down flat. She will need longer time."

"That actually makes a lot of sense to me," Mark said. "Besides, there aren't any kids at the Scarlet Cord. If the mother is willing, maybe it would be a good idea for her to stay where she'd have friends." His smile curved slyly. "Like you, right, Milo?"

Mark laughed when Milo's face took on a reddish tint. "Hmm," Mark teased. "I think I am seeing what is plain like nose on face."

"What?" John Stephens asked.

Asha turned with a smile. "It's what Milo told me when I first came back. He looked from me to Mark and said he saw what we hadn't seen yet. What was as plain as the nose on my face."

"Ah." Mark's father looked over at Milo, who was trying to be surreptitious about looking the other direction. "This will be fun."

"Sorry, little guy." Mark ruffled Milo's hair. "With me moving out, my dad's got to have someone to pick on. You're next."

"Is no plain like nose on face," Milo argued. He stood and headed for the door. "Is no good you laughing about Milo doing something nice for girl. For friend. Is not like I am singing the Bollywood love songs. Maybe I go back to my street and get the ice cream and not stay here where people think it is plain like nose on face, and . . ."

He kept talking as he exited the house and headed back to the guard shack. Asha could not help but smile. John Stephens slapped his thigh with a chuckle. "You never know what's going to happen around here!" He stood and stretched. "I'm going to head over to talk with the mother and see about the little girl sticking around here for awhile. I think she'd like getting the chance to be a kid. Probably never had that where she was."

He patted Asha on the shoulder, then slapped Mark on the back with a thud. "That wedding of yours is coming up soon. I've got it on my calendar to go pick up the little lady's parents that special morning. Sure hope their plane isn't late, because I don't want to miss the big occasion!"

Mark laughed. "Don't worry, Dad. We'd wait for you."

"Aw, I think things will work out just fine. You've waited long enough; I don't want to be the one to make you wait any longer!" He put a hand on his son's shoulder but looked over at Asha. "So where are you going on your honeymoon?"

She smiled. "I have no idea. Mark says it's a surprise."

"Well, now, you may be surprising her, but you don't have to surprise me, right?" He started leading Mark toward the door. "Let's you and I go outside and you can tell me all about it."

Mark looked back to where Asha stood by the window. He grinned. "Like I said, more than five minutes . . ."

She laughed as they walked through the door, Mark's father asking as they went, "Five minutes? Of what? How many—"

Looking out the window, she watched them walk together across the compound, Mark explaining how she had wanted to spend their honeymoon in their home, and he told her . . .

Yes, more than five minutes alone without interruptions sounded wonderful.

She did need to talk with Rahab and others about what happened, work through all she had seen and experienced. And of course her parents couldn't change their plane tickets at this point.

But aside from those things, when she just thought about her and Mark, as far as Asha was concerned, their wedding day could not come soon enough.

CHAPTER THIRTY-SIX

Amrita, Neena and Dapika hovered around Asha in the room at the side of the church foyer. "Rahab and her new baby are sitting close to the front," Amrita said, running a line of black eyeliner thick across Asha's eyelids. "She told me to tell you congratulations for her."

"And Shazari, your birth mother, is also up front. She asked me to give you this." Neena pulled something from behind her back. Asha gasped and reached out. Her hand gently touched the blanket, her baby blanket, the two torn pieces sewn together and made whole again.

"I saw your half of this in your room and mentioned it to Mark. He produced the other half."

"Neena, thank you. This is the most precious gift you could ever have given me. Please thank Mother for me."

"There are so many people here." Dapika peeked through a crack in the door. She looked back at Asha. "It's so romantic."

"I just can't believe how beautiful you look," Neena said with a happy sigh. "And Amrita, I can't believe you came today without your usual three layers of makeup."

Amrita actually smiled at the teasing. "Well, now that I've decided not to go back to Sonagachi, I figured if I was going to try to snag some Christian guy, I'd probably better lighten up on the paint." She gestured toward her arms. "See, I even wore less jewelry."

Neena laughed when Dapika touched the ten bangles still on Amrita's arms. "Oh, yes, you are definitely making huge changes."

"Okay, okay, so I'm not going completely boring and colorless. Christian guys don't want a girl who's frumpy, do they?"

Dapika ran her hands along the bangles, making them jingle against each other. "Asha *Didi* says that you don't need to have a man to be worthwhile. You have value because God loves you. And she is right. I did not believe her when she told me about God loving me. But after He sent the men to rescue us, and even rescued my mother, I know He is real."

Amrita smiled down at the girl. "I think you might be right, but it will take awhile for me to really grasp that concept enough to believe. But even if or when I do, if I'm going to be working at the salon near Sonagachi, keeping an ear out for girls who want to be rescued, I'll still have to look good. Nobody wants their hair and makeup done by someone who is—"

"Boring and colorless?" Neena laughed again. "I had heard you were considering going back near the district and being an information source. That would be wonderful! But do you think you'd be recognized? That your old madam might find out about you?"

"I thought of that, but I think it's been long enough that she's given up on me. And if I build enough rapport, the girls would warn me if there was danger. It would be worth the risk to get other girls out."

Asha had stopped listening to much of the conversation. She stared at her reflection in the long mirror Eleanor had brought from her home. Red glittering sari. Hands and feet painted with tiny, intricate designs. A bright Indian-style jewel draped down the part in her dark hair to rest on her forehead. Her baby blanket—her past now restored—cradled in her hands.

She was looking at a dream come true.

Today was her day, the day she had imagined for so long. And somewhere on the other side of the building, Mark was waiting as she was. Waiting to stand before all of his friends and loved ones and say, "I do."

Asha could not have been happier. Except . . .

"Does anyone know if my parents have arrived yet?"

Neena answered. "Last time I checked, Mr. Stephens was still not here. And I am certain that the moment your mother arrives, she will come straight to see you."

Asha bit her lip. "Dapika, could you please go check again, just in case? Maybe they are out in the courtyard and don't know what room I am in."

"Sure, *Didi*."

Music began playing and Asha's heart sped up. It was almost time. Past time really. The wedding was supposed to have started half an hour ago. Fortunately, it being India, no one expected it to begin right on time. Many of the guests showed up late.

But her dad hated being late. He would have been early.

Where were they?

Dapika returned. "The church is full of people. And more are standing outside looking in. There are many people who love your Mr. Mark. But no white parents and no Mr. Stephens yet."

Neena came to stand at Asha's side. "The music has started and that means we should go to our seats. I know they're reserved, but I don't want to risk losing them." She gave Asha a squeeze. "I want to be right up front on your most special day."

Amrita took Asha's hands. "You do look very beautiful. You're pretty on the outside, but I think most of the beauty I see comes from the love shining through your eyes."

Asha blinked back tears. "Thank you."

Neena pulled out a handkerchief. "Don't even think of crying and messing up that incredible makeup job Amrita did."

Eleanor Stephens entered the room after knocking. "Are you about ready?"

"I am," Asha answered. "But my parents aren't here yet."

"Well, we shall just have to wait a little longer then, won't we?" She turned to the girls. "If you want to go, I will wait with her."

Leaving congratulations and good wishes behind them, the two women left the small room, followed by Dapika. Eleanor turned to Asha. "You look radiant, my dear. My grandson will be so proud."

"Oh, *Didi-Ma*, I feel like I could just burst with happiness right now." Asha hugged her then pulled back. "But I'm worried about my parents, and Mark's dad. What if something has happened?"

"Well, worrying about it won't help a thing, so let's pray about it instead, shall we?"

With a grateful nod, Asha bowed her head, only to quickly lift it again as a loud knock sounded on the door. "They must be here!"

Eleanor opened the door to a wide-eyed, pale-faced John Stephens. He came inside the room and shut the door behind him.

Eleanor's face flushed. "Son, what are you doing? You aren't supposed to be in the bride's room!"

"I'm so sorry," Mark's father said. "I had left my phone charging on the kitchen counter."

"Oh dear." Eleanor put her hand to her head. "What has happened?"

"I waited and waited at the airport, but their flight arrived without them on it. I remembered your dad said he was bringing his phone that had international calling capability. I had his number written down in case I needed to call them. But I was in such a rush to get to the airport on time I forgot to get my phone and take it with me! I usually leave it in my pants' pocket so I don't forget it." He looked at Asha. "Please don't tell me you won't marry my son just because his father can't remember more than two things at a time." He grimaced. "Oh, man, now is not the time to joke. I'm sorry."

Asha shook her head. "Wait, back up. You said my parents weren't on the flight?"

He nodded. "When I got back to the compound to get my phone, on my way back to the airport I got a message from them. They had a delay on the flight just before this one. They said they were trying to get another flight as soon as possible, maybe they've even gotten one by now, but even if they arrived at the Kolkata airport this minute, they'd still not make it to the church in time."

"Oh no," Eleanor breathed out. "What are we going to do?"

CHAPTER THIRTY-SEVEN

Asha fought tears, but this time they were not happy ones. This was the most important day of her life. Her parents needed to be there.

John Stephens was punching numbers on his phone. "I knew you'd want to talk to them, so I didn't bother calling them on the way here to see if they'd found another flight yet. Here." He handed her the phone. "It's dialing."

Both John and his mother quietly stepped from the room and Asha stood alone in front of the mirror, staring at herself in her beautiful sari.

"Hello?"

"Daddy?"

"Asha!" She heard him speak to someone nearby. "It's Asha, hon."

Her mother's voice on the phone had Asha again willing herself not to cry. "Mom, what happened? It's past time for the wedding to start."

"I know, honey. I can't believe this is happening. I'm sure Mr. Stephens told you the details, but I can't tell you how awful I feel about this whole thing. I'm supposed to be there helping you into your dress! Your dad is supposed to be there walking you down the aisle!"

Asha could hear her mother's voice tightening up. Her own kept her from speaking.

"You talk to her for a minute," she heard her mother say. "I have to find that paper."

"Your mother keeps talking about the big ceremony we're planning at the church when you come to America in six months. I'm glad she keeps reminding me about it. Makes it feel not so bad that we're missing your big moment today."

"But Daddy, you need to be here! Maybe we can cancel it, or put it off. Did you find another flight?"

"We did, and it's leaving soon, but that still has us getting in a couple hours from now. Then we have to get from the airport to the church, and you know how traffic can be. You can't keep everyone waiting that long. Lord willing, if all goes well, we'll be there for the better part of the reception."

"But—"

"Here, I found it," her mother's voice stated in the background. "Can I talk to her again?"

A pause gave Asha the chance to swallow some of her words before she said them. She should have known something like this would happen. Especially in India. Why hadn't she told her parents to get tickets that had them arriving the day before? She thought she'd worked everything out so perfectly.

Asian culture seemed to enjoy crumpling up her plans and tossing them to the wind.

"Asha, are you there?"

"I'm here, Mom. This is terrible. You can't miss my wedding!"

"Honey, I spent the past couple hours saying those exact two sentences to your father here."

"And crying," she heard her father say.

"Yes, and crying. I admit it," she responded. "But then I thought of two things, and I need to tell them to you. No, three, the first being that if we weren't planning this big reception for you and Mark when you two come to North Carolina, you can bet the ranch I'd be telling you to wait for us, big crowd or no big crowd. But I'm going to make that event so amazing, it will be like another wedding and reception, so I can live with us missing this one since we have that one to look forward to."

"But Mom, I—"

"No buts yet. I have to tell you the other two things."

Asha sniffed. "Okay."

"First of all, after I got over my crying bit, I started blaming the airports and the schedules and the fact that sometimes it seems like nobody is in charge around here. Then God reminded me that this is where He called you, and if He called you, then you need to accept that this is where you are. Just like marriage is two very different human beings needing to live together in harmony—which is sometimes hard and takes adjustment—"

"You've got that right," she heard in the background.

"Yes, thank you, dear." Asha smiled at her mother's exasperated tone. "In the same way, you need to accept this new culture, with its beautiful strengths and frustrating weaknesses, because it is where God has placed you."

Asha felt her eyebrows raising. Was this her mother talking?

As if she heard Asha's thoughts, Maryanne Rogers said, "I know it's probably hard to believe I would say that; you know how I don't like branching outside my comfort zone. But God has taught me a lot over these past weeks. Especially when you were captured, and we were so helpless, and I couldn't come and do anything to find you or rescue you."

Asha's throat constricted.

"I was forced to put you entirely in God's hands and ask God to protect you. And He did. Since then He's been trying to get me to let you go in other ways. I have wanted to keep you close by, to keep you where I feel you would be safe and where I would feel comfortable, but my comfort should not be the most important thing. If God wants you there, then there you should be. And I am learning to accept that. Someday I might even be happy about it—though you know if you have children you have to bring them to see me at least every—"

Her voice was cut off by Asha's father, mentioning she might want to cut it short to save the battery in case they needed to call again.

"Oh, right. Well, the last thing is—" She stopped and Asha could hear tears in her voice again. "I have been reading about Amy Carmichael. You know, the missionary to India who was your hero as a child? I started studying her life after you left. I guess it made me feel closer to you. Did you know that she used to rescue girls who were sold as temple prostitutes? She was a missionary to trafficked girls! Isn't that incredible? You probably didn't even know that."

"No, I didn't." Asha was pleased at her mother's excitement, but . . . "But what does that have to do with ya'll missing my wedding?"

"I read something she wrote that hit me so hard I wrote it down to tell you after we got there. But we aren't there, so I need to tell you now. Here it is. It says,

"In India the eyes which watch us are not deceived. They look through what is shown to what is. They are quick to detect tinsel. It is gold they seek. Happiness, especially the kind which does not depend upon circumstances, is gold."

"That's beautiful, Mom, but—"

"Stop with the buts until I'm finished!" Excitement drifted in where tears had been. "I know this is a disappointment. I would do anything to be there right now. But we aren't. It's nobody's fault. But instead of just feeling sorry for myself, I realized that how you react to this, and how I react to it, really matters. We're supposed to have the joy of the Lord, and if that joy falls in a heap to the floor when things don't go the way we want, then how can we represent Christ to the world?"

She sighed into the phone. "I don't want my attitude to mar your beautiful day. So I have decided to be joyful that we might make it for the reception, and even more so that we will be there after you come back from your first night together. And after all, for awhile there we were terrified we would never see you again, so being delayed is not such a difficult trial."

Asha did not fight the tears this time. She caught them with a tissue before they could damage her makeup. "Mom, I—thank you—I wish you were here."

"So do I, honey. But for some reason God allowed this, so don't you let it ruin any part of your day, okay?"

Asha sniffed.

"Okay?"

"Yes, Mom."

"Your dad is telling me to get off the phone and let you go get married. And they just called for our flight, so I'm going to skedaddle so we're the first ones on. We'll get there as soon as we can!"

"I love you, Mom."

"Your dad and I love you, too. Bye for just a little while."

"Bye."

Asha hung up the phone. Her emotions were still reeling when she opened the door and motioned for Eleanor.

"What is it, dear? How can I help?"

"My parents aren't going to make it for another couple hours at least," Asha said, choking over the words.

"Oh no! I'm so sorry."

"Me too. They said they're planning another ceremony in the States, so I guess my dad can walk me down the aisle then, but . . ."

"I'd be honored to walk you down."

She looked down to where Milo stood, his face solemn. He looked more and more like a man every day. "Thank you," she said warmly. "But we need you to be the ring bearer, remember?"

He scowled. "Yes. First I think this is great honor. Then I find out Dapika is flower girl. I think it is only Mark *Dada* doing the teasing like his father."

Asha felt her face break into a smile. "No, Milo, it truly is an honor from us to you. We chose you and Dapika because you are very special to us." She put an arm around his shoulders. "And if you don't want to walk down together, that is just fine. You can go separately."

His scowl softened. "If it is like that, then okay, I walk together with her. But I am not having to throw any flowers, right?"

She laughed as he took his place behind the closed doors to the auditorium. "No, no flowers for you. Just the rings."

Dapika joined him, a basket of red rose petals in her hands. "Getting to be the flower girl is more of an honor than being the ring bearer."

Milo's chin went up. "Is not."

"Is too."

"Is not."

"Children, this is not the time to be arguing." Eleanor opened the doors just enough for the boy and girl to slip inside and start down the aisle. "Do you want me to ask Mark's father to walk you down the aisle, dear? I know he would be glad to."

Asha snuck a look through the slight opening. John Stephens had gone to stand at his son's side. Mark's side. Mark was already standing at the end of the aisle.

Waiting for her.

The crowd shifted with restless energy.

"I'm sorry. No one told Mark about your parents not arriving. He's been standing there for quite awhile now. This hasn't been as organized as I'd planned. I do apologize."

"Don't." Asha touched her arm. "It's okay." She took in a deep breath. Her mother was right. If this was where God had called her, then she needed to learn to accept all of life here, not just the parts she loved.

Okay, Lord, I will choose to be joyful regardless, and let You be in charge of this day.

To Mrs. Stephens she said, "Thank you for the offer of Mark's dad walking with me, but it just wouldn't be the same. I think . . ."

"I understand, dear." Eleanor sighed. "But to have to walk alone down the aisle on your wedding . . ."

"It will be okay," Asha reassured her, but the moment Eleanor slipped through to walk down the aisle herself, Asha's calm face came undone for a moment.

Would it be okay?

CHAPTER THIRTY-EIGHT

The double doors opened and the music changed enough to alert the congregation. Eyes and heads turned as Asha stood in the doorway.

Alone.

She felt her heart racing, but for all the wrong reasons. Did this somehow represent her future? She took in a deep breath.

Everyone was staring. Some whispered to each other. She heard a few of the comments from the back row.

"Where is her father?"

"I thought her parents were coming from America."

Asha's hands tightened on her bouquet of red and yellow roses. She felt her bangles dig into her arms as she clutched them close to her body.

Mark's eyes lit up at the sight of her. He looked with approval and love over her sari, her painted hands, the decoration painted across her forehead in an arch over each eyebrow.

When his gaze locked onto her eyes, however, his face changed from delight to concern. She tried to smile sincerely enough to keep the disappointment from her eyes, but even across the auditorium he saw it.

It was then he looked to her left and right and saw that she was alone. Awareness dawned. His eyebrows rose and his eyes questioned her.

"Where are they?" he mouthed.

Asha knew she was supposed to be walking down the aisle. Everyone was waiting, eyes on her. But she could not tear her gaze away from Mark's face as his father leaned over to whisper something in his ear.

Mark's eyes quickly looked to his father, then across the congregation all the way back to her.

Then he moved. Away from his own position at the front of the room.

He was walking down the aisle. To her.

A gasp arose from the crowd. Asha's joined it.

He was coming. For her.

She vaguely heard the murmur sweep across the room. Caught one voice saying, "How beautiful."

Another whispered, "That is the most Christ-like thing I have ever seen."

His stride was not rushed, not embarrassed, not even uncomfortable. As if his tread was not followed by the combined sigh of every woman in the congregation, he strolled toward Asha, his eyes never leaving hers.

"Mark," she whispered when he was within feet of her. She herself had not taken one step.

He came closer, until they stood face to face. His eyes smiled and his lips followed. "Hello."

She thought of a long-ago moment, when she had arrived back in India after a year in America. When they stood facing each other after so many months apart. His eyes had smiled and his lips had followed. "Hi," she said.

"I thought you might not like to walk alone." He moved to stand by her side and held out his arm. "May I escort the bride?"

"Oh, Mark." She slipped her hand through the crook in his arm. "You came to rescue me, again."

His eyes had not left hers. "As long as I live, as long as I am able, you will never walk alone."

She swallowed down the threatening tears. Joyful tears now. Together, steps in sync, they slowly walked down the aisle.

This time, Mark took the time to look and smile at friends and family along the way. Asha also looked. She had expected the church to be full of people who loved the man she would soon call husband, but realized many of the people were her dear friends as well. Neena and Rashid. Rahab and Boaz with their precious baby, Ruth. Paul and Silas. Milo and Dapika. The missionaries from the compound. Rescued girls from the Scarlet Cord.

She had hoped to someday make this place her world, her home, but as they walked she realized it already was. And it was fitting that they start their lives together this way. Him coming for her, then leading her forward.

She looked up into Mark's eyes and everyone else disappeared from her vision. A sacredness hallowed the moment as the pastor read the verse in Ecclesiastes about a three-fold cord not being quickly broken.

God, Mark and her. Bound together for life into something strong that would over time become stronger. Something beautiful that would be nurtured into something even more beautiful.

A future and a hope.

"You're here!"

The car had just pulled in, but Asha was watching for it. "Thank you, Mr. Stephens—I mean father-in-law!—for being willing to miss some of the reception to go pick them up." She grinned up at him and whispered, "There's plenty of *biryani* and curry left, and we saved you some cake. Mark has it."

"Now that's good news!" Mr. Stephens made a beeline for the head table.

"Mom! Dad! I'm so glad to see you!"

"Oh, honey." Maryanne Rogers looked over her daughter with awe. "How beautiful you look. I thought all the Indian getup would look out of place to me for a wedding, but it is just perfect on you."

"You are beautiful, my dear." Asha's father reached around and hugged her so tight Asha struggled to breathe. "I'm sorry I wasn't here to walk you down the aisle."

"Oh, it was the most inspiring thing I have ever seen." Eleanor Stephens joined them by the car. "She stood there, all alone, and then suddenly Mark was walking down the aisle to get her. It was just breathtaking."

"He walked down to get you?" Asha's mother waved her hands in front of her face. "Oh gracious, how gallant."

"It was. Or rather he was," Eleanor agreed. "The Bible says a man and wife are meant to represent Christ and His bride, the church. I have to say I can't think of a better way to start that picture than what Mark did today."

"Are you saying what he did was like Jesus?"

Asha turned to see Amrita joining the conversation, reaching up to give the Indian greeting to Asha's parents.

"I am."

"Jesus treats us like that? With that kind of love?"

"Let's go sit down and I'll tell you more about it." Eleanor waved and led Amrita toward a quiet table.

Asha hugged her parents again. "I'm just so glad you made it in time to enjoy some of the reception. There are so many people I want you to meet."

"I need to get in on this, don't you think?"

She turned with joy at Mark's voice, wishing she could throw her arms around his neck. They had not even been able to kiss at the end of the ceremony. Asha was having a hard time feeling like she was really married.

Then his eyes trailed over to hers and all doubts faded. Yes, she was his.

Mark reached his hand out to shake, but was soon enveloped in an affectionate hug. Asha's mother spoke first. "My dear boy, you look quite resplendent. And I am particularly impressed at the romantic gesture everyone here seems to be talking about."

"Thank you for taking my place and caring for my daughter," her father added. "I assumed that would happen after I gave her away, but we were a little late." This time he stuck out his hand to shake. "Officially now, I give you my daughter. Take care of her."

"With God's help, I will, for the rest of my life."

"We know." Asha's mother hugged him again. "We know because you already have. Thank you for rescuing my baby girl. I will never forget that. And it may sound strange, but after what happened, I feel better about leaving her here, knowing she has you."

"She has me alright. For life." Mark grinned over at Asha.

Again, Asha fought the urge to throw her arms around the man. "Yep. No changing your mind now."

"Never."

"Well, I think you should show us how to eat this wonderful-smelling food I keep seeing on people's plates." Maryanne Rogers smiled at the incredulous look on her daughter's face. "I know last time I was here I wasn't too keen on trying anything new, but I've decided to stop being such a ninny and add some adventure to my life."

"Well, that is good news," Asha said with a laugh. "In that case, once we get back tomorrow, we have a whole list of places we want to take you and things I want you to try. We've got to show you our banyan tree, and the river, and—"

"Food first, young lady." Her father was practically beaming with pride as he looked over at Asha and Mark. "We not only missed our flight, but we missed breakfast too. I don't care how spicy this stuff is!"

Asha laughed. "Well, follow us then, Dad. You too, Mom."

They loaded their plates, and Asha and Mark enjoyed watching them both try to eat curry and rice with their fingers for the first time.

"Now, Asha, you aren't expecting me to have anything like this at your reception in North Carolina, are you? I was thinking of going a more traditional route, with homemade Southern food. Maybe some barbeque pulled pork with baked beans and potato salad at the rehearsal dinner, and—"

"Here she goes again." Asha's father sent her mother a benevolent smile. "I've been hearing about this for hours on the plane already."

"Well, I want it to be a special event, and—I—oh my goodness, this is spicy!" Mrs. Rogers waved a hand in front of her mouth. "Oh gracious, where's some water? Oh my hand is covered in this red sauce. What do I do?"

Asha smiled up at Mark after she handed her mother a napkin and a glass of water. She was about to speak when Milo approached and announced, *"Didi,* somebody say it is time for you to be throwing bouquet. Why you spend so much time making beautiful bouquet if you will throw it away?"

"From one side of the world to the other in less than a minute," Mark commented. He stood and pulled Asha's chair back for her. "Can you handle it?"

Asha just smiled. She gestured for her parents and Milo to follow, then looked back over her shoulder at Mark. "Stick around and find out."

CHAPTER THIRTY-NINE

He held out a sure hand. "You ready, Beautiful?"

Was she? Was she ready to face the future, forever, with this man? Her husband?

Asha's heart smiled. She placed her hand in his.

"Yes."

He opened the car door for her. She turned to smile and wave one last goodbye to the loved ones and well-wishers behind them. She sent a special wave to where her parents stood beside John and Eleanor Stephens. As she leaned to step into the rose-covered car, Mark bent to say, low enough so only she could hear, "This Asian hand-holding ceremony is nice, but I'm really looking forward to kissing the bride."

Her face flamed and she bit down a smile. A peal of thunder warned of coming rain.

Before they could even cross town, it was pouring.

"Oh no! My beautiful roses!"

"As Milo says, 'I shall save the day!'" Mark turned a quick left, surprising Asha by pulling into the familiar missionary compound.

"I know you said you were surprising me with our honeymoon destination, but . . ."

"Well, this would be a surprise, wouldn't it?"

He was grinning. Asha tried a meager smile. *Please tell me you're joking.*

Mark pulled under the first driveway overhang and suddenly they were cocooned in a private world. Rain poured all around the awning, so thick nothing else could be seen.

He turned to her, chuckling. "You know I'm just kidding, don't you?"

Her relieved sigh made him laugh.

"I thought we could hide out here until the rain lets up. Maybe we can salvage some of your precious flowers."

Asha put a hand to her heart. "You amaze me."

He trailed a soft touch down her cheek. His eyes called her closer. "I planned stopping here anyway, but it's nice to have the rain. Now I don't have to rush since it will keep everyone waiting inside the church till it's over."

"Don't have to rush what?"

His hand lowered from her face and he traced the designs on her painted hands. She shivered.

"You know I'm not much for performing before people," he said softly.

She nodded, her skin coming alive beneath his touch.

"The big, official ceremony is important, and I'm glad everybody came." He paused, then continued. "But I really want to make those promises here, just you and me."

She stopped watching his fingers pattern across her hands and looked up into eyes filled with love. Her own sparkled with tears.

"So . . ." He smiled at her. "I, Mark," he began.

"I, Asha," she responded softly.

"Promise to love and cherish you always."

"For better or worse."

"For richer or poorer." He smiled wryly.

Her heart constricted at the memory of him lying ill and in pain. "In sickness and in health."

His eyes held hers. "Till death do us part."

A tear slipped from one eye and drifted down her cheek. He caught it with his touch, then reached to cup her face in both hands.

"I now pronounce us man and wife," he whispered.

She leaned in close to whisper back, "You may kiss the bride."

His lips claimed her and she sighed against him. The rain poured a waterfall from the awning all around them.

Asha slipped closer and he pulled her fully into his arms. Her heart sang at the gentle desire of his kiss, at how her skin seemed to burst into tiny explosions wherever he touched her, at the beautiful knowledge that soon she would be completely his.

The waterfall around them slowed, then ceased. Late-arriving raindrops dripped and dribbled, catching the sun and sparkling into tiny wet rainbows as they fell.

Mark looked out the windshield, far past the gate toward their future. His hands again reached to frame her face and he leaned his forehead to touch hers.

"The sun is back out. Your roses are safe."

She smiled at him, her heart in her eyes. "Shall we go then?"

They rode in a silence that felt like a happy sigh to Asha. As mile after mile of rice fields faded into the distance behind them, she became vaguely aware of the area. "Isn't this out near the House of Hope?"

He nodded.

Surely they weren't going there for their honeymoon, were they? It was already housing several people. Asha wanted to ask but she kept quiet, her toes curling into her beaded sandals.

Mark pulled into the driveway of a simple mud home. Asha turned to him. "Why are we stopping here?"

He only grinned. "Come, I want to show you something."

She followed as he opened the door and led her inside a nondescript dwelling. "Does someone live here? Are you picking something up?"

"Wait and see."

"You know I hate waiting."

His grin widened. "I know."

He walked from the main room into a hallway and she followed. Her eyes widened when he showed her very nice rooms in the back made of concrete. Each was tastefully furnished. They even had ceiling fans.

After they'd toured the amazing kitchen, American-style bathroom and even a basement with a ping-pong table, Asha could contain herself no longer. "Mark, what are we doing here?"

He grasped her hand and led her up the stairs again, then to the left room. He opened the door wider, revealing a collection of photos hung on the wall.

Asha gasped. She saw faces she loved: her mother and father, Shazari and Neena, Milo, Eleanor Stephens. The largest photo in the center showed her own smiling face next to Mark's the day they got engaged.

She turned to look up at her husband. His smile weaved its way into her heart to settle there forever.

"Mrs. Mark Stephens," he said, holding out his arms, "welcome home."

Is this not the fast that I have chosen:

To loose the bonds of wickedness,

To undo the heavy burdens,

To let the oppressed go free,

And that you break every yoke?

…Then your light shall break forth like the morning,

Your healing shall spring forth speedily,

And your righteousness shall go before you;

The glory of the LORD shall be your rear guard.

Then you shall call, and the LORD will answer;

You shall cry, and He will say, 'Here I am.'

Isaiah 58: 6-9

I have loved you with an everlasting love.

God, Jeremiah 31:3

CREATING CIRCLES
OF PROTECTION
IN THE NAME OF CHRIST.

Women At Risk
INTERNATIONAL

"Every 2-4 years the world looks away from a victim count on the scale of Hitler's Holocaust." Women in this world of ours face nothing short of a hidden gendercide.

—The Economist

800,000 *people are illegally trafficked against their will every year...***70%** *of the women are sold into sexual slavery chained to beds of horror.*

—US State Department

THE NEW SLAVERY...HUMAN TRAFFICKING IS THE FASTEST GROWING SEGMENT OF ORGANIZED CRIME. **100,000** ARE TRAFFICKED INSIDE AMERICA.

—FBI

HOW CAN YOU HELP RESCUE
WOMEN AND CHILDREN?

READER CLUB/DISCUSSION QUESTIONS
PART ONE: Chapter 1-9

1. If you were Asha, would you want an American-style wedding or an Indian one? How would you feel about so many of the traditions being different?

2. Would you enjoy the Indian idea of being pampered on your wedding day, to the point that you aren't even allowed to feed yourself? Or would you prefer having more say and being more in charge?

3. When Ahmad talks to the madam in chapter 2, the madam says she owns the women in the building. Back in the days when Americans had slaves, they, too, talked about owning people as property. What does God have to say in His Word about who owns us? (see 1 Corinthians 6:19-20, Psalm 95:7, John 10:11-16)

4. 1 Corinthians 7:23 implies that we choose who owns us. What are ways even we "free" people can become enslaved to others?

5. Asha sets aside her own desires for the good of others when she chooses the second site construction over having a home of their own by the wedding. Do you think God rewards us when we put others before ourselves? If you haven't read the entire book yet, how could you see God rewarding Asha for her choice? (Or sometimes, is His biggest reward peace and contentment even in lesser circumstances?)

6. As Mark and Asha near their wedding, the chemistry between them grows stronger. Do you think it was good or bad for the author to portray them desiring each other and needing to set boundaries? Do you think sometimes the church communicates to unmarried people that the physical aspect of marriage is bad out of a desire to help them remain pure till marriage? How can we teach about purity while also sharing that God created sex, and within His boundaries He intends it to be a beautiful gift?

7. In chapter 7, when Neena was attacked with acid, how did it make you feel to know this is a common event in some countries? Does

it make sense that in places like that, girls would be required to cover up more, to protect themselves? In your opinion, is that right?

8. How would you feel about Rashid being on the compound? Do you think Mark is too trusting, Asha is too suspicious, both or neither?

9. Young Dapika feels completely trapped. We know she could have been honest with the missionaries and they would have helped, but Dapika doesn't know that. Is it understandable that she trusts no one? Should we expect people to trust us, or does trust need to be earned? How do we do that?

READER CLUB/DISCUSSION QUESTIONS
PART TWO: Chapter 10-19

1. What do you think of Amrita? Is it safe to assume that even if you are ministering and helping others, there will be some who are ungrateful and unappreciative? What would your natural reaction tend to be? What do you think your reaction should be?

2. Do you like Mark's idea of having an Indian-style house from the front, and American from the back? Do you think missionaries should make an attempt to live like the people they live among, or do you feel everyone should understand that they are Americans and have a different standard and style of living?

3. Why do you think it is harder for Asha to forgive Rashid than her father?

4. Asha is so wrapped up in her own feelings, she does not notice Mark's illness. Do we sometimes miss important information about how our loved ones are really doing because we are so focused on ourselves and how we are feeling? Do you think that is the source of a lot of our misunderstanding in relationships?

5. How do you feel about Amrita? Can't stand her? Empathize with her plight? Something else?

6. Both Rashid and Neena feel inadequate and unlovable because of things they have done or things that have happened to them. Have you ever pushed someone away from loving you because of your own feelings of unworthiness? What would you have told Rashid and/or Neena about their value? What do you need to tell yourself? (see Psalm 139)

7. Asha apologizes to Rashid for not being an example of how a Christian should act. According to the two Biblical models in Matthew 5:23-24 and Matthew 18:15-17, who is responsible to start reconciliation, the one who sinned or the person sinned against?

8. If we keep things inside, thinking only of our own perspective of the problem, how does that damage relationships? Do you think sometimes we avoid going to the person, not so much because we fear addressing issues, but we do not actually want to be reconciled? How is God's way of addressing and dealing with issues better than our natural way?

9. Do you think it is reasonable that Asha feels threatened by Amrita? Would you? How can/should we deal with a person who is threatening us in an area we already feel vulnerable?

10. What do you think of Rahab's words that she has learned to pray for God to help her husband face temptation rather than trying to keep it from him? What happens when we try to be responsible for our loved ones never facing any test or temptation? Do you tend to want to do that more out of love or out of fear? Do you really think praying is more powerful than doing?

READER CLUB/DISCUSSION QUESTIONS
PART THREE: Chapter 20-29

1. Do you really believe Jeremiah 29:11 is true? How can it be true for the trafficked women? How can it be true for you right now?

2. Do you ever feel overwhelmed by the vast amount of evil in the world? What do you tell yourself when you feel weighed down by all you cannot change?

3. Were you surprised when Mark bought a gun and willingly disobeyed his father? Mark has always found it easy to walk with the Lord. Now he is tested on whether he will obey against all his own desires. Do you remember a time in your life when your walk with the Lord was tested? Maybe, like Mark, God allowed something to happen to someone you love. Or maybe God did not answer an important prayer the way you thought He should. What do you do when God does not act the way you think is right?

4. Have you ever had a time when what was happening around you made you feel like God must not care? That He must have forgotten about you? Or He must be punishing you? Can you share a time when you felt that way, then saw God come through and surprise you with His love?

5. When Mark is rationalizing his actions, verses come to his mind refuting what he tells himself is justice. Does that happen to you? What are some verses you find coming to your mind most often—the ones you need to hear to remind you to think and act according to truth?

6. Proverbs 3:5 says, *Trust in the Lord with all your heart, and lean not on your own understanding.* How do you think Asha and Mark could have applied this verse throughout this section?

7. What do you think will happen?

READER CLUB/DISCUSSION QUESTIONS
PART FOUR: Chapter 30-39

1. Both Asha and Mark have times when they give up hope. Were you ever in a situation where you gave up hope? Did it bother you if those closest to you had not? Do you think God helps us by giving us others who might struggle at different times than us, so we can hold each other up? (see Ecclesiastes 4:9-12)

2. What might have happened had Mark continued on his path of personal counter-revenge? How was God's way better?

3. Had you been Asha, would you be the type to keep trying to escape yourself, or would you be more likely to wait on someone else to rescue you? What are the pros and cons of each way?

4. Ahmad finds the truth of Numbers 32:23, *Be sure your sin will find you out.* Do you think it often happens that the very sin a person does to others comes backs on them? (see Proverbs 26:27, Galatians 6:7)

5. Were you upset when Asha's parents were not going to make it to the wedding? How do you tend to react when something you really looked forward to goes awry?

6. What did you think of the Amy Carmichael quote about people seeing through tinsel and looking for gold? Do you think the world is watching how we act and react? Do you think our reactions can either draw people to Christ or push them away?

7. Did the story end the way you expected? What do you see happening in Asha and Mark's future in India? Do you think they will have a good marriage? Why or why not?

8. What was your favorite part of the book?

ROMANCE FACT OR FICTION: Interview with the Author

A lot of people want to know, is Mark like your husband?
Oh, definitely! Basically Asha and Mark are based on me and Brian (my husband), just in further directions. I am naturally creative, passionate, empathetic and tend to lean too much on my feelings. Brian is solid and stable, loves reason and doesn't trust feelings.

So are their arguments based on yours?
No, but it was fun to write them! =)

What about the romance?
Well, I admit to being much more of a romantic than my husband. Nevertheless, I've always disliked books where the guy character gushes like a girl—you know, the kind that you know are written by a woman and say what a woman wants to hear. So if I read a scene to Brian and he said, "No, most guys wouldn't say (or think) that," I almost always fixed it to sound more realistic. Almost.

Are the big romance scenes fact or fiction?
A little of both. In Stolen Child, the proposal scene is very loosely based on our proposal misadventure. The wedding scene when Asha stands alone and Mark comes for her actually happened to a friend of mine. She came from a difficult family situation and stood alone at her wedding. I felt so sad for her but then he walked down the aisle and got her and it was one of the most beautiful things I had ever seen. So of course it had to end up in a book! The scenes of Mark and Asha at the banyan tree (Stolen Woman), in the rickshaw in the rain (Stolen Child) and the last chapter vows in the rain (Stolen Future) are all fiction—have to give my imagination credit for something!

How do you feel about the Stolen Series being finished?
I'm going to miss the characters from this series. Call me crazy, but they've become like a great group of imaginary friends. And I loved writing about Asian culture. Fortunately for me, I get to do a lot of speaking on trafficking, culture and missions, so I'll get to revisit the series often. But as far as writing, I'll have to make a new set of imaginary friends and move on to the next story. It's

already in my head and has some very interesting characters, so…on to the next adventure we go!

OTHER BOOKS BY KIMBERLY RAE

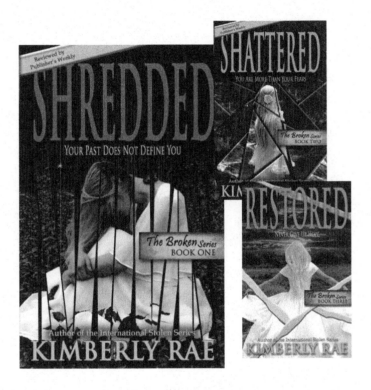

Jean has been called Blue Jean since childhood, but not because of her clothing. She wears nondescript colors and avoids people when she can. Her world is unhappy but predictable, until the new pastor and his handsome brother move into town. A chance encounter brings the town prostitute to church that Sunday, starting a chain reaction that will shake the church to its core.

Will Jean embrace the truth that will set her free, or will fear keep her captive forever?

Find out what happens to Asha, Mark, Amrita, Milo, Dapika, and more!
Jasmina and her brother, Samir, are sold by their father to a man promising them an education and good jobs.
They soon discover the man is providing an education, not in a school, but as a slave in his sweatshop garment factory. While Samir quickly submits to his new life of misery, Jasmina never stops planning an escape.
She comes to realize that escape doesn't always mean freedom.
(Series age-appropriate for ages 10-14)

269

ACKNOWLEDGMENTS

First, thank You, God, for giving me this series and for taking it and using it in ways I'd never dreamed. You've created quite a buffet out of my little basket of loaves and fish!

Thanks to the group of ladies at Lower Creek Baptist Church, who had me come for an 8-session Reader Group on Stolen Woman and Stolen Child. It's largely thanks to you that I had discussion questions for a 2nd edition. I'm looking forward to our Stolen Future group. And also to the Pennell Mission Group, who got me started speaking to ladies missionary groups again, which I love.

Thank you, Shawne, again, for your great cultural insights, Jeannie Lockerbie Stephenson for working through an edit while actually in Kolkata despite your busy schedule (and the heat), and Aunt Kim Olachea for cheering me on even before you knew if the books were any good!

Thanks to my group of readers who help find all those typos I miss, and help me know what readers want. That added ending where Asha got to see the house was because of you!

Thank you to every person on Facebook who passed the word about my books—it's thanks to you I'm an Amazon Bestselling Author.

Lastly, of course, thanks to Brian, my Mark, who puts his expertise into making my covers, listens to every word, and grins when I write about Asha's quirks because he knows they're really mine. I love you.

ABOUT THE AUTHOR

Kimberly Rae has lived in several countries overseas. She has been published over 200 times and has work in 5 languages.

Rae's first book, *A Trip to Where?* takes children on a 5-day story adventure to Bangladesh. Her current projects include the *Sick & Tired* series of books on chronic health problems (Rae has Addison's Disease, hypoglycemia, asthma, scoliosis, and a cyst on her brain), and a new series for teens on human trafficking.

A stay-at-home mom, Rae lives in North Carolina with her husband and two young children. She loves being a writer. "With writing, you never know who you are going to touch, and that's really exciting to me. I love putting something on paper, handing it over to God, then watching what He does with it!"

Go to Rae's website, www.kimberlyrae.com, for her blog, info on human trafficking, resources to use in ministry, or to order autographed books.